The Cottage at

DARCIE BOLEYN

The Cottage at Plum Tree Bay

CANELO

First published in the United Kingdom in 2019 by Canelo

This edition published in the United Kingdom in 2020 by

Canelo Digital Publishing Limited
Third Floor, 20 Mortimer Street
London W1T 3JW
United Kingdom

Print ISBN 978 1 78863 852 4
Ebook ISBN 978 1 78863 120 4

This book is a work of fiction. Names, characters, businesses, organizations, places and events are either the product of the author's imagination or are used fictitiously. Any resemblance to actual persons, living or dead, events or locales is entirely coincidental.

Look for more great books at www.canelo.co

Printed and bound in Great Britain by Clays Ltd, Elcograf S.p.A.

For my husband and children, with love always.

Chapter 1

'What the hell is going on in here?'

Jamal Wilson's cockney accent cut through the warm Saturday morning haze that had enveloped Catherine Bromley and dragged her back to reality with a bump.

'She's having a head massage.' Bradley Jones-Wilson replied without pausing the delicious, hypnotic movement of his fingers.

'Well, it sounds like she's having way more than that from the moans and groans and we have other customers out there. They're getting quite jealous, you know, Bradley.'

Catherine peered up at Jamal. She couldn't move because she was reclining with her head over the sink at Jamal and Bradley's salon, Hairway to Heaven. Bradley was washing her hair and giving her a complimentary head massage, and she'd been really enjoying it – perhaps a bit too much, according to Jamal.

'Sorry, Jamal.' Catherine reached out a hand to him and he took it, holding it between both of his. 'It's just been a while since someone else has washed my hair.'

Jamal nodded. 'I know, and you should have come in for a cut weeks ago. Your ends are like rats' tails and as for your roots…'

He shuddered dramatically and Catherine laughed.

'I'm sure you can make me look better.'

She had been friends with Jamal for over five years, ever since he'd moved to Penhallow Sands with Bradley and opened the doors of Hairway to Heaven. Catherine had come in for a haircut, and they'd got talking and made each other laugh. It had led to a friendship that Catherine didn't know how she'd ever managed without.

'We'll do our best.' He squeezed her hand. 'Bradley, make sure you use the conditioner for mature hair. She needs the extra moisture.'

Catherine winced inwardly. Mature was a word she seemed to hear more and more as she got deeper into her thirties, as if somehow, leaving your twenties behind created some dramatic transformation in you overnight.

'Look, Jamal, just because you haven't yet entered your thirties, it doesn't mean you need to describe everyone over thirty as mature.' Catherine tutted.

'Quite right, Catherine,' Bradley agreed. 'Also, my darling husband, you don't need to remind me which conditioner to use every time I wash hair, you know.'

Jamal sniffed loudly. 'I know that... it's just that Catherine's hair is in need of some serious TLC.'

'And that's what she's getting.' Bradley winked at Catherine.

'Right, I'll leave you to it. I need to get back to Mrs Tipperton's perm.' Jamal sashayed away.

'How's the water for you?' Bradley asked as he ran the warm spray over Catherine's head, tickling her scalp and the nape of her neck.

'Perfect.'

She closed her eyes again and floated as Bradley ran his long fingers through her hair, clearing away all traces of conditioner, and all too soon, he was done. Catherine sat up and Bradley wrapped a towel around her shoulders. She felt light-headed and weak, as if she'd just woken up from a nap on the beach after a day in the summer sun.

'You okay, darl'?' Bradley asked.

'Yes, thanks. You just completely relaxed me.'

'You've had a tiring time recently, what with the ridiculous hours you work at the school,' Bradley said as he led the way through to the front of the salon. He gestured for her to sit down in a black swivel chair in front of one of the large mirrors. 'I'll get you a coffee and some magazines.'

Catherine sat down and propped her feet on the footrest then gazed at her reflection in the mirror. She did look tired, exhausted even, but then the summer term at school was always a busy one with trips and Year 6 leavers' events, as well as tying up all the loose ends before the holidays. She'd need to go into work a few times over the summer, but for the next week or so, she was going to relax and recover.

Catherine loved the first week of August. It was when she felt that the summer holidays had truly begun. The final week of July, after the children had finished school, was when she went into work to finish whatever she hadn't had time to do during the busy school days, so for her, the summer holidays began that precious first week of August. Of course, she knew she was lucky, because she worked in the village where she lived, so she didn't have a long commute morning and evening. She also knew that she'd find a longer journey quite difficult after so many years of working in Penhallow Sands where she had grown up.

Some people found it strange (and had told her as much, in their friendly open way) that the only time Catherine had ever been away from Penhallow Sands was when she went to Exeter university for her History degree and then for her teacher training. She had chosen to live in Exeter during that time because she didn't want to commute over an hour each way through the week, and because she had hoped to be able to immerse herself in university life. However, her sense of duty to her mother had drawn her back to Penhallow Sands at weekends, and her weekday evenings had been her time for study, so Catherine hadn't actually got involved in campus life at all, or really been able to appreciate the whole living away from home experience. It was another reason why Jamal's friendship was so important to her. He had grown up in the East End, moved to Cornwall five years ago and never looked back. As the eldest of three brothers, Jamal had been expected to join the family plumbing business, and had horrified his father when he expressed a desire to be a hairdresser instead. Then, when he'd also told his parents that he was gay and in love with Bradley, they had turned their backs on him and never spoken to him again. Jamal had told Catherine that yes, there were other places out there, but the warm community of Penhallow Sands had accepted him and Bradley in a way that his own family never had, and Catherine knew what he meant.

She lifted the corner of the towel that sat on her shoulders and dabbed at her right ear to clear the water away. She was thirty-four now, and although she enjoyed her job and liked most aspects of her life, she sometimes worried that time was slipping away and that before she knew it, she'd be the same as Ms Jowanet Tremayne, Head

Teacher at Penhallow Sands Primary School. Jowanet had worked at the school her entire career, going from class-room teacher to deputy head teacher to head teacher in a career that had spanned forty years, and would – Catherine had no doubt – span another ten years at least. Catherine admired her senior colleague's dedication to the children of the school and to the community, and she strove to emulate it, but some days, she also wished that there was something else in her life. Some days, she was aware of feeling incomplete and, though she hated to admit it, a bit lonely. She loved seeing how close Jamal and Bradley were, and had been overjoyed when she attended their low-key wedding eighteen months ago – honoured to be one of the few guests invited – but at times, their devotion to each other did make Catherine more aware of her own single state.

'What are you looking so gloomy about?'

Jamal had appeared behind her. He placed his large hands on her shoulders; every finger had a silver ring and his nails sparkled with glittery lilac polish.

'I'm not gloomy.'

'No?' He tilted his head, causing his mid-length spiky dreadlocks to bounce. 'Considering it's the summer holi-days and you've got the glorious month of August ahead of you, I'd say that you're looking pretty gloomy. This should be the time to smile.' He raised his eyebrows. 'I almost hate to ask, but is it because you're not going away… again?'

Catherine lowered her gaze to her hands. Her own nails were short and sensible, free from nail varnish, and she wore no rings. The only jewellery she wore on a daily basis was a watch that had lived on her left wrist for about five years. The leather strap was frayed and the screen was scratched, but she could still read the time, so couldn't see the point in buying a new one. After all, when and where would she wear it?

'Catherine?'

She raised her eyes to meet his in the mirror.

'It's fine, Jamal. I'm happy staying in Penhallow Sands. Besides which, I can hardly leave Mum behind can I?'

'Take her with you if she won't let you go alone.'

'Jamal… you know full well it's not a case of her not letting me go. It's not like that.' Catherine sighed. 'I just… I can't take her away… you know how she is about money and leaving the village… But we never talk about that, do we?'

'What?'

'About my mum and her… frugality and selective agoraphobia.'

'No!' Jamal shook his head furiously. 'I have absolutely no idea what you're talking about.'

'Good. Thanks.' They smiled conspiratorially at each other. Jamal knew her mother well and how challenging she could be. Having had his own bad experiences with his own parents, he had always been very understanding of Catherine's difficulties with her mother. However, whereas his parents turned away from him, Catherine's mother clung to her like a limpet to a rock.

'But you could pay? Treat the old dear and tempt her with the promise of, I don't know… a foreign lover.'

'Jamal… One, please don't refer to my mum as an old dear, and, two… she doesn't like going away as she gets anxious and, finally, three, Bob Scratchit is quite poorly at the moment, so she won't even go to the supermarket in case anything happens to him while she's gone.'

'Poor Bob's no better?' Jamal asked.

'Nope. It's terrible to see him so unwell.' Catherine's stomach lurched as she thought of how Bob had declined of late.

'How old is he now?'

Jamal gently squeezed the ends of her long blonde hair with the towel.

'Eighteen.'

'That's a good age for a cat.'

'He hasn't got a tooth in his head and his breath stinks. He's stiff with arthritis and the sofa cushions are whiffy from where he's dribbled on them but he's still... well, he's Bob, you know?'

Jamal nodded his understanding.

'Has Jamal been telling you about *his* morning breath?' Bradley placed a glass mug of coffee on the counter in front of Catherine then added three glossy magazines.

'Cheeky!' Jamal nudged him and Bradley grinned in response.

'It's worse if he's had garlic.' Bradley ran a hand over his shiny bald head.

'Well, stop making so many Italian dishes then, Bradley. You know I can't resist your lasagne or your creamy mushroom penne.'

Bradley blushed with pleasure at his husband's praise.

'Anyway, we were actually talking about poor old Bob Scratchit.' Jamal started combing through Catherine's hair. 'Sounds like his days are, sadly, possibly... numbered.'

'The vet actually said he could live another year or longer if he's this well looked after,' Catherine replied. 'As long as his kidneys keep functioning and he keeps eating.'

'Your mum's still hand-feeding him?' Jamal raised his eyebrows.

'Yes. Three times a day. He gets the best bits of fish and chicken and he's happy enough.'

'Good.' Jamal smiled. 'However, it doesn't solve the problem of getting you away for a bit does it?'

'Aren't you planning to take a holiday?' Bradley asked, meeting Catherine's eyes in the mirror.

'No. But I never go away, as you both know, and I'm fine with it, so stop worrying, you two.'

'Well… perhaps you'll meet a hunky tourist this summer and fall madly in love.' Bradley clapped his hands then smoothed them over his head as if flicking back imaginary locks.

'Perhaps.' Catherine returned his smile, but if she did meet a hunky tourist, she knew she wouldn't do anything about it, even if the man was interested in her. It hadn't happened for the past eleven years, so why would this summer be any different? And, of course, she had no intention of risking her heart, lonely as she might some-times feel.

'Damon Looe is not the only man in the world, you know?' Jamal leant forwards and wrapped his muscular arms around Catherine then kissed her cheek. She leant on him, appreciating the affectionate gesture from her friend.

'I know.' Catherine nodded, but deep inside she knew he was the only one she'd ever cared about and the only one who'd cared in return. But it just wasn't meant to be and she'd been convinced since the day their relationship had ended that she was destined to be alone.

'Damn the words! Why won't they come?'

Mark Coleman slammed the lid of his laptop shut and folded his arms across his chest. This move to Cornwall was meant to be a fresh start for him, a change of location that would kick-start his creativity again and put an end to the writer's block that had plagued him for the past few months. Well, more than a few months, but in that time he'd been completing his structural edits on the last book as well as copyedits, although he'd been unable to think of any new story ideas. And since he'd sent those edits back to his publisher, his hoped-for muse had remained elusive.

He pushed the chair away from the kitchen table and went to the open door that led out to the back garden of the rental cottage. He took some slow deep breaths and forced himself to focus on the pretty garden. Although forcing himself was, he felt sure, counterproductive to relaxation and meditation. He'd read plenty about how important it was to exist in the moment and to appreciate what he could see, hear, smell and so on, so that was what he would try to do.

The garden was enclosed with a four-foot wooden fence that looked quite new. The borders surrounding the lush green grass were bright with red and pink roses, golden and copper marigolds and the purple star-like blooms of asters. In the one corner was a summerhouse complete with wicker furniture and colourful curtains and beyond that, the sky grew gradually lighter as the land gave way to the coast. When the breeze blew in the right direction, as it did right now, he could smell the sea, fresh and briny, and it did lift him with the promise of warm sunny days ahead.

He'd been lucky to find such a perfect cottage to rent at short notice. When he'd emailed the estate agent at Penhallow Sands and asked if there was anything available for the summer months, he'd been stunned – and delighted – when the woman had told him that she'd just added a lovely property to her books. She'd sent him the details for Plum Tree Cottage and he'd quickly looked through them then phoned her to say that he'd take it. Part of him had been worried that he might change his mind if he didn't just go for it, and hanging around in London any longer, sofa-surfing at friends' homes because he had no idea what to do next, was not helping his state of mind. After all, how was he supposed to write when Brian's four-year-old son tried to use his laptop for cartoons or when Ashley's girlfriend had her single mates around for drinking games? Neither helped his focus, and although it was nice to have company, he also felt that he was imposing upon their generosity, and it couldn't continue. He could have found somewhere to rent in London, but the excruciating rental prices that some landlords charged for a decent square footage and the fact that everywhere he went he saw his past, weren't helping him to move on. The other option had been a return to his parents and sister in Surrey, but at thirty-eight, that really seemed like going backwards and he didn't want to worry them. A break by the coast seemed like the ideal escape he needed, and Cornwall had been his first choice. At least then he could tell everyone (including his agent and his editor) that he was heading off to a writing retreat and no one would think it was strange.

When he'd first arrived two days ago, he'd been expecting there to be a catch, something unsavoury about the property that hadn't been mentioned on the estate agency documents – like an outside toilet or a garden rented out to a pig or sheep farmer – but he'd been pleasantly surprised. Plum Tree Cottage was set within its own land, far enough away from the village to allow for privacy but close enough should he need bread, milk or anything else, and not far away there was also a vineyard. The estate agent had told him that the vineyard owners were renting him the cottage and that they would leave him alone unless he had any problems or extra requirements during his time there. She also said that they were very pleasant people and that a trip to Greenacres Vineyard to take a tour and to sample the delicious wines was well worth it.

As he gazed out across the land, he realised that he didn't know what lay beyond the fields that bordered the fence. The village lay in one direction, the vineyard in the other, but out there behind the trees, he could make out the sea. As he squinted, he thought he could see a path at the far end of the field. He could be wrong, but it was certainly something he'd like to investigate and soon.

Being here was exactly what he needed right now – to be left in peace so he could think, so he could start writing again and so he could recover after what felt like the worst year of his life. He was bruised, battered and bereft and he hated what he had become. Mark had always thought of himself as a positive person, as someone who got up and got things done, but losing the life he'd been comfortable with for so long, the life he'd expected to carry on living, had almost broken him completely. However, time was a healer, or so they said and he was really hoping to heal and move on.

He made himself a coffee, stirred in two sugars, then took it out into the garden and sat on the sofa in the summerhouse. He smiled as he sipped the sweetened coffee. Two sugars – exactly how he liked it. For years, he'd drunk his coffee without sugar because Ellie had said he didn't need it. She'd insisted that sugar ruined coffee and that it meant he was adding unnecessary extra calories to his diet. Well, look who was having all the sugar he wanted now, Ellie Warner!

He shook his head.

Bloody Ellie with her perfect tennis coach physique, her red hair in a pixie cut that accentuated her long slender neck and twinkly hazel eyes. His heart plummeted to his flip flops. This time last year, his life had been very different, then Ellie had gone and turned it upside down, taking away his settled comfortable existence – and the relationship he'd been in since they were both sixteen – and, it seemed, his ability to write anything decent enough to submit to a publisher, too. He'd heard of authors who were inspired by heartbreak, of those who found writing cathartic and the perfect form of escapism, and while he had to admit that writing was many of those things, it didn't seem to be the way out of his current slump. His confidence had been knocked and he'd been left needing something to fix him but he had no idea what that something was.

He drained his coffee then stood up. He'd had a quick stroll around the pretty village yesterday morning, and he'd spotted the local library, as well as plenty of independent shops and places to eat, so he'd head down there and see if he could find some inspiration within the shelves.

If the words wouldn't come to him, he'd go to the words.

Chapter 2

'Make sure it's wholemeal bread but not with the grainy bits because they get stuck in my teeth, and don't forget to pick up milk, too, as we've already used what the milkman delivered this morning and I need it to make a sauce later. The skimmed one though, not the semi-skimmed gloop. I can't stand the taste of it. *Catherine!* Are you listening?'

Catherine nodded at her mother as she slid her feet into her sandals. She picked up a tote bag then tucked it into her handbag.

'I'm listening, Mum. Skimmed not semi, and whole-meal but not grainy bread. It's the same every time I go shopping.' She suppressed a sigh and instead, forced a smile to her lips.

Her mother stood in the lounge of the fisherman's cottage they shared, her hands on her slim hips, her face blank. She looked good for seventy-five, if a bit thin, but Catherine put that down to the anxiety that meant her mother couldn't sit still. Diana Bromley was always doing one of two things – cleaning or gardening. Catherine couldn't put a mug down on the coffee table unless she'd finished her drink because her mother would zoom past and take the mug away, straight to the sink to be scrubbed. The cottage always smelt of bleach and air freshener, and even in winter, the windows were left wide open to let the sea air blow through. Catherine knew her mother hadn't always been quite so meticulous about keeping house and home scrubbed and shiny, but after Catherine's father had left when she was twelve, her mother had become obsessed with keeping everything absolutely spotless. It was almost as if she was trying to clean more than dirt and grime away.

'Okay. Thank you. Be careful, won't you?'

'Of course, Mum. Are you sure you won't join me? We could have a walk along the front, get an ice cream, take a paddle in the sea.'

Her mother shook her head. 'No, thank you, Catherine. I need to wash that kitchen floor, and you know I don't like to leave Bob for long.'

Catherine nodded, accepting the same excuses her mother always offered, then watched as her mother went through to the small kitchen. She heard the bucket being pulled from the broom cupboard and the tap running, so she knew any further conversation would be lost as Diana got to work with the bleach. At times, Catherine had thought her mother's blood must be fifty percent bleach because Diana had used so much of the stuff over the years.

She let herself out the front door and onto the sunny street. Surely a walk in the fresh air would be more beneficial than bleaching the kitchen floor for the second time in two days, but she knew that once Diana had something in her head, she should be left to get on with it. Catherine had tried many times to wash the floor, windows or sheets before her mother got to them, in the hope that it would free Diana from her need to tackle chores, but Catherine never got it right according to her mother, and there were only so many times she could be told how to ensure that she didn't leave smudges on the glass or to fold the sheets so they didn't crease. It had become clear that while Catherine liked a clean and tidy home, she also liked to do other things, and her standards were never going to be high enough for her mother.

Catherine walked briskly, enjoying the feel of the breeze in her hair – that she'd left down for a change, seeing as how it was the summer holidays – and the warm sun on her face and shoulders. It was a beautiful August day and she was free for an hour or so. She would pick up milk and bread from the small grocery, but first, she knew where she wanted to go.

The village library. Her sanctum. Her perfect place.

And it was only five minutes' walk from her front door.

Outside the library, Catherine waved at some of the children she knew then headed into the old building. A long time ago, it had been the village school, before the new premises had been built around fifty years ago. Fifty years was a long time but locals still thought of the school as being new. The library was a solid stone Victorian structure with white painted sash windows and two entrances, one with *Boys* carved in the plinth above the door and the other with *Girls*. These days, the one door was blocked off, and everyone used the girls' entrance, which some of Catherine's pupils found funny when they had their weekly walk down to the library for reading time or creative writing sessions.

Catherine smiled as she entered the place she had loved visiting for as long as she could remember. The smell of books was the first thing to greet her – old, new, hardback and paperback. It was a woody, smoky scent with a hint of vanilla, one that she couldn't quite describe unless mixing a variety of aromas, and even then, she knew she could never explain to someone how uplifting she found the familiar smell. Whether in the library, a bookshop or on a supermarket shelf, books would always raise Catherine's mood, giving her hope. It was the knowledge that authors had taken the time to create each story, that every book was different, that she could open the cover and be transported to new worlds, meet new characters and escape from her own life for a while. She could feel what the characters felt, live vicariously through them as they laughed and loved, travelled, got married and had children, as they aged and lost loved ones. She had learnt so much from reading, and experienced things she would never otherwise experience first-hand. Reading unlocked doors that she would never tire of opening; it had enriched her life.

Inside the sanctum, she enjoyed the familiar respectful hush with just the hum of the air conditioning and the gentle tapping of keys in the computer area where locals came to write emails, CVs and to use the internet. There were still some elderly residents of Penhallow Sands who didn't have their own computer at home, so they used the ones at the library, and then there were the tourists staying locally and those on day trips needing to use the speedy WiFi.

Catherine nodded at the chief librarian, Maggie Chan-Dyer, as she passed the desk, and Maggie smiled back. Catherine did have a book in her handbag to return but she'd do that when she took her new selection to the counter.

She wound her way through the sections, passing Biography, Science and Nature and True Crime. She could have closed her eyes and her feet would have carried her to her desired destination because she had been there thousands of times before.

Romance.

Her heart gave a small leap and her stomach fluttered with excitement. This was her favourite section and had been since she was a teenager. She had spent hours standing in front of these shelves, browsing the titles until she could recite them along with the names of their authors. Catherine loved romance novels, from regency to billionaire, from light-hearted romcoms to deeper, darker paranormal tales which left her gazing at the full moon, and (almost) wishing werewolves really did exist, but only so that one would choose her for a mate and she would feel fulfilled.

Fulfilled.

After all, if love was fated, then how could she resist it? There would be no turning away a mate who told her their love was written in the stars, who professed undying love and devotion, who swore to love and honour her for the rest of their lives.

She shook her head now. The sensible Catherine Bromley, the deputy head teacher who knew the cost of love and had felt the pain of a broken heart – her own and her mother's – scoffed at such fantasies. But the softer, gentler Catherine, the teenager who'd retreated to a far corner of her mind and who dreamt of finding *The One* and of being loved with passion, intensity and devotion, never scoffed. When Catherine treated herself to a romance novel, when she ran her fingers over the cover, read the blurb then turned to that all-important first chapter, the Catherine who normally hid from the world emerged. Slowly. Gradually. Cautiously. But she was there, waiting to be found. Waiting for love to find her. Waiting for her destiny.

Catherine ran her gaze along the spines, wondering if today she would choose a new title – one she hadn't read before. Not that there were many of those, but she did try to avoid reading certain titles until the school holidays came, just so that she could give them her full attention, so she could fully savour the delicious contents of their pages. It was her treat to herself. Catherine couldn't go away, she couldn't leave her mother alone in their cottage, but she could escape through reading. It was an escape that she loved. Real men might let their lovers down, but the heroes between the pages never did.

Twenty minutes later, Catherine approached the counter with three books under her arm. She waited in line until her turn came, then she placed the books on the counter.

'Hello, Catherine. How are you today?'

The diminutive dark-haired librarian smiled at her from behind the counter.

'Hi, Maggie. I'm very well, thank you. How are you?'

She took in the other woman's glowing skin and sparkling eyes then felt her gaze lower to the woman's middle and the neat baby bump that sat under her white maxi dress. Maggie was two years older than Catherine and had four children already. She'd confessed to Catherine that this latest one was unexpected, but welcome nonetheless.

'I'm good, thanks. Big as a house but not long to go.'

'Hardly big, Maggie.' Catherine shook her head. 'End of August you said you're due, didn't you?'

'That's right. Fred is on pins because I've planned a home birth like last time. It went so well but he still worries that there could be unforeseen problems followed by a hospital dash. I've told him it will all go fine, as usual.'

'Good for you.' Catherine smiled. 'Are the children enjoying the holidays?'

'Oh yes. They're having a great time. My poor mother-in-law promised them she'd get the paddling pool out today because she can't manage the four of them at the beach on her own, and Fred had to go into Newquay for a meeting.'

'She's a force to be reckoned with, so I'm sure she'll be fine.'

Maggie laughed. 'She certainly is. I don't know how I'd manage without her during the school holidays. It would be a struggle to find childcare for all of them.'

Maggie accepted the book Catherine was returning, then picked up the top book from Catherine's pile and scanned it before doing the same with the other two.

'Ah… two you haven't read before and an old favourite, hey?'

Catherine's cheeks glowed. She wasn't ashamed of her penchant for romance novels but knew that some people, some of the local parents perhaps, might well judge the deputy head of their school for reading them. She glanced around, but apart from a tall man who was currently browsing in Biography, there was no one within hearing distance.

'I can't help myself with Alex Radcliffe books. They're just so good and every time I reread one, I find even more within the pages than the last time.'

'I love them too.' Maggie nodded. 'What amazes me is how the author has kept her identity a secret for so long. I mean, it's known that Alex Radcliffe is a pen name, but that's all her publisher will reveal.'

'I find it quite exciting. There's so much out there on social media about authors these days and we know them inside out, from where they went to school to what they like to eat and drink and sometimes even what allergies they have, but this kind of secret identity is kind of... old school, isn't it? There's a mystery to it that adds to the romance.'

Catherine glanced around again, hoping no one had heard her. She knew that Maggie wouldn't broadcast her reading tastes to the community, and that even if she did, it wouldn't really matter, but she did like the librarian-reader confidentiality that Maggie upheld. It added to the enjoyment of the whole process of choosing books and taking them home.

More than anything, Catherine didn't want her mother to find out what she read. It just wasn't worth the lecture that would follow – and last for agonising weeks – about being realistic when it came to men and love, and look what happened between your father and me and how badly that all turned out. Catherine found those conversations so difficult and knew from past experience that her mother disapproved of anything romantic, from novels to movies to cards to TV. It was all to be avoided as far as Diana was concerned and she believed that the same should apply to her daughter too.

She tucked the books into her tote bag, knowing that she'd get them up to her bedroom before Diana could see them. She always kept a few biographies and thrillers on her bedside table to show her mother if she ever asked what Catherine was currently reading. Not that Diana paid that much attention to anything other than cleaning.

'Excuse me… Did I just see you putting an Alex Radcliffe novel into your bag?'

The voice was deep and unfamiliar, the accent quite posh, rather like Hugh Grant or Jack Whitehall. It reverberated in her stomach and made it flutter.

Catherine raised her eyes slowly and met the intense dark green gaze of the tall man from Biography. Her shoulders tightened instantly and her breath caught in her throat. In black combat shorts, a white T-shirt that was stretched across a muscular chest and white deck shoes, this stranger wasn't exactly dressed like Hugh Grant in one of his romcoms and he was certainly broader than Jack Whitehall. He had the physique of a hero from a romance novel and for a moment she wondered if he had ever modelled for a book cover. For a fraction of a second, she even wondered whether her imagination had conjured him and he was about to disappear.

As she stood there silently, a tiny line appeared between his brows and he coughed as if to fill the silence. Catherine swallowed her confusing sense of disappointment as reality dragged her back down to earth. This man was obviously just a tourist, likely here with his family or even more likely with his surf buddies if his golden skin was anything to go by. His thick light-brown hair was flecked with white at the sides hinting at his age (probably thirties or older) and he had a few freckles over his nose and cheeks that gave him a boyish edge. He might sound like Hugh Grant but he looked more like John Krasinski. Catherine had watched the American version of The Office on her laptop in bed, because her mother wouldn't let her watch it downstairs in peace – she hated the way they glamorised the Jim–Pam romance and gave a running commentary about how it was far too Hollywood for her liking. Catherine had adored their burgeoning love affair and rooted for them all the way. She'd also developed a bit of a crush on Jim. And as she looked at this man, she realised that he had an uncanny resemblance to the actor.

'Well? Did you?' He smiled warmly, a dimple appearing in his right cheek as the frown disappeared.

'I'm sorry… what?' Catherine tilted her head.

'I asked if you have an Alex Radcliffe novel in your bag.'

'Oh… yes. Yes, I do.'

The heat that had been swirling through her chest now crawled up her throat and into her cheeks. For something to do, she hooked the tote bag over her shoulder and cleared her throat. The stranger's unflinching gaze was unsettling her. Why did he want to know what she was reading? Why did he keep staring at her like that? Why was he so good looking?

'Good choice.' He nodded.

'Uh… thanks. Yes. I know.'

Catherine peered at the book in the man's hands.

'*Three Hundred Inspirational Quotes From Across the Ages*,' she read. 'Nice.'

'Yeah…' He laughed. 'I know, right. A bit of light reading to get the old cogs whirring.' He tapped the side of his head.

'Well, uh… good luck.'

Good luck? Had the art of conversation deserted her completely?

Catherine turned back to Maggie, who was gazing at the computer monitor, apparently oblivious to everything except for the screen in front of her and willed her blush to fade.

'See you soon, Maggie.'

'Of course! Have a great day!' Maggie smiled then turned to the stranger. 'Right, sir, are you a member?'

As Catherine walked away, she heard him reply that he would be local for the summer at least, then Maggie told him he'd need to fill in some forms in order to take books out.

Catherine felt a strong urge to turn around and get one last look at him, but she fought it. Even if he was staying in Penhallow Sands for the summer or longer, it didn't matter. He was probably with a partner and their children, and even if he wasn't, Catherine was not at all interested in him. Not in the slightest. He might be attractive in a tall, broad shouldered kind of way, with a rather sexy accent and eyes that made her insides melt, but it made no difference at all to her. He was just passing through and Catherine had commitments that meant she had no time for men in her life. No time for fate or destiny...

Besides which, she also had three gorgeous books in her tote bag that she would enjoy over the next few days. In fact, once she'd taken the bread and milk home, she might well head down to the beach or the quiet bench at the top of the cliff path, and spend the afternoon with a fictional hero.

She straightened her shoulders and forced herself to focus on the positives of her situation: at least a fictional man couldn't let her down as her mother had convinced her that a real man was sure to do. At least a fictional hero wouldn't stare at her while she blushed profusely and became as awkward as the teenager she had once been.

Although, much as she hated to admit it, no fictional hero had made her heart beat as fast as the handsome stranger in the library.

—

Mark thanked the librarian then strolled out of the library with his chosen book under his arm. It was full of inspirational quotes and he hoped that at least one of them would help to get his brain working again. If not, at least the quotes might help to lift his mood. He'd intended on taking out more than one book, but he'd been distracted by the very pretty blonde woman at the counter, and before he'd known what he was doing, his feet had carried him over to her side and he'd spoken to her. He had surprised himself because it was unusual for Mark to approach a woman he didn't know, especially an attractive one but he had been drawn to her as if pulled by some invisible magnetism. The thought made him smile; it was like something out of a romance novel…

The woman hadn't seemed very comfortable when Mark had asked about her reading selection and she'd turned bright red, so he'd instantly regretted his impetuous attempt at conversation. And yet, something about the woman had intrigued him and made him want to find out more about her. Something in her eyes reminded him of something he often saw in the mirror and he wondered if she too was nursing some secret hurt, if she was hiding a part of herself away from the world to avoid getting hurt. Of course, he could just have irritated her and she might have been keen to get on her way, so perhaps the writer in him was inventing stories about her blush being caused by her instant attraction to him and the flash in her bright blue eyes happening because a primitive part of her being was reacting to him. It wouldn't be the first time Mark's imagination had got carried away, but usually it was when he was writing and not when he was trying to make conversation with a beautiful flesh and blood woman.

He wandered along Dolphin Drive and sniffed appreciatively. The most wonderful aroma of baking and coffee filled the air and he could see why. Just before the junction, set back from the road, was a cafe called Shell's Shack. Mark didn't feel like going straight back to the cottage; he wanted to stay in the village a bit longer. Of course, while he was here, there was always the chance that he might bump into the lovely blonde again, although he had no idea what he would say if he did see her. But he'd hopefully think of something, so why not stop and have a drink and a bite to eat? At least that way, he'd be able to refuel before heading back to his desk.

He walked under the flower-heavy pergola, savouring the sweet heady scent of summer roses, and into the cafe. It was darker inside, and it took his eyes a few moments to adjust, but when he could see properly again, he realised it was like he'd walked into a fisherman's cottage. The tables were small and round, ideally suited to two people and no more, which gave it a cosy, intimate feel. Dried herb bouquets filled the sea glass vases that sat at the centre of each table, and similar bouquets hung from the low ceiling beams that were also draped with fishing nets and shells. There was an impressive fireplace adorned with lobster pots, and an anchor and a driftwood mirror above the hearth. Against one wall, two elderly women sat on a small sofa covered with a patchwork blanket. They were deep in conversation, pausing only to reach for their pottery mugs and large muffins from the driftwood table in front of them.

Something inside Mark fluttered, as gentle as a butterfly's wings, but it stopped as soon as he realised he'd felt it. He knew what the feeling was... It was the writer inside him, inspired by his surroundings. Not only did this lovely village have a small library housed in an old school building that was clearly rich with history, but it had a cafe that smelt of freshly baked bread and cakes, and locals who could easily have been characters from one of his stories. It was a location that could inspire an author to write a whole series, to pen a number one bestseller perhaps!

Movement caught his eye and he spotted a rosy-cheeked woman smiling at him from behind the counter, so he returned her smile and headed over to her.

'Hello there.' She gave a small nod. 'Would you like to take a seat and have a look at the menu?'

'Yes, thanks, that'd be great.'

Mark decided to take the table near the window that had a view of the pergola and the narrow street beyond. He sat down and placed his library book on the table then picked up a menu. As he tried to decide what to order, the door opened and a couple came in with a buggy and a dog and the cafe owner greeted them warmly. He made an effort not to stare but it was hard as he found people watching quite addictive.

Five minutes later, the woman from the counter came over to him. She had a small notebook and a pencil in her hands.

'Have you decided what you'd like?' Her blue eyes were kind and her smile lit up her face.

'I'll have a cappuccino, please, but I can't decide what to have with it. What do you recommend?'

'Well, as the owner of this establishment and the one who baked the cakes, I'm biased, but how about a slice of freshly made carrot cake or a big, fat scone with jam and clotted cream?'

'I'll take a scone, thank you. Uh… Shell then, is it?'

'Yes, I'm Shell.' She held out a hand and Mark shook it.

'Mark Coleman. I'm staying at a local rental cottage for a few weeks.'

'You'll love it here, especially during the summer. Penhallow Sands is a beautiful place and I'm sure you'll find the locals warm and welcoming. There are a few grumps around but most of us are nice.' She giggled. 'Anyway, back to your order… You can always have the carrot cake later if you have room, or take a slice home with you.'

'That's a good idea.' Mark nodded.

While he waited for his coffee and scone, Mark gazed out of the window. The woman he'd seen in the library kept popping back into his thoughts. She'd been blonde and blue eyed like Shell, but whereas the cafe owner seemed bubbly and friendly, the woman at the library had seemed guarded and wary. That and her manner had stirred something inside him. She seemed so different from Ellie; the confidence in his ex-girlfriend's eyes had been akin to coldness at times, but the strange woman had an air of vulnerability and he wanted to know why. He'd been surprised to see that she was checking out an

Alex Radcliffe novel but when he'd asked her about it, she'd seemed almost embarrassed. He wished he could have spoken to her for longer just to find out more about her reading tastes and what other romances she liked to read – it was good to keep an eye on the market – but as soon as she'd thanked the librarian, she'd shot off out of the library and was long gone by the time Mark had emerged.

'Here you go, lovely.' Shell placed a large pottery mug in front of him and a plate holding a scone, a pot of jam and a separate one of clotted cream. 'If you need anything else, just let me know.'

'That looks fabulous.' Mark licked his lips. 'Uh… Do I put jam or cream first?'

Shell gave a throaty chuckle. 'Now, that is entirely up to you. It's been widely debated, I know, but you just enjoy it the way you like it.'

She turned and went to the doorway where a couple dressed in hiking gear waited to be served, leaving Mark to his scone. He glanced around but no one was looking, so he cut the scone in half, added jam then cream to one piece then cream followed by jam to the other. At least by mixing it up, he'd get it right with one half of the scone.

–

Catherine had picked up milk and bread and was making her way home along the seafront, when on the opposite side of the road she noticed a small figure behaving strangely. The person, dressed in a yellow raincoat with the hood up – even though it was warm and dry – was peering into the window of Hairway to Heaven then crouching down intermittently as if trying to avoid being seen.

Catherine stopped walking and placed her bags on the pavement then leant against the rail that overlooked the beach. She turned sideways so she could watch the figure discretely, and she started to giggle. It was like watching a meercat bobbing up and down. What on earth was the person doing? Was it some kind of game?

The door to the salon opened and Jamal appeared, causing the figure in the raincoat to jolt, turn and run along the street. But in such a hurry, the person didn't look properly and crashed straight into a signpost. As Catherine picked up her bags and hurriedly crossed the road, concerned that whoever it was might be badly hurt, Jamal waved at her in greeting. Confusion crossed his face as Catherine ran past him and towards the figure who was folded over on the street corner.

'Goodness me, are you all right?' she asked, crouching down too.

'Uh…'

Up close Catherine could see that there was a woman under the hood who couldn't be older than her early twenties. She had bright blue hair, brown eyes and a small hoop through her septum. 'Yeah… I think so.'

'Can you stand?'

Catherine helped the woman to her feet just as Jamal arrived at her side. She kept hold of the woman's arm in case she was dizzy after the collision.

'What happened then?' he asked, towering over them both.

The woman's eyes widened as she raised them to meet Jamal's face.

'Nothing!'

'She was peering into your window, then you came out and she turned and ran but she crashed straight into the signpost and kind of bounced off.'

Jamal leant over so he was face to face with the stranger.

'Do you need to go to hospital? To see a doctor? Or perhaps come into the salon for a cup of tea or a glass of water?' He spoke slowly, as if to a child.

'I'm fine!' the woman snapped, snatching her arm from Catherine's grasp. 'Now leave me alone.'

With that, she dusted herself off and marched away, heading in the direction of the car park just off the main road.

'Do you think she's really okay?' Jamal asked.

'No idea, but we can't exactly force her to come with us, can we? That would be great, wouldn't it? "Deputy Head Teacher of local primary school denies kidnapping charges and insists she was just helping an injured stranger out."'

Jamal laughed then his expression turned more serious. 'Did you say she was peering into the window?'

'For quite some time, I think.'

He frowned. 'Bradley thought he saw someone doing that yesterday and at some point last week but every time he turned around, whoever it was had disappeared. In fact, he wasn't sure that there had been someone there and said he was worried he was being haunted by the ghost of an ancient mariner or his Great Aunty Ethel.'

'His Aunty Ethel? I don't think you've told me about her before.'

Jamal nodded. 'She didn't approve of him being gay or getting married to me and she said she'd haunt him if he didn't see the error of his ways and marry a woman.'

'Oh dear.' Catherine grimaced. 'Well, at least you can reassure him now that it wasn't her.'

'I can. But if it was that woman who just ran off, why would she be spying on us?'

'Because she fancies you or Bradley?'

'I know we're a hot couple, Catherine, but I doubt it's that and what I could see of her haircut was quite cute and trendy… so I doubt she was trying to decide whether to get it done at Hairway unless she's considering coming here next time. However, it is also possible that she was checking us out in other ways.'

'How?' Catherine shifted the bags from one hand to the other as the thin handles of the paper bag from the grocery were digging into her palm.

'As competition.' Jamal folded his arms across his chest and nodded. 'I bet it's that.'

Catherine shook her head. 'You've got the only salon for miles.'

'True. But she might be taking part in Beach Waves, in which case she could be checking us out to see what styles we're practising.'

Catherine nodded. Beach Waves was an annual competition held at Penhallow Sands, where hairdressers from surrounding areas came together to compete for a trophy and a monetary prize of five thousand pounds. The prize was donated by a former resident of Penhallow Sands named Portia Pemberton. She'd gone to London and set up a successful salon chain and wanted to give something back to the community. The prize was highly coveted by those who wanted to make a name for themselves in the hairdressing world, and Jamal had won it twice in the past five years. He'd put the money into the business and used it to support apprenticeships of local teenagers. Catherine really admired him for helping out the local youths, but he told her that the warm community had given him and Bradley so much in terms of the love and acceptance that they hadn't received from their own families, that they wanted to give something back.

'You'd better up your game then.' Catherine nudged him.

He nudged her back, almost knocking her over and she staggered until he grabbed her arm and steadied her.

'Well, you know... I really could do with a model with long hair. Something I could work with and completely transform.' He pressed a forefinger to his chin and pursed his lips thoughtfully.

'No way.' She shook her head and laughed. 'You know me and my hair. It stays the same as it's always been. I don't mind a trim and some highlights but I'm not one for dramatic transformations. Anyway, it would unsettle the pupils when I go back in September.'

'We'll see, Catherine. We will see. Now come and have a coffee with us.'

'I can't. I need to get back to mum.'

'One coffee won't hurt. I'm sure your mum can wait a bit longer. Besides which, the kitchen floor won't be dry yet.'

Catherine shrugged, knowing that her best friend was probably right.

Chapter 3

Catherine dropped her towel onto the sand then kicked off her sandals. It was the perfect time of day to go for a swim. She'd set her alarm early, though she had already been awake when it went off, then she'd donned her plain black swimming costume, pulled a kaftan over the top, slipped her feet into a pair of sandals and made her way down to the beach.

She had always loved the beach at this time of day, before it filled up with holiday makers and day trippers, when it was just her and a few other swimmers or dog walkers. The sun was just rising above the black expanse of the sea and the sky was pink, the few clouds dusky mauve cotton puffs. The tide foamed up over the sand, its rhythm regular as a heartbeat.

Catherine pulled her kaftan over her head then padded over the grainy sand to the water. Goosebumps rose on her arms as she let it lap at her toes, cool and refreshing, then she waded in up to her chest. The water's embrace was cold and she shivered as it caressed her skin, but she knew she'd soon become accustomed to it, so she pushed off the seabed into deeper water. She swam for a while, her heart rate increasing with the exertion, then turned over and lay on her back.

All sounds were muted as she gazed up into the sky, floating effortlessly, supported by the water. This was the ultimate moment of serenity for her, when she could focus on feeling, could exist in the moment, when she could just be. Thoughts drifted by like colourful balloons and she let them, not allowing anything to enter her mind and sit there. This was her timeout, her brief escape from all worry and anxiety, her time to recharge and rebalance.

She closed her eyes. Focused on her breath. Found peace.

–

Mark had run down to Penhallow Sands, keen to wake himself up and to get into some sort of routine. Yes, he was here to relax and to find his muse once more, but he also wanted to establish a daily writing pattern, and in the past he'd found that exercise helped him create a more efficient routine. A run or a swim was a good way to wake up and it also helped burning off some of the calories that he consumed when he was in front of his laptop. Writing could lead to an unhealthy lifestyle if it wasn't balanced with exercise and healthy eating, and Mark believed that a sluggish body led to a sluggish brain.

He jogged down to the sand and removed his trainers then headed for the sea. He hadn't worn his swimming shorts because he hadn't intended on swimming this morning, suspecting that the sea would be a bit chilly, but looking at it now, sparkling in the morning sunlight, he wished he had done. He could have thrown a towel in his small rucksack and a fresh pair of shorts, gone for a swim then run back to Plum Tree Cottage again. He'd make sure to remember to bring them next time.

It was early-morning quiet on the beach, calm and peaceful, and other than a few people walking dogs, he couldn't see another soul. Just before he reached the water's edge, he paused. There, on the sand, was a floaty piece of material that looked like a summery dress, a pair of sandals and a towel. He looked around but couldn't see the owner.

He set his trainers down a little way from the items then walked right up to the frothy tide and into the water up to his ankles. Even if he couldn't go for a swim, he could enjoy a paddle. The water was cold and goosebumps rose on the back of his neck, but it was a good sensation – it made him feel alive.

He peered out across the water, appreciating the shades of pink and mauve that painted the sky. The open horizon seemed endless and he wondered what it would be like to move here permanently, to always be able to enjoy this beautiful location. If he did, would he appreciate the view for the rest of his life? He thought so. How could someone fail to see the sheer beauty of nature, especially a writer?

Then something caught his eye.

Something was floating on the surface of the water… white, lifeless…

'What on earth!' He looked around but there was no one within shouting distance.

He peered out again, but still couldn't see any movement from what appeared to be a body.

There was nothing he could do other than dive in and try to help.

He pulled his T-shirt over his head, flung it onto the sand behind him, waded in a bit further, took a deep breath then dived in.

As the cold water rushed over him, he pushed forwards. His heart was pounding with the fear that he might be too late and his limbs weighed heavy with anxiety, but he was a strong swimmer and he knew he would make it. He ploughed through the water, instinct driving him forwards, his body trained to swim at speed from hours spent in the water as a teenager when he worked as a lifeguard at his local leisure centre.

He surfaced when he could make out the shape of the body above him and popped up right beside the woman. As quickly as he could, he took hold of her chin then started to swim back to shore, holding her in the classic life-saving position. The training he'd received all those years ago kicked in, and when the woman started to cough and struggle, he held her tight, murmuring what he hoped were reassurances that she would be fine and that they'd get her help as soon as they got back to the beach.

In the shallows, he planted his feet on the sand, then finally relinquished his hold on the squirming woman who rolled herself over before standing up and glaring at him.

'What do you think you're doing?' Her blue eyes were cold, the tilt of her chin haughty and imperious.

He rubbed his eyes, trying to clear the salt water away, and pushed his hair back from his face.

'Rescuing you.'

'Rescuing me! Why? I didn't need rescuing!" She planted her hands on her hips. 'In fact, you almost drowned me by frightening me half to death then dragging me through the water.'

Mark opened his mouth to speak, but embarrassment was fighting confusion in his mind. Had he been mistaken?

'I thought you were in trouble. That you needed saving.'

Dismay started to seep into him. In one of her harsher rants, Ellie had claimed that he always wanted to help and save things, whether a butterfly that had got caught indoors and was fluttering against the window, desperate to be free, or an elderly lady who couldn't reach the pickles on the top shelf of the supermarket. Ellie had said that his need to be a hero was a weakness, but Mark hadn't seen it that way. It wasn't that he wanted to be a hero, more that he liked helping people and creatures in any way he could. Was that so wrong? Judging by the fury on the face of the woman in front of him, it hadn't been right this time.

She shook her head then pushed her hands through her long hair, squeezing the water out of it. Even in these circumstances, Mark couldn't help noticing that in her black swimming costume with her wet hair plastered to her head, the woman was very attractive. And kind of familiar. Then he realised where he'd seen her before.

'The library,' he said.

'What about it?'

'I saw you at the library... taking out an Alex Radcliffe book.'

His heart sped up as the realisation filled him. This was the beautiful woman he had hoped to see again. The woman who had popped into his thoughts more than he'd like to admit.

She scowled at him. 'Oh! It's you.'

'Yes, it's me.' He held out a hand. 'Mark Coleman.'

She stared at his hand for a moment as if debating whether to shake it, then her expression softened a little. 'Hello, Mark Coleman, I'm Catherine Bromley.' They shook hands. 'Do you make a habit of accosting female swimmers and almost drowning them?'

'I really am sorry.' His lips twitched. Yes, it was awful that he'd saved her when she didn't need saving but even so… And her irritation was making her eyes sparkle and her cheeks glow and she just looked so good…

'It's not funny, you know. This is my time out and I don't get a lot of it. I come here to swim and to have some peace and quiet before the beach fills up for the day. I was floating and relaxing, meditating as I do, and then I was grabbed and dragged to shore.'

'I hardly dragged you. I was as gentle as I could be.'

'Didn't you notice me struggling and trying to prise your hand from my chin?'

'Swimmers in trouble always struggle if they're conscious.'

She waved a hand. 'Well… do me a favour if you see me out there again? Don't try to save me.'

'Okay. I'll make sure I don't.'

He turned away so she couldn't see his smile – now part amusement and part uncertainty – and waded out of the water. He crossed the sand to where he'd dropped his T-shirt. He was soaked and he'd have to walk back to the cottage in wet shorts, but at least his trainers were dry.

As he squeezed as much water as possible from his shorts, Catherine appeared at his side. She picked up her towel and held it out.

'Here, use this. It's the least I can do… seeing as how you just tried to rescue me.'

'No, it's okay, thanks. It's just my shorts. And it's my fault for trying to save someone who didn't need saving.'

'But you're soaked.'

She eyed his torso, her gaze sweeping over him, then quickly glanced away but not before he had the chance to see something flicker in her eyes. It was something he hadn't seen in a woman's eyes for a long time, and it sparked something inside him that warmed him right through He hadn't been wrong at the library then; there was something between them, even if it was just physical attraction.

'I'll be fine. I'll dry off as I jog back.'

'Are you staying in Penhallow Sands?'

He nodded. 'Up at Plum Tree Cottage.'

'Ah, right. That's Rich and Holly's cottage isn't it?'

He frowned. 'I think the estate agent said it belonged to a Rich Turner.'

'That's right. Rich and Holly live up at Greenacres Vineyard.' She gently towelled her hair then wrapped the towel around her waist and picked up what Mark could now see was a floaty kaftan. As she pulled it over her head, the towel slipped to the sand and he looked away, feeling as though he was intruding by staring at her beautiful curves, although he'd have happily carried on looking at her all day. 'Have you been to Greenacres?'

He shook his head; his voice had temporarily disappeared.

'It's a lovely place. They recently developed the vineyard and the whole of the property. They now offer wine tasting tours, as well as hosting events up at the barn and they have a lovely little shop onsite where you buy wine and art and… Oh, look at me babbling on. Sorry.' She smiled and her blue eyes softened. 'I'm used to talking a lot at school.'

'You weren't babbling. It's nice to find out more about the area. Since I arrived a few days ago, I haven't spoken to many people. Except for the librarian and Shell at the cafe.'

'People around here are very nice. It's a warm and welcoming community.'

'They seem friendly. And you work at the school?'

'Yes.' She nodded. 'I'm the deputy head.'

'Wow! So I just saved the deputy of the local primary. I guess that's one to write home about.' He laughed and she joined him. When she smiled, her whole face lit up and he could see exactly how pretty she was. Not that he'd had any doubt about it before, but her smile was something he knew he'd want to see again, just like the sunrises at Penhallow Sands.

'That really would get the children talking. In fact, it might inspire their creative writing and we're always grateful for anything that gets them writing.' She bent over and picked up her sandals and towel. 'Are you staying in Penhallow Sands long?'

He shrugged. 'I'm renting the cottage for the summer initially, but who knows. It depends how I feel and how certain things go.'

'Oh, right.' She nodded. 'Well… it was nice meeting you, Mark. I'd better head home now or my mother will get worried and send out the coastguard.'

'You live with your mother?'

Her smile dropped and her eyes changed, as if she'd just raised her defences.

'I do.' Her tone had also changed, becoming colder.

'Nice.' He smiled, keen to show that he wasn't judging. There were lots of reasons why adults lived with their parents, from caring for them to saving money, or simply because they got on well. Mark couldn't imagine living with his parents now, but what worked for one didn't have to work for everyone.

'Goodbye then, Mark.' She lifted her chin and strolled back to the path that led up from the sand.

Mark wanted to call after her but sensed that he shouldn't. He watched as she made her way along the front and crossed the road, then he turned back to look at the water. The sky had brightened, the former purple hue long gone, and the bright blue promised a gloriously sunny day ahead. But for some reason, Mark didn't feel quite as uplifted by that thought as he'd expected to be. For a moment there, he'd thought he'd felt a hint of a connection with someone, the suggestion of a spark that could well turn into something more – hopefully friendship, possibly something else. Then he'd asked the question about her living with her mother and everything had changed in an instant as if he'd flicked the wrong switch. People could be so difficult to read.

He exhaled slowly and shook his head. Falling for another woman wasn't part of his plans, although if Catherine had been a bit warmer, a bit less guarded, then he might even have asked her to go for breakfast. That thought surprised him, and not just because his shorts were soaking, but because he actually wanted to get to know her better. But he wasn't really here to make friends;

he was here to work and to finally get over Ellie. To try to rebuild his life and his writing career.

That was what he needed to focus on, so that was what he'd try to do.

But as he headed back to Plum Tree Cottage, he couldn't help smiling at the thought that he'd tried to save a beautiful woman who didn't need saving. A woman who had stirred him in ways he hadn't experienced for some time. A woman he could easily have scooped up into his arms and kissed passionately.

Now that was something he could certainly write into a story…

–

Catherine folded her legs under her on the sofa and smiled as Bob Scratchit stiffly climbed up next to her and curled up at her side.

'Hey, Bob, how're you feeling?'

She gently ran a hand over his soft fur and he started to purr, a sound that was all the more wonderful as he got older. Poor Bob had been unwell for a while but he still liked to show his humans his appreciation for their care and attention. Bob had been around long enough to have seen them through some tough times. He was very intuitive, always seeming to know when Catherine or Diana needed a cuddle and some company. Catherine knew losing him would be awful and she had no idea how her mother would cope, because Diana was completely devoted to the cat. It was almost as though he was her second child, but a far more perfect one than Catherine had ever been in Diana's eyes, she felt sure.

Catherine reached for the mug of coffee that sat on the side table next to the sofa. She had her Alex Radcliffe library book with her too, tucked behind the cushions in case her mother came down, but Diana had gone to take an afternoon nap, which meant Catherine had an hour or so to read her romcom in peace. She slid the book out of its hiding place and onto her lap. Soon, she was lost within the pages, her heart pounding as she read the beautiful descriptions of the exotic location, the pretty but vulnerable heroine and the strong yet flawed, handsome hero. As the couple shared their first kiss, Catherine felt longing rise in her chest and she looked up, gently closing the book for a moment to better savour the passion and intensity of the scene. She would reread it in a moment, but she wanted to let the words sink in. Surely, to write such love and desire, an author would have to know what true love felt like? Otherwise, how could Alex Radcliffe create such gorgeous scenes where two people were drawn together, where they fought all obstacles in their way to become one? The author had an alchemy with words; they were truly magical and all of Alex's books transported Catherine to scenes she could only dream of. And dream she did, though she didn't always admit it, even to herself. What if there was one special man out there who could be Catherine's one and only? Who could stir the passion in her that Alex's heroes roused in her heroines? Who could love her from dawn until dusk and beyond?

She reached for her coffee and gazed out of the window at the bright blue sky. The beautiful morning had turned into a glorious afternoon and she knew that the beach would be packed now.

The beach…

The scene of her rescue.

How many times, over the years, had she imagined being swept up by strong arms and laid down on the sand? When no one was around, of course. Probably at sunset as the sky turned dark purple and the stars emerged. It might be clichéd, but as much as Catherine loved her job and her independence, she still had desires and yearnings. She had known briefly how it felt to be held by a man, to have soft kisses showered over her skin, to feel the exquisite heat of the moment when lust turned into making love.

And she wanted to feel it again.

She lived in a beautiful part of the world and didn't have an overwhelming urge to go anywhere else. At some point, it would be nice to travel a bit perhaps, but ultimately, her heart would always belong here. She had her career; it was fulfilling and it took up a lot of time and she loved working at Penhallow Sands Primary School, and wanted to be Head Teacher one day. She also loved her mother and worried about her and wanted her to be happy. Jamal and Bradley were great friends and the majority of people in Penhallow Sands were very nice. But there was something missing from her life, and the further along into her thirties she got, the more she felt it and the more she tried to ignore it. Yet it was there. Catherine had cared for a man, she had become very fond of Damon Looe, loved him in fact, and enjoyed their time together, but it had ended and left an empty space in her heart. It hadn't been the grand passion of Alex Radcliffe novels but it had been warm and sensual, comfortable and reassuring while it had lasted.

Catherine could survive without love, her whole life if need be, but she'd prefer not to. She was still young; she could still have children of her own if the right man came along; she could still fall madly in love.

But… as much as she might enjoy the fantasy of what being loved could be like… her mother's voice was always there, in the back of her mind, reminding her that men were unreliable, that men cheated and men left and life could be a struggle if you gave someone your heart and they let you down.

She finished her coffee and set the mug back on the coaster.

Catherine knew that most of the time, she got on with things. She was so busy with work and her mother and even Bob Scratchit, that the hole that asked to be filled with love and companionship didn't bother her. Or she didn't let it. The holidays were always harder because there was time to think then, and as she saw the tourists flock to Penhallow Sands, couples and families – those who had people in their lives – she felt her own single state all the more harshly.

This morning, she'd been taking an innocent swim when Mark Coleman had come along, out of the blue, and – as he put it – rescued her. It had been like a scene out of the novels she liked to read, and although she had pretended to be outraged, deep down, a part of her had quite enjoyed the whole experience. Mark was certainly an attractive man, tall and broad shouldered with a toned physique, and being so close to him in the water and then on the beach had awoken feelings in Catherine that she'd been trying to suppress for a long time. The only time she really indulged them was when she read romances, in particular, Alex Radcliffe novels. But when Mark had stood before her on the beach, she had enjoyed running her gaze over his broad chest, over his toned stomach and wondered how it would feel to be held tightly by him, to be pressed against his hard, male body.

She knew she couldn't allow herself to fall in lust or love. She had responsibilities and her time wasn't her own, but she could enjoy spending time with a man, couldn't she? Even as a friend? Of course, it would all depend upon the man in question; for all she knew Mark could be married (no ring though) or staying in Penhallow Sands with his partner and family (but he hadn't mentioned them). There was also the important factor that he might not be attracted to Catherine, and even if he was, how would she conduct any kind of friendship (or romance) with her mother and the rest of the villagers around? Even if she hid a potential friendship/relationship from her mother, other people would likely see her and word would get back to Diana – through an innocent enough comment, most likely – and then all hell would break loose.

She shook her head at her own musings. This was real life, not a romantic novel, and much as she liked toying with the idea of a summer friendship, possibly romance, it was highly unlikely to happen. It was not written in her stars…

'Looks like it'll be me and my cat, right, Bob?' she rubbed behind his ear and he rolled over onto his back and purred loudly. 'And plenty of reading. That way I can at least enjoy a vicarious love affair through the characters. It's far safer anyway.'

But she didn't pick up her book for a while. Instead, she continued to gaze out of the window, replaying the moment of her rescue, but in her imagination, it ended not with her walking away, but with a tender kiss.

Chapter 4

Mark had resisted the urge to return to the beach in
Penhallow Sands for the past two days. It wasn't that he
didn't want to bump into Catherine again, because the
idea of seeing her and talking to her again appealed enormously, but he didn't trust himself not to dive back into
the sea and save her again if he saw her swimming, or
floating or even paddling. The idea of it actually made
him smile because it was good to feel positive emotions
towards a woman again, to feel desire for a woman other
than Ellie, and to have that delicious sense of hope that
had been missing from his life for some time. Yes, he
barely knew Catherine, and yes, she might not be attracted
to him, but she was there in Penhallow Sands and Mark
wasn't far away. He was convinced that there was something between them and would like to find out what it
was, but he also didn't want to push things. He had learnt
over the years that he needed to take his time and to think
things through before he reacted, so he wouldn't rush
down to try to bump into Catherine again. He wanted
to give his own emotions some time to percolate first so
he could find out if they were real, if they were more
than just lust. He knew how powerful lust could be and
something inside him told him that it was more than this
with Catherine, but even so, he wanted to take his time.

So, instead of heading down to the village, he decided to explore closer to Plum Tree Cottage. He packed his rucksack with water and snacks then headed out into the balmy morning. He needed some air and some exercise before he sat down to write, so he'd go for a hike first.

In his hiking boots, T-shirt and cargo shirts along with a baseball cap and sunglasses, he was prepared for the sunny day that the forecast had promised, and he'd covered himself in sun cream too. Just before he left, he threw his swimming shorts and a towel into the rucksack – just in case. After all, the direction he'd decided to walk in did appear to have a sea view.

He set off across the field behind the cottage, hoping that it was okay to walk across the land, and when he got to the far side, he saw the path he'd spotted from the cottage garden. It was so overgrown that he doubted anyone had used it for years, but then with the British weather – often a mix of sunshine and rain – greenery grew quickly, so it might not have been that long after all.

He started to make his way carefully along the path, stepping over brambles and avoiding stinging nettles, although a few times his legs did get scratched and stung. The further along he walked, the more the trees thickened, and soon he was heading underneath a canopy of branches and leaves that shaped a cool archway through which the light created a dappled carpet on the ground. The aromas of flora and fauna were strong here and it reminded him of a time when he'd visited a hothouse at a zoo. Above him birds tweeted and warbled, and off to his right something charged through the undergrowth, making him wonder if it was a fox, rabbit or badger.

Whatever it was, he hoped it was more scared of him than he would be of it should he encounter the creature.

After walking for about ten minutes, he could see a clearing at the end of the path. He forged ahead and soon the sunlight warmed his face again and he removed his cap, glad to have the fresh sea breeze on his face and head.

He gasped as he looked around him, because the path had brought him to the cliffs of the next bay along from Penhallow Sands. To his right, he could see across the land to the small village and make out familiar shops and buildings. He could also see the beach where he had rescued Catherine then tried to avert his eyes from her appealing curves. Lust shot through him and he forced the image from his mind. This was not the time to allow desire to consume him. He had exploring to do.

He looked left and saw that the path continued, so he followed it until he came to a stile set in a fence. There was an old wooden signpost with three thin pieces of wood nailed to it. The first was too faded to read; the second said Penhallow Sands and pointed in the direction he'd just come from; the third pointed across the stile and towards a path that disappeared over the edge of the cliff. He wiped a cobweb from the sign and saw that it read Plum Tree Bay.

Beyond the fence, in the adjoining field, were lots and lots of trees, and as he looked closer he could see that they were heavy with fruit.

'Plums!' he said aloud, delighted by the sight, wondering if it was why his rental property was named Plum Tree Cottage. Perhaps the cottage had been linked to this land at one point in time; it certainly wasn't far away.

He climbed over the stile and made his way carefully to the top of the path and looked down. The path was steep but it was wide enough for two people to descend side by side, so he'd be safe to use it. He shrugged; he'd come this far so why not keep going?

He descended carefully, keeping his eyes on his feet in case he encountered a stone that could trip him or a bramble that could catch his lace and cause him to fall. When he reached the bottom, he turned and gasped, because spread out before him was the most beautiful little bay he had ever seen.

And it was completely deserted.

He dropped his bag and hat on the sand, stepped out of his clothes until he hadn't a stich on, and ran, laughing, excited and carefree as a child, towards the sea.

Then he dived into the water of the secluded, and seemingly forgotten, Plum Tree Bay.

–

'Good afternoon, gorgeous!'

Jamal kissed Catherine's cheeks as she entered Hairway to Heaven.

'Afternoon, Jamal.'

'You are looking *good*, Catherine. Have you been swimming a lot this week?'

She nodded. 'Every morning, bright and early.'

She hadn't seen Jamal for a few days as he'd been working and she'd been settling into her summer holiday routine of swimming, baking, reading and napping. It was bliss. The only thing that had disappointed her so far about the week was that she hadn't seen the handsome Mark since his rescue attempt five days ago. Every morning, she'd found herself hoping that he might appear at the beach – after all, she went for a swim at the same time every morning – but there had been no sign of him. Perhaps he only ran once a week or perhaps he'd decided to steer clear of the beach after what had happened. She hadn't exactly been brimming with gratitude towards him; she had, in fact, been a bit cold and ungrateful. The thought that she might never see him again left her feeling extremely disappointed, even though her common sense told her that it was probably for the best. After all, what could possibly happen between them?

'I'll just finish up here...' Jamal glanced behind him at the woman sitting in front of one of the salon's mirrors, her head down as she scanned her smartphone. 'This woman is being a pain in the backside. She's bleached her mop so many times it's fit to fall out, but still she insists on being blonde.' He rolled his eyes. 'It has taken some industrial strength conditioning treatment to soften the wiry mess she created. If she's not careful, it'll be a wig next.'

Catherine bit her lip, hoping that the customer couldn't hear Jamal's whispering, but she didn't raise her head so she must have been engrossed in the world of social media.

'Coffee, Catherine?' Bradley peered around the wall that separated the salon from the sinks and small kitchen.

'Please.'

He nodded then disappeared again.

Catherine took a seat on the purple leather sofa in the window and picked up a celebrity gossip magazine. She leafed through it, scanning the articles but not really finding anything of interest, until she came to a section titled 'What's in a Pen Name?' She read through, surprise filling her that some of the authors out there whom she'd assumed were male, were actually female, and vice versa. Sometimes, it was deliberate and others, it was down to reader assumption. She shrugged. An author's gender didn't matter at all, as long as their books were good. But her mind strayed to some of the authors whose books she read and she ran through their names. Some had websites featuring photographs, many were on social media sites like Instagram and they posted personal photos and details of their lives. But not Alex Radcliffe. She had never seen a photo of the author and had no idea what she looked like. Or what *he* looked like. Now what if Alex Radcliffe was a man? A man who wrote such romantic sensual stories. A man who clearly understood what it was like to love and be loved in return. A man who must have a romantic soul, because otherwise, how would he have such a deep understanding of love and passion? He must be... a wonderful man.

'What're you smiling about?' Bradley asked as he set a glass coffee mug on the table in front of the sofa.

'Just thinking about something I read.'

'Anything interesting?'

'An article in here.' She tapped the open magazine. 'About pen names.'

'Thinking about writing, are we?' He raised his perfectly shaped black eyebrows that always caught Catherine's attention because his head was completely hair free.

'Goodness, no!' Catherine laughed. 'I have enough to do without trying to write as well.'

'That you do.' He nodded. 'Are you enjoying the holidays?'

'I've settled into them now and yes... it's bliss. It always takes me about two weeks to unwind and to feel that I don't have to be busy every minute of every day.'

'I know, doll, it can be difficult to relax. I find wine helps. Talking of wine makes me think of parties. And talking of parties... You still want me to bring the cake later?'

'Yes, please! I'm relying on you, Bradley.'

'I hope you're going to like it.'

'I'm sure I'm going to love it.'

Bradley leant over and gave her a hug. 'See you later. Around six?'

'On the dot!'

Bradley swanned away, his skinny jeans clinging to his slim hips, the back of his tight T-shirt featuring the shop's logo of a staircase with a woman at the top, her long hair tumbling down to touch the bottom step like Rapunzel.

It was Catherine's mother's birthday, so she was heading up to Greenacres with Jamal to purchase some wine for the small party they were holding at home. It was a surprise party that Catherine would tell her mother about an hour before it started. She couldn't tell her any sooner as Diana would want to cancel it, but she had to tell her before guests arrived, otherwise Diana would be too surprised to handle it. Catherine took a deep breath then exhaled slowly. It was so challenging and tiring trying to navigate around her mother's emotions and her ups and downs, but Catherine did her best to be a caring and thoughtful daughter. She loved her mother so much and all she wanted was to see her happy. It was why she'd never really made more of an effort to have a life of her own. Other people might think Catherine was strange for that, she'd endured enough snide comments when she'd been a pupil at school and a few later on too, but the ones she'd heard as an adult had been uttered out of concern and pity. She knew that some people in Penhallow Sands pitied her, thinking she was held back by her mother, but they just didn't understand. No one could understand someone else's life unless they experienced it first-hand. They hadn't lived Catherine's life, witnessed Diana's sadness, or held her as the dark clouds had descended and left her at rock bottom. How could Catherine live her own life when her mother needed her so badly? How could she enjoy herself knowing that Diana had no one else, that Catherine and Bob Scratchit were the only reasons Diana got up in the morning? Loving someone meant that you were at least partly responsible for them and Catherine had never been one to shirk her responsibilities.

Thankfully, Diana's very low times didn't tend to last for more than a few weeks at a time and she was able to continue with her daily routine. Catherine had tried to persuade her mother to seek medical help, but that only led to Diana becoming angry and believing that Catherine wanted to be rid of her, so it was easier to keep quiet and just… be there for her. After over thirty years of living with her mother, Catherine had developed strategies for dealing with her moods and she was lucky enough to have a job that she could escape into, and good friends in Jamal and Bradley. She had so much to be grateful for in her life and she always tried to focus on the positives.

Her mother was seventy-six today; she needed Catherine more than ever.

That was how it was. That was how it would always be.

It was the life Catherine had been given when her father had walked away when she was twelve, leaving her to care for her mother, to miss out on the life she might have otherwise had. She had resented him for a long time, had struggled to deal with her anger towards him throughout her teenage years, but she had read self-help books and spoken to Jamal about it, and at some point, she had been able to make a kind of peace with the situation. She wasn't happy about what had happened and never would be. In fact, she was still incredibly sad about it, but she had been able to let go of the vile black anger that could have soured her existence. It was what it was and no amount of sadness or regret would change that. Although she was no fool and she was aware that it had impacted upon her life choices and the way she had handled her romantic life. How could such abandonment not leave scars?

Movement in the mirror opposite, which reflected the street outside, made Catherine turn to look out of the window, and as she did, she caught sight of a figure bobbing up and down. She stood up to get a better look but the figure darted away, so Catherine went to the door and opened it. As she peered out onto the street, she saw a yellow raincoat darting through the crowds on the pavement then disappearing around the corner. It was the same colour as the raincoat she'd seen earlier in the week. Was it the same woman? The one who'd run into a signpost?

'What's up, Catherine?' Jamal asked over the noise of the hairdryer that he was using on his customer.

'Oh… I thought I saw something. Doesn't matter.' She didn't see the point in telling Jamal as he'd likely chase after the person and it was probably a false alarm. Hopefully, anyway.

She shook her head and sat down, taking a sip of her coffee.

There was definitely something strange going on in Penhallow Sands at the moment.

—

Mark stood back and stared at the results of his labours.

The lounge window was sparkling.

It was amazing what procrastinating could do for an author. He might not have written anything substantial this week, but today he'd cleaned the rental cottage from top to bottom (not that it needed it, as it was already spotless), he'd mowed the grass and weeded the flower beds, and he'd done all his washing and ironing.

After his encounter with Catherine Bromley earlier in the week, he'd thought he'd felt a spark of inspiration and he'd rushed back to Plum Tree Cottage to make some notes. His head had been filled with images of a beautiful woman, of a mutual attraction and a dramatic rescue that had led to romance. But that was all that his spark had led to and since then, he'd had nothing more. Not a paragraph, not a sentence, not even a word… Then he'd discovered Plum Tree Bay and he had spent the past two days there, swimming, enjoying picnic lunches complete with some plums that he had picked from the trees, hoping that no one would mind since they seemed to be quite wild and neglected now, as if people had forgotten they were there, and lying on the sand as the sun shone down on him, turning his skin a golden amber. He'd reasoned with himself yesterday that he could have another day down at the bay as long as he made up his word count over the weekend. The freedom he'd felt skinny dipping in the waves and being the only person on the beach had already had a restorative effect upon him and his spirits had lifted considerably. This was life and he was living it, grabbing it with both hands and delighting in it.

And now it was Friday and he'd made a deal with himself that after he'd cleaned and done his chores, he would head up to Greenacres and purchase some local wine that he could enjoy with his homemade plum crumble.

It was a glorious summer day: the air was sweet with the fragrance of roses and honeysuckle, and below that was that salty tang of the sea. Plum Tree Cottage was perfectly placed – within walking distance of the beach and pretty village of Penhallow Sands, but off the beaten track so he could avoid the swarms of tourists and enjoy the peace and quiet of the countryside. He had been frustrated by his lack of writing but he had to admit that he was starting to unwind and his two trips to Plum Tree Bay had helped with that, as had the location and the solitude, being surrounded by greenery and by nature. In the mornings he woke to birdsong and in the dark of night he could hear the hoots of owls and the calls of foxes. Last night, he'd heard a different noise, a kind of snuffling and purring, so he'd got out of bed and gone to the window. At first, he hadn't been able to see anything, but then, a small shape had appeared from the undergrowth and shuffled out along the path and another had followed soon after. Mark hadn't even realised that hedgehogs made any noise.

He peered down at his T-shirt. If he was going anywhere, he'd better take a shower and put some clean clothes on. He didn't want to meet his landlord and land-lady smelling of sweat and window cleaner.

–

'Which do you think she would prefer?' Catherine held up two bottles of wine and Jamal read the labels.

'Will she even drink any of it?'

Catherine shrugged. Her mother didn't drink much alcohol because she said it made her feel worse, but now and then – on special occasions – she did enjoy a glass of good wine, so Catherine wanted to make sure she got one that her mother would approve of.

'Why don't you get them both? Then she'll have red and white to choose from.'

'They're both very tasty, Catherine.' Holly Dryden smiled at her from behind the counter. 'I know I'm biased, but…'

'Okay, I'll take them both.' Catherine placed the bottles on the counter.

'How's everything going with the vineyard these days?' she asked Holly. The vineyard had been developed earlier in the year and if it was as busy there throughout the rest of the summer as it was today, then they must be doing well.

Holly leant forwards over the counter. 'It's going fabu-lously. We're really pleased.'

'I'm so happy for you.'

Holly wrapped both bottles in tissue paper. 'Thank you. I'm really enjoying being home at Greenacres again and... well, you know, it's wonderful being here with Rich and Luke and the shop is doing well too.'

Holly was glowing with happiness. Catherine knew that things hadn't been easy for Holly this past year and that Holly and Rich had split up for a while, but now they were back together, living at Greenacres, proud parents to their baby son, Luke.

'And, of course, Fran's work is selling faster than she can paint.' Holly gestured at the wall behind her where four watercolour landscapes had SOLD stickers underneath them.

'I'm not surprised,' Catherine said. 'They're wonderful.'

Fran Gandolfini was a local artist who sold some of her paintings and pottery via the vineyard shop. Her watercolours of the vineyard and surrounding scenery were very popular. She was also Holly's best friend and had been for as long as Catherine had known them.

The old-fashioned bell above the shop door tinkled and Jamal let out a low whistle. 'Who is that?' he muttered.

Catherine turned around and met the dark green eyes of Mark Coleman. Instantly, heat flooded her cheeks and her heart fluttered. She quickly turned back to the counter and took a few deep breaths. Was this man destined to turn up everywhere she went this summer?

'It's Mark something or other.' She tried to sound nonchalant even though blood was racing through her veins. 'I bumped into him at the beach the other day.'

'I wouldn't mind bumping into him. He looks just like that John Krasinski.' Jamal leant casually against the counter, affecting his flirtatious pose, and Catherine nudged him.

'You are taken. Remember?'

'That I am, sweetie, but a man can look as long as he doesn't touch.' He leant closer to her. 'Besides which, I'm more interested in that shiny dark hair of his. Imagine what I could do with that! In fact, he'd be perfect for Beach Waves. You think he'd want to model?'

'I barely know him so I have no idea.'

Catherine realised that Holly was staring at her quizzically.

'Would you like anything else, Catherine?'

'No. No, thank you. These are perfect.' She paid for the wine then picked up both bottles.

'Hope your mum has a great birthday.'

'Thanks, Holly.'

Jamal went to the door and opened it. As Catherine crossed the shop to join him, Mark was standing in front of the shelves of bottles reading the labels. She was debating whether to say hello when he turned to face her.

'Hello, Catherine. How are you?'

'I'm good, thanks.' She wished the raging heat would leave her face and neck but knew there was no chance of that happening anytime soon. 'How are you?'

'Not bad. Thought I'd treat myself to some wine. Any suggestions?' He glanced at the bottles she was holding.

'No.' She shook her head. 'Uh… what I mean is, yes.' She tucked one bottle under her arm then held up the other one. 'I can't remember which one I picked up. Hold on.' She fumbled with the tissue paper, trying to unwrap the bottle but her palms were clammy and her cheeks were burning and all she wanted to do was get out in the fresh air.

'Here, let me.'

Mark went to take the bottle from her at the same time that Jamal did and it slipped from Catherine's fingers. The sound of the bottle smashing was followed by an aroma of rich berries and oak and Catherine looked down at the floor in dismay.

'Oh no!' she gasped.

'It's all right. I've got it.' Holly appeared by her side with a dustpan and brush. She deftly swept up the mess then returned to the counter for a cleaning spray and cloth.

'I'm so sorry about that.' Mark chewed his bottom lip. 'It was completely my fault.'

'Or mine,' Jamal's deep voice rumbled next to Catherine.

'Let me replace it.' Mark pulled a wallet from his pocket.

'No, it's fine. Don't worry.'

'I insist.' Mark waited until Holly returned to them then said, 'I'd like to replace that bottle of wine, please. And I'll take another one too. I'm really sorry for the accident. It wasn't exactly how I wanted to introduce myself.'

Holly smiled at him. 'Introduce yourself?'

'Yes… are you Holly Dryden?'

'I am.'

'I'm Mark Coleman. Your new tenant.'

'Of course! Wonderful to meet you.'

They shook hands.

'We should be going,' Jamal said to Catherine. 'We need to collect the pastries from the bakery before it closes.'

'Yes.' Catherine nodded. 'Sorry about that, Holly, I really am. Uh… Mark, there's really no need to replace the bottle. I've got white wine here, so the red doesn't matter.'

'Why doesn't he come to the party and he can bring the replacement wine then?' Jamal asked, causing Catherine to turn and scowl at him. 'The more the merrier, right?'

Catherine turned to Mark, knowing that her face would now be a blotchy, red mess. 'He's probably busy. Aren't you, Mark?'

'Actually, no. Not really. But I wouldn't like to intrude.'

'Nonsense!' Jamal shook his head. 'Let me give you my number then you can text me and I'll send you the address. I'll put it straight into your phone if you like.'

Catherine looked from Jamal to Mark to Holly. The vineyard owner was grinning but trying to hide it, and Catherine's blush deepened while her armpits tingled uncomfortably. This was just great! Her best friend had invited this very handsome stranger to her mother's party. At her home. Where her mother would be. Where Jamal would be. Where they would have to make small talk and she would have to pretend that she didn't find this man very attractive and that was going to be a challenge indeed.

'That's settled then.' Jamal handed Mark's phone back to him. 'See you at about six thirty.'

'Fabulous.' Mark smiled. 'See you later.'

'Yes.' Catherine forced her lips into a smile. 'See you then.'

They left the shop and crossed the yard to the car park. Catherine's legs were stiff; her feet felt like lead weights as she tried to lift them and walk normally and she stumbled once and stubbed her toe. She didn't say a word until they were inside Jamal's white Jeep.

'Why did you do that?'

He turned to her and raised his eyebrows.

'Do what?'

'Invite him to the party.'

He gave a throaty chuckle.

'Please, Catherine, tell me you don't fancy him and I'll go back in there and tell him he can't come after all.'

'What the... What on earth makes you say that?'

'It was obvious from the moment you locked eyes with him in the shop. Holly could see it too, I reckon. You started behaving strangely and you went the colour of the wine you spilt.'

'I do not fancy him.' Catherine set the bottle of white wine on the floor between her feet. 'And I have no idea where you got that from.'

'He fancies you too.'

Jamal's shoulders were shaking with laughter. Catherine tapped his arm.

'Cut it out. I am a grown woman with a career and responsibilities and even if I did fancy him – which I don't – it wouldn't matter. There is no point in him coming to the party.'

'There's every point.' Jamal took her hand and squeezed it. 'I've known you for years and I've never seen you react like that to a man. You like him a lot. There's something between you two and if I'm not mistaken, it's attraction. Perhaps it will come to nothing, but I wouldn't be a good friend if I didn't try to set you on the right course.'

'The right course? For what?'

He started the engine and the air conditioning came on. Catherine tilted the vents to make the most of the lukewarm air. It would soon cool down and soothe her heated cheeks.

'For true love.'

'Jamal… just get us to the bakery and stop talking nonsense.'

'Your wish is my command!' He gave a small salute then drove them away from Greenacres and back to Penhallow Sands.

Catherine knew that he meant well. He was a good friend and he was right about her feeling something towards Mark Coleman. But she wasn't even sure what it was, and it made her nervous. But also a bit excited. Catherine liked being in control of her situation, her surroundings and her circumstances. It was something she'd learnt from her mother. For some reason, although she'd only met him a few times, Mark Coleman made her feel as though that control could slip away at any moment. It was unsettling, unnerving and unacceptable. It made her heart beat faster and turned her palms clammy. It did funny things to her core, things that made her think of Alex Radcliffe's novels.

If Mark did bother to turn up at the party later, she'd keep her distance.

Anything else would never do.

Not even a summer fling. No matter how tempting the idea was…

–

Mark paid for two bottles of red wine then gently tucked them into his rucksack. He didn't want to risk dropping them and making more mess on the shop floor. He felt really bad about what had happened with Catherine's wine. He would have spared her that embarrassment if he could have. So far, they didn't seem to be having much success around each other at all, although they did keep bumping into each other. Was it coincidence or something else?

'Right, I need to pop up to the house for a moment, so would you like to come and meet Rich?' Holly asked as she pushed her short blonde bob behind her ears.

'Yes, that would be great, thanks.'

Holly locked the shop door behind them and they walked up towards the big house that dominated the vineyard.

'Have you lived here long?' he asked.

'All my life, apart from a few months when I spent some time… away. My grandparents owned the house and vineyard and when I was born, my mum and dad brought me up there too. My granny still lives there but my grandpa passed away earlier this year, and my mum… well, she passed away when I was a teenager.'

'I'm sorry.'

She smiled at him.

'It's okay. I mean, obviously I miss them both but I also have a lot to be grateful for. Rich, my partner, actually bought Plum Tree Cottage for us to live in. He secretly renovated it and made it beautiful. But as much as I love the cottage, I didn't want to leave Greenacres. My granny and my dad live here and it's nice having our family together under one roof.'

'I can imagine that it would be.' Mark nodded. 'Family is important.'

'Very! Ah, there's Rich!'

Holly waved to a tall, dark haired man who was standing on the doorstep. He waved in return then walked through the small rear garden and let himself out of the gate.

'Rich, this is our tenant, Mark Coleman.'

Mark shook Rich's proffered hand.

'Pleased to meet you.' Rich smiled. He had to be about Mark's age, possibly a bit younger and Holly looked younger again. 'We would have come down to Plum Tree to say hello but we wanted to let you get settled in first. Besides which, I'd hate to be the nosy landlord, appearing without notice and making you feel on edge.'

Mark laughed. 'Oh there's no danger of that. You'd be most welcome, but thanks anyway. It's a fabulous cottage and I've settled in very well.'

'Do you think you'll stay longer than you initially thought?' Rich asked and Holly cleared her throat.

Rich shook his head. 'Sorry. I know I shouldn't ask. It's just that it would be great to have a long-term tenant. We could let it as a holiday cottage, but we already have two here at Greenacres, and with running the vineyard too, we have our hands full. Obviously, the agent takes care of the paperwork now, but even so… it's good to have tenants that we know and can rely on.'

'I'm not sure what my long-term plans are yet,' Mark said, wanting to be honest with this warm and friendly couple, 'but I'll let you know soon. It depends how my writing goes, to be honest.'

'The lettings agent said something about you being an author,' Holly said. 'What do you write?'

Mark paused, wondering how much to say. He wanted to be honest about the work he loved but he also didn't want to go through the whole pen name discussion, not yet at least.

'Fiction. A mixed bag really.' And that was true, because he had written thrillers and romcoms, he just preferred to focus on romcoms now.

'Lovely.' Holly smiled. 'Just imagine, Rich, one day we'll be able to put a plaque on the cottage wall that says "Famous Author Lived Here".'

Mark chuckled. 'Now that would be something. I'll have to ensure that I only write Sunday Times Bestsellers from here on in.'

The couple laughed.

'Is Luke okay?' Holly asked, turning to Rich.

'He's napping in the lounge and your granny is keeping an eye on him.'

'Great. Well, I'd better pop inside… just to give him a kiss… then get back to the shop.'

'What about me?' Rich asked.

Holly shook her head then stood on tiptoes and kissed Rich's cheek.

'There!' She grinned at Rich. 'See you again, Mark. Don't forget to call if you need anything.'

Mark could see that the couple were very much in love. They had that way about them that spoke of trust and intimacy, of a bond that wouldn't be broken. It was heart-warming to see but it also made him aware of what he didn't have, of what he'd lost. He'd thought that he'd have a wife and a perhaps a family of his own by the time he was forty, but at thirty-eight, that seemed unlikely now. Ellie had taken his dreams and his world and everything he'd thought he'd known and dashed them against the rocks. Sometimes, it was hard to stay positive, especially with his author life taking a nosedive too, but although he knew he had to let Ellie go, he couldn't do the same with writing. It was a part of who he was and no matter what else changed in his life, he knew he would always need to write. He just wished he could get going again, but right now he had no idea what it would take to achieve that. However, since meeting Catherine, he was also aware of a flicker of hope. He hadn't so much as noticed another woman since his split with Ellie, at least until Catherine. That had to be a positive thing.

'Are you in a hurry or do you have somewhere you need to be?' Rich asked.

'Not at all.' Mark shook his head.

'Well, seeing as how I have the day off... I'm on holiday this week from my accountancy job... How do you fancy a quick tour of Greenacres?'

'I'd love to take a look around,' Mark replied.

'Let's start with the winery building, shall we?'

They set off around the vineyard, and Mark listened to Rich's clear and enthusiastic explanations of how the vineyard ran efficiently and how long the family had been there and about their hopes for the future of Greenacres. It was fascinating, and Mark wished he'd brought his notepad with him, because he felt sure there must be a novel in there somewhere.

Chapter 5

Catherine checked the downstairs of the cottage for what felt like the fiftieth time that hour. She was worried that she might have forgotten something or that she'd have left something out that shouldn't be there, in spite of Diana's obsession with tidiness – like a stray bra over the back of the sofa or a smelly sock tucked behind a cushion, or that Bob Scratchit would have done a secret poo behind the TV stand (which he only used to do on the odd occasion, but lately seemed to do every other day as he became increasingly elderly). Poor old Bob. But he was still eating and drinking and enjoying cuddles and neither Catherine nor her mother could bear to think about letting him go until there was no other feasible option.

She shook herself. This was no time to be dwelling on Bob's demise. It would upset her and she didn't want that when guests were about to arrive. She popped upstairs and checked that he was settled on her bed, gave him a kiss on his soft head then pulled the door behind her just enough to give him some peace, but wide enough for him to get through should he need to go downstairs for the toilet or a drink.

Thankfully, Jamal and Bradley were already here, both looking smart in jeans and new shirts and filling the house with the smell of expensive cologne. All that was needed now was to tell her mother about the party so she could mentally prepare herself. Not that they'd invited many people, less than ten in fact, but all the same, Diana would need to know before they all arrived.

Catherine steeled herself, peered through the front window to check that no one had got here early, then went through to the kitchen. The French doors were wide open and the sweet summer evening air filled the kitchen, mingling with the scents of cakes and pastries from the bakery owned by Lucinda and Rex Turner. She was pleased to see that her mother was sitting outside on the wicker furniture speaking to Bradley. So far, Diana thought that she was going to celebrate her birthday with Catherine, Jamal and Bradley, and she'd been fine with that.

Bob appeared in the kitchen, took a drink from his bowl then sauntered out into the garden and Catherine shook her head. She had hoped he'd stay upstairs where it would be quieter, but he did love spending time in the garden, so perhaps he'd be all right out there. He jumped up next to her mother and stretched out then rolled over onto his back, his paws bobbing in the air as he relaxed. It was a sight Catherine would never tire of seeing.

'All ready to break it to her?' Jamal asked.

'I guess we have to do it now.' Catherine bit her bottom lip.

'She'll be fine. I encouraged her to have a glass of wine, so she'll be more susceptible to suggestion.' Jamal smiled.

'That sounds terrible, Jamal… like we're trying to take advantage of her.'

'When all we're really doing is trying to give her a good birthday.'

'Come on then, let's do it.' They held hands and went out into the garden.

Ten minutes later, Catherine had told her mother that they had some guests coming and her mother had expressed her shock, stating that she was happy just having Bradley and Jamal there. However, after a few moments of silence, she'd surprised Catherine by draining her wine then asking for another glass, seemingly embracing the change in plans. Jamal had quickly poured more wine then put some music on.

So far, so good.

If the rest of the evening went as well as this, then they should have a good time and Catherine might be able to relax.

Might…

–

Mark stood outside the front door of a small fisherman's cottage. He could hear the gentle hum of conversation and jazz, which he suspected were coming from the garden at the rear of the cottage. He ran a finger under the collar of his white linen shirt. Even though he hadn't done up the top button, he still felt as though it was choking him because he'd got so used to wearing T-shirts. It was a while since the last time he'd been to a party, a while since he'd been out socialising at all, so he wasn't sure what to wear. But he had wanted to make an effort for this evening. He hoped he'd gotten it right.

He took a deep breath then knocked on the door.

It swung inwards and there she was.

Catherine.

She looked radiant in a sleeveless navy-blue maxi dress with thong sandals exposing glittery painted toenails. Her blonde hair was loosely pinned up with a few curls hanging down, just in front of her ears, and he had a sudden urge to wind one of them around his finger. As she smiled at him, the pupils dilated in her big blue eyes and his heart stuttered as if realising how beautiful she really was. He had thought her attractive, of course, but every time he saw her, his inner reaction was so dramatic that it was like seeing her again for the first time.

'Mark! It's good to see you. Come on in.'

He'd timed it so he was a bit later than Jamal had suggested in his text message but not too late. He didn't want to be the first one to arrive but neither did he want to be the last. Again, he wasn't sure what the correct protocol was. Ellie had always dealt with arrangements and known what was right and when to do it – in terms of timing arrivals and gifts. He was on a learning curve, and although it was, at times, a bit daunting, he found that he was also enjoying himself.

He held up the gift bag containing the two bottles of wine he'd bought at Greenacres.

'I brought wine. One to replace yours and the other is a gift for you.'

'You didn't need to do that.' Her cheeks flushed slightly as she accepted the bag.

'I also brought flowers for the birthday girl.'

He held out the bouquet of roses and gypsophila that he'd picked up at the grocer's in the village. The shop looked small from the outside but was actually rather large and they seemed to stock everything a person could want, which was handy, as you never knew when you'd need a pack of cards, some baby wipes, a nose hair trimmer or a Phil Collins CD.

'Come on in and you can give them to her yourself.' Catherine waved him inside.

He followed her through a cosy lounge with an open fireplace, a TV, a sofa and matching chair, and through a short hallway that had a staircase and another two doors. Catherine led him through the first door to the left and into a bright kitchen where people were talking and laughing. At the rear of the kitchen, French doors opened onto a walled garden and he could see that more guests were out there too.

'She's in the garden,' Catherine said.

They went through the kitchen and Catherine approached an elderly lady who was sitting on a wicker sofa with an old-looking cat on her lap.

'Mum, this is Mark. He's renting Plum Tree Cottage. Mark, this is my mother, Diana.'

Mark stepped forwards and held out his hand. Diana stared at him for a moment, then shook his hand limply, and although she smiled, her gaze was cold.

'These are for you.' He held out the bouquet with his other hand. 'Happy Birthday.'

She accepted the flowers.

'Thank you.' Then she turned back to Jamal. 'Why don't you see if our *late*st guest requires a drink?'

Mark wondered if he'd actually heard her put the emphasis on *late*, as Jamal nodded and stood up. What a great start! He'd already upset one of the locals with his tardiness, even though he was trying to arrive at the right time to be sociable. Would he ever get any better at all of this or was he destined to spend his time alone with his laptop? At least he didn't seem to offend his laptop. He mentally shook himself; he was learning, it was all okay.

Back in the kitchen, Jamal poured Mark a glass of wine.

'Look… don't worry about Diana. She can seem a bit… harsh, at first, but underneath it all she's a good person.'

'I didn't think anything.' Mark shrugged.

'You didn't notice that she commented on you being late. Not that you were late.' Jamal held up a large hand. 'She's just a bit… guarded, for want of a better word. Between you and me, Catherine has the patience of a saint to tolerate everything that Diana throws her way. I mean, how many women in their thirties would stay living with their mother because they worry about her being alone?'

Mark nodded, grateful that Jamal had such a friendly, chatty air. He felt comfortable with Jamal, that he wasn't being judged, and it was nice – especially in light of how cold Diana was being.

'Anyway, now that you're here and I have your attention…' Jamal took a sip of his gin and tonic. 'How long is it since you had that lovely hair cut?'

'Sorry?' Mark heard the surprise in his own voice.

'Well, you have hair to die for… or to *dye* for…' Jamal chuckled at his own joke. 'And I'm always looking for models. I'm a hairdresser, you see.'

'Oh!' Mark laughed. 'I'm no model.' He patted his hair self-consciously.

'But you could be. With your lovely skin and those dark green eyes. You have the physique too.' Jamal looked him up and down and Mark tried to swallow his embarrassment. He'd gone from feeling comfortable with Jamal to wondering where this conversation was heading.

'Don't worry, he's not hitting on you.' Another man appeared at Jamal's side and wrapped an arm around his shoulders.

'This is my husband, Bradley. Brad this is Mark Coleman.'

'So, you're Mark.' Bradley nodded.

'You say that like you've heard of me.' Mark took a long drink of wine. Had they been talking about him, then? Had Catherine?

'Jamal said he met you up at Greenacres this afternoon.' Bradley smiled at him as if he knew more but wasn't going to share it.

'Yes, that's right.' Mark nodded. 'Lovely vineyard.'

'It is,' Bradley replied. 'Did you take a tour?'

'Not an official one, but Rich Turner did show me around and told me about some of the changes they've made there recently. It was fascinating to hear about how they run the vineyard and I'd definitely like to have another look around soon and perhaps take a proper tour.'

'You should.' Jamal smiled. 'Anyway… as I was saying, Mark, you could model. If not catwalk… at least hair.' He reached out and ran a hand over Mark's head. 'It's so soft and thick, but let's be honest, you could do much more with it.'

'I could?' Mark was frozen to the spot now as Jamal's long fingers ran though his hair. He wasn't used to having other men caressing his hair, wasn't used to having anyone do it, in fact. He didn't know whether to run or stay there, to laugh or scream.

'Yes, indeed. How do you fancy modelling for me?'

'It's not something I'd ever… uh… thought about before. But… uh…'

'Catherine is going to let me loose on her curls for the competition.'

Mark glanced past the couple to the garden where Catherine was currently speaking to a woman with short dark hair, thick-rimmed glasses and big silver earrings.

Those beautiful curls? She was going to let someone cut them?

'Really?' he asked Jamal.

'Yes, so how about you accept the role as my male model for Beach Waves? You two would complement each other perfectly as my models.'

'What's Beach Waves?' Mark asked.

'It's an annual competition that most local hairstylists enter,' Bradley explained. 'Jamal has won twice before and he'd like to win again. He's so competitive.' He squeezed Jamal's cheek and they grinned at each other.

'You could help us win.' Jamal smiled. 'Please?'

'Uh…' What did he have to lose? Even if Jamal did something awful to his hair, it would grow back. Besides, it was far longer right now than he liked to wear it, almost long enough to tie back and he'd never really seen himself as a man who'd wear a ponytail or a man bun. And, Jamal had said that Catherine was involved in the competition, so it meant he'd have an excuse to see more of her. Any excuse to see more of Catherine was worth taking advantage of. Jamal had also made that comment about Mark and Catherine complementing each other perfectly. 'Count me in.'

'Yes!' Jamal high fived Bradley. 'You won't regret it. I'll text you some more details next week.'

'Great.' Mark finished his wine and Jamal refilled his glass. He had a feeling he was going to need it.

Catherine could see Jamal and Bradley speaking to Mark in the kitchen and she was getting a bit worried. Mark didn't look very comfortable, especially when Jamal was touching his hair, and she wondered what they were speaking to him about. She hoped it wasn't her. But the hair touching suggested Jamal was off on one about styles and probably trying to persuade Mark to go to the salon. He was always working, always keen to attract new customers. She hoped Mark didn't mind.

She excused herself from Fran, who went to sit next to Diana, and made her way through to the kitchen.

'Everything all right?' she asked, placing a hand on Bradley's shoulder. 'I hope these two aren't bothering you, Mark?'

He smiled and shook his head. 'No, we're fine.'

'Absolutely wonderful, in fact,' Jamal said, grinning broadly. 'Mark has agreed to be the male model for Beach Waves.'

'You have?' she asked, meeting Mark's eyes.

'So it would seem.' He raised his eyebrows slightly and Catherine realised that he'd probably been (gently) pushed into accepting the role.

'Well, at least it's not just me,' she said, patting her curls. 'I'm already worried about what he's going to do to my hair.'

'Work wonders with it!' Jamal said. 'Now… let's get the candles on the cake, shall we, Bradley?'

As they walked away, Catherine stepped a bit closer to Mark, feeling self-conscious at being so close to him, yet aware that she wanted to be closer to him.

'Are you sure you want to do it?'

'I don't think I have much choice.'

'Jamal is great with hair. He won't do anything too dramatic, as long as you ask him not to.'

'That's good to know.' Mark's eyes widened and he grinned.

'Here we go!' Jamal reappeared carrying a large rectangular cake on a silver tray. The candles on it formed the number 76 and there was a photo of a cat in the corner of the icing.

'She loves Bob Scratchit… a lot,' Catherine explained, wondering if Mark would think they were mad for having a photo of their old cat on her mother's cake, but he smiled broadly and nodded.

Bradley started to sing Happy Birthday and everyone joined in as they all filed out into the garden.

Diana stood up and wobbled slightly and Catherine hurried to her side. She knew she shouldn't have let Jamal refill her mother's glass more than once. But then, who was she to tell her mother what to do? Her mother was an adult and if she wanted to have a few glasses of wine – at any time, and not just on her birthday – then that was her prerogative.

'You okay, Mum?' she whispered as she gently took Diana's arm.

'Yesh!' her mother smiled back but her eyes were glassy.

'Go on then, Diana, blow out the candles and make a wish.' Jamal set the tray down on the table in front of the wicker sofa and Catherine held her mother's hand while she leant forwards and puffed at the candles. They flickered but didn't go out. So she tried again and this time three of the flames went out. Catherine leant forwards quickly blowing the rest out and everyone cheered.

'What's your wish, Diana?' Bradley asked.

'No, don't tell us,' Jamal said. 'It won't come true.'

Catherine's mother turned to her and took her face between her hands. Catherine winced as her mother's fingers dug into her jaw, her hold a bit too tight. It must be the alcohol affecting her fine motor skills.

'My wissshhh… is that my daughter will NEVER… and I mean NEVER! EVER! fall in love.' Silence fell in the garden. 'Becaushh… men only hurt you and leave you, and my Catherine desherves sho much better than that!' She gave a chuckle then slumped down onto the wicker sofa and belched.

Catherine glanced around at their guests. Most were staring down into their drinks, clearly uncomfortable at Diana's comments, but Fran met Catherine's eyes and mouthed, '*You okay?*' Catherine nodded.

'I guess it's time for cake!' Jamal announced loudly. He brandished a large knife that he went to hand to Diana, but he seemed to have a change of heart as it was in mid-air and he pulled it back to his side, then knelt in front of the table. 'I'll serve, shall I?'

Cake was cut and placed onto napkins then handed out to guests while Catherine slunk inside as soon as she could. Very quickly after that, people started making their excuses to leave, and her spirits sank. Even Fran's warm hug didn't comfort her as it usually would, or the offer of a girls' night out with Holly so they could put the world to rights. Catherine had never been one for going out drinking and she doubted that it would make her feel any better anyway. Her mother had just revealed to the world what they had always suspected. Catherine had heard it enough times growing up: how people thought she was odd for moving back home to live with her mother after university and for not having a relationship and moving out. Catherine was Deputy Head Teacher at the local primary and the last thing she needed was people gossiping about her, but then, what could they say, really? She allowed her mother to dominate her life. And why? Because she couldn't bear to hurt her by standing up to her. Catherine believed that her mother had already been hurt enough for one lifetime by her father; why would she make it worse? She'd happily say this to anyone who tried to suggest otherwise.

In the kitchen, Catherine found Mark drying his hands.

'Have you just washed up?'

He nodded. 'There wasn't much to do.'

'But we have a dishwasher.'

'Oh!' He smiled. 'Never mind. They're done now.'

'Thank you.' She glanced outside where her mother was dancing around on the patio with Bradley to Cyndi Lauper. Jamal was collecting glasses, his gaze flickering towards Diana, his eyes filled with concern. 'Uh… my mother… she's um…'

Mark shook his head. 'No need to explain.'

'But what you saw and heard… she's not normally like that.' And by 'that' she meant that she didn't say things like that *in public*. It was usually reserved for Catherine and occasionally for Jamal and Bradley. 'She's just… she was hurt by my father a long time ago and she never got over it.' She wasn't sure why but she wanted Mark to know why her mother had behaved that way. She had a feeling that he'd understand. There was something about him that suggested that he was empathetic, possibly more so than lots of other men Catherine had encountered in her life – except for Jamal and Bradley, that was.

'It's okay, honestly. People have their reasons for what they do and she didn't hurt anyone else, did she?' He met her eyes. 'Well, I mean… she didn't hurt you, did she?'

'No, no.' Catherine shook her head vigorously. 'I'm used to it. She says things but she doesn't mean to upset me. She's just… hurting inside, I think. It's like she never really got over it all.'

'Well, as long as you're okay.'

He reached out and gently touched her arm, a simple act of reassurance, but one that made goosebumps rise on her skin. Her breath caught in her throat as she wondered what he would do next. Would he hold her close? Press her to his strong chest and kiss the top of her head. Such reassurance would be so good to have. It would be wonderful to have someone to lean on when things got tough, because Catherine had never really had that from a partner; she'd always been alone, caring for her mother and for herself.

'I'm fine.' She nodded, pulling herself together and pushing the thought of being held from her mind.

'I'd better be going,' he said, but he didn't move. 'Unless you'd like me to stay a bit longer?'

She found she did want him to stay so they could talk more, so she could tell him all about what her mother had been like while Catherine was growing up, and about how she missed her dad and about how sad she sometimes felt. Why she suddenly wanted to share that with him, she wasn't sure, but there was something in his eyes that was so kind and understanding. Most people would have run a mile as soon as her mother opened her mouth, but Mark was still here. Cool and calm. Seemingly not judging. But how could she ask him to stay? She didn't know him, not well, and it could be that he was just a very polite man. In reality, he probably wanted to leave as soon as possible and she might not see him ever again.

'No, it's fine. You head on home.'

She walked him to the door.

'Thanks again for the invite, Catherine. I appreciate your hospitality.'

His words seemed so formal but his tone was warm, and once again she found herself longing for a hug. But she knew that if he reached for her now, it would be her undoing and she would crumble. She had to stay strong.

'You're welcome... although, it was Jamal who invited you really. Not that I'm not glad you came, because I am and... Goodness, I need to stop talking.'

'See you again?'

Was that hope in his voice?

'Yes.' She smiled. 'That would be lovely.'

But the smile fell from her face at the bloodcurdling scream that tore through the cottage and echoed through the evening air.

Chapter 6

Catherine ran back through the cottage to the kitchen.

'What is it? What's wrong?' she shouted.

Jamal was holding her mother up as she sagged against him and Bradley was opening cupboard doors.

'She thinks Bob has gone.' Jamal looked up at her, his eyes filled with concern.

'What? Gone where?'

'We don't know but Bradley said perhaps he's crawled into one of the cupboards.' He grimaced. 'He's not outside or upstairs and I checked the lounge while you were seeing Mark out… Hello again, Mark.' Jamal flashed a smile at Mark, who'd followed Catherine, probably as alarmed as she was by the awful screaming.

Jamal helped Diana into a chair then stood behind her with his hands on her shoulders, clearly worried she might fall off.

'Mum, don't worry, we'll find him.' Catherine knelt down next to her mother and touched her arm. 'It's okay.'

'No! It'sh not okay…' Her mother's eyes were already puffy; her face wet with tears. 'Bob has gone and it's all your fault, Catherine. What were you thinking? All those people coming and going scared him and he's run off somewhere. He never goes out the front way anymore but now… he… HASH!' She turned on the chair and wailed into Jamal's shirtfront.

'Try not to worry, Mum. I'm going to do a full check of the cottage and if he's not here, I'll go and search for him.' Catherine's stomach was churning and bile burnt the back of her throat.

'I'll help,' Mark said.

'You!' Diana glared up at Mark. 'Coming round here… shniffing around my daughter like she's yours for the taking. Well, she doesn't want to know. You hear me? So shod off and find yourself another woman!'

'Mum! That's enough.' Catherine folded her arms over her chest. 'Just… stop this now. Please!'

She hurried from the kitchen before she said anything she might regret and climbed the stairs. She searched the bedrooms and the bathroom then came back down and searched the lounge and the small cellar that led off the hallway. But Bob was nowhere to be seen.

Ice-cold fear wrapped itself around her heart. Poor, lovely old Bob. Friend. Confidante. Footwarmer. Heart-breaker.

In the lounge, she sank onto the sofa and buried her face in her hands.

She felt the sofa move as someone sat next to her and a hand touched her arm.

She looked up, expecting to find Jamal or Bradley, but it was Mark.

'It's okay, Catherine. We'll find him.'

He was here. In spite of everything. Offering reassurance and kindness.

She inhaled shakily.

'What if we don't? He must have run out the door when it was open and… he never does that so he might have…' She didn't want to say the words she'd heard from her mother just days before, but they circled in her head regardless: *We have to keep a special eye on him now, because sometimes, when cats get old and unwell, they go off somewhere to die.*

'Do you have a photo of him?' Mark asked.

'Yes. Lots.'

'Well, grab one for me and you'll probably have some on your phone, right? We'll go and look for him. He won't have gone far.'

Catherine went to the dresser in the kitchen, avoiding looking at her mother. She opened it then pulled out the old tin where they kept photos. With smartphones, they didn't print so many anymore, but they always printed their favourites. She chose three photos of Bob then grabbed her cardigan off the peg in the corner.

'We're going to try to find him,' she said quietly, more to Jamal than her mother.

'Okay.' He nodded. 'Take care.'

Jamal was such a good friend and she didn't know how she'd manage without him. He'd seen her and her mother through some tough times and she was lucky that Bradley was just as kind and understanding. If Jamal had married someone else, it could have been a different story. Catherine saw Jamal and Bradley as an extension of her family and she loved them both dearly. But even though she knew they were there for her, they had their own lives and concerns. They weren't there in the way a partner would have been and it was at times like this that she felt more alone than ever.

Back in the lounge, Mark was waiting by the door, his face pale and his eyes filled with concern. She handed him one of the photos.

'Mark… I don't want to sound ungrateful, because I'm not… I am incredibly grateful for your help. But… Why are you doing this?' she asked quietly.

'I want to help you.'

'But my mother just said some awful things to you and yet… you're still here.'

He held her gaze and her heart pounded uncomfortably. She was so emotional right now that she was afraid she might disintegrate.

'Catherine, I'm sorry that your mother feels I'm some sort of predator but—'

'She didn't mean it. She's just—'

'Hey, it's okay. We need to go and find your cat. But I want you to know that I'm here as a friend. A new friend, but a friend nonetheless. I want to help. You need help right now, as we all do at times. Try not to overthink it. I'm sure you'd help a friend in need.'

She nodded because she would. Mark was right.

'I'm so sorry.'

'Your mother isn't your responsibility, Catherine. She's her own person. What she says and does is not a reflection upon you. Okay?'

'Okay. Thank you.'

Catherine had said those words to herself hundreds of time before, tried to reassure herself that she was not responsible for what Diana said and did, but she had never really believed them. Never thought it could be the truth.

Until now…

As they marched up and down the street, Mark tried to keep his expression neutral. He had been shocked by Diana's behaviour but the last thing he wanted to do was to make Catherine feel worse. She was clearly carrying a lot on her shoulders and didn't need his disapproval adding to that. People said mean things. People behaved badly and hurt the ones they loved. Being angry and resentful about that could lead to damage, as Mark knew first-hand. Seeing Diana treat Catherine badly this evening and hurt her, then expect her to come running back was something he'd been through himself – but with Ellie, not his mother. He'd loved Ellie and taken quite a lot from her over the years but she'd been the one to sever ties. For Catherine it was different; this was her mother and it must be hard to walk away from a relationship like that, however much it was hurting you. Society told people that family was everything – it was instilled into the human race from birth – but it wasn't always true. Sometimes, family behaved badly; sometimes they treated you worse than they would treat a stranger.

He found that he wanted to help Catherine, not just with finding Bob, but in any other way he could. He recognised something in her that he had seen in his own eyes in the mirror. It was a deep and secret emotion that she kept hidden most of the time but one that occasionally rose to the surface. It could wear a person down over time and he would hate to see that happen to Catherine. Loneliness was one of the worst feelings imaginable.

They stopped at the end of the street and Catherine turned to him.

'I don't think we're going to find him.'

Her eyes filled with tears and Mark fought the urge to hug her. He wanted to pull her into his arms and tell her he'd be there for her, but he worried about how she'd react. Instead, he squeezed her arm gently.

'Why don't we go a bit further down the hill? Perhaps he's wandered down to the library or even to the beach.'

She nodded but her bottom lip was trembling, so Mark compromised with himself over the desire to hug her and reached for her hand. He closed his fingers around her soft skin, and for a moment she didn't move, but then she curled her fingers around his and held on tight.

Sometimes human contact was the best way to show someone that you were there for them. A way of giving support without saying a word.

–

Catherine slumped onto the sand and pulled her knees up to her chest. They'd been searching for Bob for a while but had no luck. She'd called his name until she was hoarse, knocked on doors in every street and left a message on the vet's voicemail to let her know that Bob was missing. He was chipped and had a collar with a nametag on it, but she knew it was best to cover all angles. He was old and she didn't think he would have gone far, but the thought of going home and finding that he hadn't returned was one she wasn't quite ready to face just yet. She also didn't know if she was ready to deal with her mother. It had been a difficult evening and she wanted to feel more composed before she had to shoulder Diana's grief too.

Mark sat next to her and stretched out his legs in front of him. Dusk had fallen and the sea was a dark carpet stretching away to the horizon. The sky was burnt orange with slashes of mauve and flamingo pink. It was a beautiful evening but she knew it would turn cold when night came. Poor Bob would be out there all alone… cold and afraid… unless…

She covered her mouth with a hand as a sob escaped.

'Hey…' Mark placed a hand on her shoulder. 'It'll be okay.'

She shook her head. How could it be okay?

'I'm so worried about him. I just want him home. Even if… the worst is going to happen, then at least if he's home… it will be… better for him.'

'Of course.'

Mark sat with her, as the colours of the sunset faded and stars emerged above them, twinkling in the endless black. She was grateful for his company, knew that being alone would have been harder, and she found comfort from his presence. She was also grateful that he didn't utter platitudes trying to reassure her, because right now, nothing could. Until she saw Bob again, she wouldn't feel right.

Her phone buzzed in her cardigan pocket so she checked the screen. It was a message from Jamal to say that he'd managed to get Diana to go to bed and now, as long as she was okay, he was going to head home with Bradley. Of course, they needed to go home. They had a full day at the salon tomorrow, with Saturday being one of their busiest days, so she could hardly expect him to stay with her mother any longer. She thanked him and told him she'd be home soon, so he wasn't to worry.

'That was Jamal. I should go back now. Mum's gone to bed but she might wake and I need to be there.'

'Of course.'

'There's no one else around us, you see. I do have an aunt who lives in Devon. She's my mother's older sister by two years but they rarely speak. When I was younger, before my dad left, Mum and I used to visit her a few times a year but they were never really close the way that some sisters are.'

'That's a shame.'

'Well… yes, it is, I guess. My mother said they had a falling out over something when they were younger and there was always some residual tension there. As Mum has aged, she's been less inclined to leave the village or even the house, and so she hasn't been to see my aunty, nor my aunty her for years. Jane has a son, Henry, and he has three children I've never even met. People drift apart.'

He nodded.

'Do you have any siblings?' she asked.

'I have a sister called Summer, who's twelve years younger than me. She was what my mum called a surprise baby. They tried for years after me but had a few miscarriages and thought they were destined to have just the one child. They were loving and supportive and I know I was very lucky, probably a bit indulged at times. Then, along came Summer… one summer, funnily enough.'

'What's she like?' Catherine watched him carefully. His frown had disappeared and a smile played on his lips now.

'She's… frustrating but very sweet. I think that because she was so longed for, she was a bit spoilt, by me as well as my parents, and so although she's very affectionate and funny, she can be a bit stroppy if she doesn't get her own way.'

'Where does she live?'

'With my parents in Surrey. She's twenty-six and still lives at home.' He shrugged. 'But hey… so do lots of people these days.'

'What do you mean?' Catherine bristled, wondering if he was drawing a comparison between Summer and her. 'I'm not living off my mother.'

His eyes widened a fraction, suddenly realising his mistake.

'No, sorry… I wasn't suggesting that for a minute.'

'The cottage is actually mine. Mum worked as a cleaner at the local caravan park after Dad left. She worked really hard to support me and to help me through university. When I qualified as a teacher, I swore to do the right thing by her and I hope I have. I bought the cottage for us.'

He shifted position on the sand and turned to face her. 'Catherine, I wasn't suggesting that you were in any way sponging off your mother. I was merely saying that for my sister, who's an artist on a low and often unreliable income, it's easier to live at home.'

She exhaled slowly. 'I've always supported myself and I always will. I never want to rely on anyone for money or accommodation or… anything else for that matter.'

Being independent was so important to her. As long as Catherine was independent then she'd never need anyone else and she could never be hurt. She knew this. Why let it slide from her mind just because she felt lonely sometimes? Just because she thought it would be nice to be hugged?

She pushed herself up and dusted off her dress.

Mark gazed up at her. In the light from the street behind them, she could see his face but his eyes were dark hollows, so she couldn't read him. She wasn't sure if she'd misunderstood him but she was tired now and the wine she'd drunk at the party had given her a headache. She was also still worried about Bob.

'I need to go.'

'Okay.'

He stood up and sand fell from his jeans.

'I'm sorry if I upset you, Catherine. I really didn't mean to.'

She nodded.

'Thanks for coming tonight and for helping me look for Bob.'

'Take my number and let me know if he turns up, okay?' he asked, pulling out his phone.

She typed her number in and saved it.

He raised a hand as if to touch her cheek then shook his head and tucked it into his pocket instead.

'Take care.'

'You too.'

Catherine walked up the beach to the sea front and shook off her sandals then headed for home. Tonight, had been an emotional maelstrom. Her mother had got upset, Bob had run off, and Mark – a seemingly nice guy – had shown that he might well be like most other men according to Diana. Catherine didn't need the likes of him complicating her life. She couldn't allow anyone to complicate her life; it was confusing enough as it was.

When she reached her street, she slowed her pace, keen to breathe in as much of the night air as she could before she went inside. It was cold and refreshing, cleansing, and she wished it could clear away all of her negative emotions. If only that were possible. If only she could have a clean slate and start all over again.

She reached the cottage and pulled out her phone then removed the case where she tucked her key. A cry from the shadows on the doorstep made her heart leap.

'Bob?'

She turned on the torch on her phone and shone it into the deep doorway.

And there he was.

Sitting up, his tail wrapped around him, his eyes squinting in the torchlight.

But he wasn't alone.

'Oh Bob!' She knelt down and swept him into her arms then buried her face in his soft fur. 'I've been so worried about you. I thought...' Her voice came out strangled so she swallowed hard. 'And who's this with you?'

She crouched in front of the smaller cat and held out a hand. The cat sniffed it then rubbed her chin against Catherine's fingers.

'Let's get you into the warm, Bob. And your new friend too, I guess.'

She had no idea whose cat it was, but Bob seemed to like it, so she'd let it inside for now and try to find out who it belonged to in the morning.

She unlocked the door and carried Bob into the cottage then set him down gently on the sofa. As he gave himself a wash, the other cat wandered around sniffing the furniture and rubbing its chin on surfaces.

Catherine crept around the downstairs of the cottage, turning off lamps and checking that the French doors in the kitchen were locked before returning to the sofa, grabbing the fleece blanket off the back and snuggling up next to Bob. His new friend jumped onto the sofa and curled up by Catherine's feet.

Bob lay next to Catherine, his smelly breath puffing into her face, occasionally patting her chin with his paws, and his familiar purring soon sent her off to the welcome escape of sleep.

–

Mark let himself into Plum Tree Cottage and kicked off his shoes then went to the kitchen and ran the tap. He drank a glass of water down in one go then refilled it and carried it upstairs.

He would never understand women, or people in general for that matter. This evening had been an especially strange one, granted, but he'd thought that he and Catherine were getting on well. He'd seen her mother behave erratically, and knew that there were clearly issues there, but he'd been torn between feeling that it was none of his business and wanting to offer Catherine some comfort. Especially when Bob Scratchit had run off.

Mark hoped that the cat would return home because not knowing what had happened to him was the sort of thing that would haunt Catherine and Diana forever. He also hated to think of animals suffering and the idea of the old cat outside all night was one that he found troubling.

He opened the window and let the cool night air into the bedroom. It was fresh and sweet with the scent of the honeysuckle that grew along the fence outside, and of the roses that climbed up the cottage walls. Beneath it was the earthy scent of flora and fauna from the fields and a hint of woodsmoke. Penhallow Sands was a wonderful location and part of him was starting to think that he could settle here. But then, properties were probably hard to find as why would residents move away? He'd been lucky to find the cottage to rent, but perhaps he would speak to the estate agent about extending his contract, just in case he wanted to stay on. Holly and Rich were clearly keen for him to do so. He also didn't like the thought of leaving Catherine, even after this evening. She'd been tired and emotional and his instincts had screamed at him to help her, to hold her, to stay with her. Manners and socially acceptable behaviour prevented him from doing two of those things, unfortunately, but he wanted to be around for her for the foreseeable future. Catherine had not had an easy time of it and yet she was still a sweet, kind and caring person.

Mark undressed and crawled into bed, enjoying the sensation of the cool sheets against his warm skin. He lay on his back and stared up at the ceiling, listening to the sounds of the animals outside. An owl hooted in a nearby tree and somewhere, in the distance, a dog barked – or was it a fox? He loved being in the countryside.

His muscles relaxed and his breathing slowed along with his thoughts.

Life was complicated – *people* were complicated – and sometimes it was exhausting trying to navigate around them. For years he'd tried to be what Ellie had wanted, but he could never get it right. In fact, by the end of their relationship, according to her, he'd got it really wrong – just by being himself. Perhaps it was better to stay single, to hide away in a countryside cottage and to shut out the rest of the world. To be surrounded by nature and nothing more.

Perhaps…

As he drifted into sleep, Catherine's tearstained face was the last image he saw, and the main one he dreamt about through the night.

Chapter 7

Catherine opened her eyes. The lounge was hazy with early morning light. Her neck was stiff and she was cold. She pushed herself up onto her elbows and saw that the blanket she'd pulled over her on the sofa was on the floor. Next to her, Bob was still fast asleep with his little chin resting on his paws, his tail curled between him and Catherine.

She smiled and gently ran a hand over his fur and he wriggled in response.

Then she froze…

Because she couldn't move her right leg. She peered down at it, wondering why it was completely numb, and when she saw the fluffy ginger cat lying on it, she knew why. She'd let the cat come in last night and it had clearly settled in well.

She eased her leg out from under the cat then waited for the feeling to return before getting up and going to the kitchen. She put the kettle on then opened the French doors and went out into the garden. Birdsong and the scents of the flowers in the pots and beds filled the air. Bob loved the walled garden where he was safe to lounge around and, when he was a kitten, to play as he chased butterflies and bees. He was such a big part of their life and she was so relieved that he was home. He'd been a friend, a housemate and a precious companion. And now he had brought a friend home.

Catherine knew that her mother felt the same about Bob and telling her was that he was home safe would be a huge relief, although she wasn't sure how Diana would feel about his new friend or if she'd let the cat stay. Diana had gone to bed thinking that Bob was still missing and Catherine hadn't wanted to wake her.

A high meowing made her turn and smile, because Bob and his little friend clearly wanted some breakfast.

-

'He does seem very fond of her,' Diana said.

Catherine and her mum were sitting on the garden furniture that afternoon, both watching Bob and his friend as they groomed each other. They'd established that Bob's friend was female earlier that day.

'When I saw that he'd brought her home last night, I couldn't turn her away. He never goes out the front way anymore, so it's as if meeting her was meant to be.'

'I've always said I wouldn't want another cat, but looking at them now, I do hope she can stay. It's like she's given him a new lease of life.' Diana smiled.

The phone started to ring inside.

'I'll get it,' Catherine said, as she got up.

She returned to the garden a few minutes later holding the phone with her palm covering the mouthpiece.

'It's Aunty Jane. Shall I tell her you're in the bath?'

That was the usual routine if her mother's sister ever rang. Catherine would ask if her mother wanted to speak to Jane, her mother would say no, then Catherine would make some excuse up and Aunty Jane wouldn't ring again for a month.

Diana took a deep breath, closed her eyes, opened them and looked across at Bob and his friend again then shook her head. 'No, it's okay, love... I'll speak to her.'

Catherine bit back her surprise.

'Are you sure?'

Her mother nodded, stood up and took the phone then went into the cottage.

Catherine was surprised. She knew that her mother and Jane rarely spoke these days, in spite of Jane's efforts. Catherine did sometimes wonder though if Jane rang to ease her own conscience, as she knew her younger sister would decline to speak to her – with an excuse, of course, that made it easier for both of them. It seemed to work for them both.

But today was different.

Catherine sat back down and picked up her mug of tea. They'd drunk numerous mugs of tea today, trying to cleanse away the memories of the previous evening. What was it about tea and difficult situations? The act of making tea gave them something to do, and there was something comforting about the drink itself, she couldn't deny it, but even so...

Her mother had dealt with the news that Bob had a friend better than Catherine had expected. She'd patted her daughter's hand, apologised briefly for her behaviour the previous day – if in a roundabout way, by saying that she apologised for anything that *might* have upset Catherine – and gone to give Bob a cuddle.

Catherine had texted Jamal first thing to let him know that Bob was home, and when she'd told him that he'd brought back a friend and that she'd need to find out whose cat it was, he'd asked if she needed him to come round. She'd told him she'd be fine. He had a salon to run, after all. Besides which, she thought it would do her and her mother good to have some time alone to talk things through and to solve the mystery of where the cat was from.

Just then, it dawned on her that she'd promised to let Mark know if they found Bob, so she quickly sent a text explaining what had happened then placed her phone on the table. She hoped that Mark was okay and that she hadn't offended him when she'd left the beach. After all, he'd been so kind and helpful, and he deserved better than her marching away like that. She'd been caught up in emotion and slightly hurt by the idea that he might think she was strange for living with her mother. Sometimes she wished things were different, but what could she do? She sighed. This was her life and she had to get on with it.

After she'd finished her tea, she lay down on the wicker sofa and closed her eyes. Yesterday had been exhausting, this morning had already worn her out, and she wouldn't mind taking a nap…

–

'Catherine?'

She blinked, aware that the sun was hot on her face and her mouth was bone dry.

'Ummm?'

'Catherine?'

She sat up.

'Yes, Mum?'

Diana sat next to her, looking thinner than ever in her yellow sundress. 'Sorry about that.'

'How long were you talking?'

'Over an hour.'

'Wow!'

'I know. I surprised myself.' Diana nodded. 'It was good to speak to her though. It's been a while since we had a proper conversation.'

'How is she?'

'Good. Very good in fact. She's so active, you'd never believe that she's seventy-eight. She does yoga and pilates and is a member of a walking club and she has three grand-children and another one on the way. Can you believe that?'

Her mother reached out and gently took Catherine's hand.

'It made me think about you and… how things are for you here.'

'I'm fine.' Catherine shrugged, feeling too sleepy and disoriented for a big conversation right now.

'But *are* you? I mean… we've been so focused on Bob and, well, me and… I sometimes worry that I've held you back from having the life you could have had.'

Catherine cleared her throat to buy some time before replying. Where had all this come from? Her mother had never suggested that she worried about Catherine being held back before.

'I'm only thirty-four, Mum.'

'But you could have a husband and a family now, two or more children of your own.'

'I could… but it doesn't always have to be that way.'

Her mother nodded. 'No, it doesn't, but if you'd been given more freedom to live your life and not so tied to me, then it could have happened that way. I mean, look at Bob. Even at his time of life, he's found a companion.'

'Perhaps. Who knows?' Catherine needed a drink but she also wanted to ask something first, while Diana seemed in the mood to open up and discuss things. 'Why didn't you and Aunty Jane speak for so long?'

Her mother worried her bottom lip. 'It's… complicated. I know you've asked me before and I've fobbed you off saying I was too busy to talk about it and that it was a disagreement but… it's actually more complex than that.'

'Okay.' Catherine nodded. 'Well, I'm here if you want to talk. If you *need* to talk. But right now, if you don't mind, Mum, I'm going to run a bath then go to bed. My head feels like it's going to burst.'

'Of course, Catherine. You go and get some rest.'

They hugged then Catherine stood up and carried their mugs into the kitchen. She glanced back outside before she left the room. Her mother was sitting on the sofa, elbows on knees, her head resting on her hands. She was deep in thought and Catherine wondered what she and Jane had spoken about.

However, even though it wasn't yet gone four, Catherine was ready to take a hot bath and to get a good night's sleep.

An hour later, even after a bubble bath and climbing into her comfortable bed, Catherine had not dropped off to sleep as she had hoped. Instead, she had gazed up at the ceiling as her mind whirred with thoughts.

Her mother had seemed to experience some sort of revelation today following Bob's disappearance and reappearance and after speaking to her sister, Jane. It could be a temporary change in her demeanour, of course, but Catherine hoped it was something more. Sometimes, it took a shock for people to realise that they were hurting their loved ones, for them to accept that something needed to change. Was that what had happened with Diana?

And Catherine's thoughts had strayed, as they often did, to when her life had changed. To that awful day when she'd returned home from school to find her father packing his suitcase as her mother alternately screamed abuse at him and begged him not to go. Diana had been red-faced and puffy-eyed, the tendons in her neck taught and the veins in her forehead throbbing. It had been emotional, ugly, devastating, and Catherine had watched from the sidelines, wanting to ask what had happened, yet afraid to find out the truth. It must have been something truly awful to cause her parents to split up.

Her father had hugged her tight, kissed her cheeks and told her he'd always love her, then he'd opened the door and walked along the path, got into his car and driven away. Catherine had sobbed, fear filling her that she might never see him again, but as she turned, expecting comfort from her mother, she'd seen that it would need to be the other way around. Diana was on the path, curled up, keening with pain and grief. Something had changed in Catherine that day and she'd grown up quickly, left her childhood behind. She'd become the adult in the emotional relationship with her mother and it had never been the same again.

Her father had stayed in touch with phone calls and visits, but it had been strained and awkward. Whenever he came to collect Catherine, her mother had been there glowering on the doorstep or shouting in the background when he rang, so that eventually it had been easier to let the visits slide to special occasions only and to leave the calls unanswered or to accidentally on purpose unplug the phone. It had hurt Catherine to do this but witnessing her mother's hurt was far worse. Catherine had become her mother's rock, and her own pain, grief and wants were pushed away. What else could she do? Her mother needed her strength, so there was nothing left when it came to Catherine's own needs.

But now, her mother had taken a step forwards in talking to Jane. It was a small step, but a positive one. Could Catherine take a step forward too? Her father had stayed in touch with emails and occasional phone calls and had asked to meet many times, but Catherine had always made an excuse about work or other commitments.

Catherine realised that she would never get to sleep if she didn't act on the impulse that was nagging at her now, so she grabbed her phone and fired off a brief email to her father, asking how he was and telling him that she'd like to see him soon – if he wanted too. It was risky, making her feel vulnerable, and she wondered how her mother would react if she found out, but it was something she had wanted to do for a long time. Life was short, people wouldn't be around for ever, and Catherine wanted to find some peace of mind – something that had eluded her for what felt like a lifetime.

She shut her phone down, placed it back on the bedside table then snuggled down under the duvet. Tomorrow would be a new day. She hoped it would be a good one.

Chapter 8

Mark strolled along the sea front, admiring the view. Penhallow Sands really was a glorious location and he was glad to be there, especially during the summer months. He wondered what it was like through the rest of the year and whether he'd have the chance to find out. Aside from the views and the lovely secret bay he'd found, the people were friendly, the village and beach were busy – but not horrendously so – and the town had everything a person could need. And, of course, he'd met Catherine.

Catherine…

She had sent him a text the day after Diana's party to let him know that Bob had come home; in fact, he'd been waiting when she'd got home from the beach. He had cuddled up to her on the sofa along with a new friend – a cat he'd brought home with him as if it was something he did every day. That had made Mark smile. They'd been worried that Bob had gone off somewhere to give up on life and instead, he'd brought a lady friend home to stay. Catherine had thanked Mark again for helping to search for Bob and said that she would speak to him soon.

Mark wished there was something he could do to help with Catherine's situation with her mother, but he barely knew her and it would be wrong of him to interfere. It was similar to his own situation with Ellie. Mark had grieved for what he'd had with Ellie. She'd always been there in his life – since he was a teenager – and that was a long time to let go of and no one could really help him with that. Although, having said that, the pain of their break-up was no longer as sharp, no longer as present in his life. Perhaps it was being in a different location, being surrounded by people who hadn't known Ellie, who hadn't known him and Ellie as a couple. Here, Mark was himself, not Ellie's 'other half', not the man she'd wanted him to be. It was liberating and he liked the freedom of being able to eat what he wanted without criticism, to speak as he wished without knowing that she was rolling her eyes if he mentioned a band she disliked or thought wasn't 'cool', and of not having to suffer the insecurity that had crept up on him in their final months together when Ellie declined his third proposal then kept dropping another man's name into their conversations. Looking back on it now, Mark could see that she'd been testing him, gauging his reaction, possibly even preparing him, as the man she'd kept naming was the one she'd later moved in with.

He shivered in spite of the warmth of the sun on his face and started to walk up towards the library. He would have liked to have dropped in to see Catherine, but didn't think that Diana would appreciate him stopping by, and even if she didn't mind, he still didn't want to make a nuisance of himself. He'd told Catherine to let him know if she needed anything, even just to talk to someone, and she'd replied to thank him. That had been two days ago – no time at all in the grander scheme of things – but he kept checking his mobile anyway, just in case.

Outside the library, he took a few deep breaths of the lovely air, savouring the scents of the flowers that seemed to bloom everywhere in Penhallow Sands. Most cottages had window boxes and hanging baskets bursting with different coloured flowers, including the library, which had two hanging baskets outside the front door. The air was also filled with birdsong and the sounds of laughter that occasionally carried up from the beach. It all combined to lift his heart and to make him feel lighter than he had done in ages.

He pushed the door and walked inside, blinking as his eyes adjusted. The library smelt, unexpectedly, of baby products, and as he walked towards the counter, he could see why. The diminutive librarian, Maggie – who had introduced herself during his last visit to the library when he'd signed up for a temporary membership – had what looked like an overnight bag on the counter and she was packing it with towels, blankets, tiny clothing, nappies and a variety of bottles of cream and baby hair and body wash, which Mark assumed must explain the smell.

'I thought I could smell babies.' He smiled at her.

'Oh!' She laughed. 'We're very quiet this morning so I'm just checking my hospital bag.'

'Do you always bring it to work with you?'

She shook her head. 'Only this past week. I take it everywhere now to be honest. This is my fifth baby, and my labours are very quick, so I want to be ready… just in case. I'm hoping for a home birth like last time, but it's always good to be prepared in case I have to go to hospital.' She grimaced.

Mark eyed her swollen belly, which was hard to miss in the bright cerise sundress. She did look as though she might need to make a dash to hospital at any moment.

'Anyway... Mark, isn't it? I'm intrigued. How do you know what baby products smell like?'

He smiled. 'Oh... I had to do some research once for a book and, being true to my art, I bought a range of baby products to smell and test.'

He ran a hand through his hair and she smiled.

'Baby shampoo is lovely stuff! I'd be lost without it. My children scream if they get water in their eyes, let alone any shampoo that might sting. And as for my husband...' Her grin was contagious.

'Yes, I have sensitive eyes too, so I did appreciate the no-sting factor.'

'And you say you're an author?' She frowned at him.

'Guilty!' He winced affectedly, as if it was something to be ashamed of, but he'd become used to a variety of reactions f rom people when he told them what he did for a living. Mostly, people were curious and positive, but a few times he'd encountered negativity from those who didn't see writing as a 'proper' job.

'That's wonderful! What do you write?'

'I... uh...' Did he out himself now? Admit that he was, in fact, an author of romantic comedies? There was no good reason not to and Maggie was a librarian, so she would be a good person to start with.

'Ouch!' Suddenly Maggie hunched over.

'Are you all right?'

She exhaled slowly then stood up. 'Yes, I'm fine. Braxton Hicks can be painful things. That one really stung.'

'Those are the practice contractions, right?'

'Yes! You're good at this. What else do you know?'

'That labour can be fast or slow, some women suffer days of contractions, which must be awful and some men apparently endure sympathy pains. And I know all the... ahem... biological stuff... and that the best way to regulate a newborn's temperature is skin-to-skin contact and—'

'Gaaaaah!' Maggie gripped the counter and stared at him, her eyes wide as saucers, a sheen of sweat covering her upper lip. 'I'm glad you know so much, Mark, because this baby is on its way.'

'What?' He held up his hands. 'Now? But... how? Why?' He looked around frantically but there really was no one else in the library. Why did it have to be graveyard quiet today of all days? 'Who can I call? Doctor? Ambulance? Midwife? The father?'

She shook her head. 'Help me over there. To the reading corner... then bring my bag!'

Mark took her arm and helped her shuffle to the corner where she clung to a shelf of self-help manuals while he ran back to get her bag. He also grabbed a bottle of water from the counter and Maggie's smartphone.

'Okay... I'm back.' He pulled a blanket from the hospital bag and opened it out then eased Maggie down to sit on it. 'Now shall I call an ambulance?'

She shook her head, her teeth pressed together as she pushed small breaths out between them. 'Not ambulance. Midwife. Number in contacts.'

Mark searched her contacts, called the midwife and put her on speakerphone then Maggie explained – between contractions, that were coming very close together – that she wasn't far off delivering. The midwife said she'd be there in ten minutes.

'Now... husband... Fred.' Maggie nodded. 'Quick!'

Fred was notified, but currently stuck in traffic on the way back from a meeting, so wouldn't be with them for at least half an hour. Mark did his best to reassure Fred that he knew what he was doing and that the midwife would be with them soon – he didn't want Fred rushing and ending up in a road accident.

'Where are your other children?' he asked Maggie.

'Mother-in-law.'

'Shall I call her?'

'No! Not her.' Maggie grimaced. 'We don't need the children running around here while I'm trying to stay calm.'

Mark's hands were clammy and his heart was racing. 'What next then? I could run outside and see if I can find someone.'

Anyone. Anyone will do as long as I don't have to do this alone.

'No! Please stay with me.' She gripped his arms and he knelt in front of her. His insides felt like they were dissolving. This was awful! He was alone with a pregnant woman in labour. He didn't want to see anything he shouldn't or to show fear because she needed him to be strong but this was like being in an actual nightmare.

'Okay… in the bag are some towels. Get them out ready.'

'It's… the baby… is coming now? Definitely?'

'She… is… coming… *very* soon.'

Mark pulled the towels from the bag with one hand, because Maggie was still gripping his other one, then he set them out in front of her and helped her to shuffle over them, while still trying to avert his eyes from actually seeing where the baby was coming from.

'Owwwww!' Maggie groaned, an animal-like sound that made the hairs on Mark's arms stand on end. Her legs started trembling uncontrollably. 'I need to get my knickers off!'

She wriggled around and somehow managed to slide them down while still holding on to Mark.

'Here comes another...' Maggie grimaced.

'Owwwww!' He uttered as her nails dug into the soft flesh of his wrists.

There was a loud pop and a gush of water that soaked the top towel and splashed Mark's shorts. 'What was that?'

'My waters broke. I thought you knew about labour.'

'I do but there's *so much* water. It's like someone just pulled the plug out of the bath.'

'You're funny.' Maggie offered a tight smile.

'Humour helps in many situations.' He grimaced. 'But not this one, perhaps.'

Maggie blew out a deep breath then met his eyes. 'She's coming... can you see the head?'

'I can't.'

'That's because you're not looking.'

'I know.'

'Look!' She shook him.

'I can't look down there.' Panic had gripped him and sweat trickled down his back, soaking into his T-shirt.

'You have to! Please!'

'Okay...' He nodded. 'Okay. I can do this. But I don't want to. Is that clear?'

'Yes!' She growled at him. 'Just look!'

He leant back and glanced downwards, keeping one eye firmly closed. Yep. There was something going on down there but he couldn't tell one thing from another.

'I think there's a head.'

'Yes... it's there. I can feel the stretching.'

'Ugh...' He shook his head.

'Don't be such a wimp!' Maggie glared at him. 'I'm the one pushing a melon out of my vagina.'

'Okay... Sorry.'

'I'm going to push now. But first, can you check that the cord isn't around the baby's face or neck.'

'Me?'

'I can't see anyone else around here.'

He reached out a hand then pulled it back. He really couldn't do this... it was a step too far coming right after a step too far.

'Fine. Support me while I check.'

He held her one arm as she moved from her knees into a crouch and checked around, then she met his eyes again.

'It's fine. Ouch! Bloody hell, I always forget how much this bit stings!'

Maggie panted a few more times.

'Catch the baby, Mark! NOW!'

He ducked and put out his hands like a rugby player diving for the ball, and suddenly, there was a small warm wet shape in his hands. He held it out above the towels, terrified it would slip from his grasp.

Maggie pulled one of the towels up and slid in under the baby and Mark wrapped it around the wriggling form just as it let out a cry.

'Should I cut the cord?' he asked, hoping she'd say no because the thought was making him queasy.

'No, it's fine. The midwife will do it when she gets here.'

Maggie wriggled around so she was sitting on the spare towel. She held the baby against her chest and gazed down at her, checking her over and speaking softly to her.

Mark sank back onto his heels and looked at his trembling blood-stained hands and arms.

'Are you okay?' Maggie asked, her pretty face flushed, her hair plastered to her forehead and her eyes filled with emotion.

Mark nodded, but he didn't trust himself to speak. He'd just helped to deliver a baby. A real baby! A new life had emerged into the world in front of his eyes and it was a beautiful baby girl. It all felt so surreal and yet so amazing.

'Thank you,' Maggie said.

Mark swallowed hard to dislodge the lump from his throat then croaked, 'My pleasure.'

And it was a pleasure. Life was a rollercoaster and no one knew what was coming next, but the ups made the downs more bearable, and this was most definitely an up. If a completely terrifying one and one he'd prefer not to make a habit of.

–

Mark had left the library that morning without any books, but with a sense of wonderment at what he'd experienced. He couldn't even recall what book he'd gone to look for, but he'd come away far richer and more enlightened regardless. The midwife had arrived as baby Molly turned five minutes old, then the cord had been cut and the afterbirth delivered – something Mark had not helped with and had avoided looking at. Instead, he'd done his best to clean up around them and made them all a well-deserved cup of tea in the staff kitchen. Molly was declared fit and healthy, and as Maggie drank her tea, Molly took her first feed.

The midwife had praised Mark and he'd turned tongue-tied and bashful, unaccustomed to such compliments. Maggie's husband, Fred, had arrived just as Mark had been closing up the library for Maggie, and Fred had shaken Mark's hand and said he owed him a pint at the pub one day soon.

Mark had picked up a sandwich and a takeaway coffee from Shell's Shack then sat and watched as the tide came in, seeing but not seeing the other people on the beach as they splashed in the water and sunbathed on the warm sand, hearing but not hearing the shouts and laughter around him. His life had not taken the direction he had once thought it would, but in spite of that, he didn't mind the direction it was heading in now.

Life was for living, one day at a time, and he felt that he was starting to learn how to do exactly that.

Chapter 9

'Your mum seems to be dealing well with things,' Jamal said as he and Catherine strolled down to the main street of Penhallow Sands.

Jamal and Bradley had gone to Catherine's cottage after work with a bottle of wine and some fish and chips. After they'd drunk the wine – which Diana had declined – and eaten the food, Catherine had felt more relaxed. It had been five days since Bob had returned and although she'd asked around and put up a sign at the vet's, no one had come forward to claim the little ginger cat. So they had decided to let her stay. Since her arrival, Bob had been different: more energetic and he seemed happier, as if having company of his own kind had helped him to find a new lease of life. His little friend snuggled with him, washed him and had even encouraged him to play with a feather she'd found floating in the garden. It was adorable to watch and had made Catherine quite choke up, as had watching how Bob gently patted Ginger, as they'd named her, when she rolled around in front of him in the patch of catnip in the flower bed.

Jamal had insisted on bringing dinner for Catherine and Diana this evening and Catherine suspected it was because he wanted to see Bob with his new friend.

As they ate, Jamal and Bradley had entertained Catherine and her mother with some anecdotes about the people they'd had in Hairway that day. When they'd cleared the plates away, Jamal had asked Catherine to go to the pub with him and Bradley. She'd been about to use her mother as an excuse, but Diana had insisted that Catherine go, telling her that Aunty Jane was expecting her to ring at eight.

'Almost losing Bob then seeing him with a feline companion seems to have changed her somehow. I don't know exactly why but she's been more reflective the past few days and she's spoken to my aunty on the phone several times.'

'The sister she never speaks to?'

Catherine nodded. 'They rarely used to speak, but now they've had three conversations since the weekend.'

'Well, that's a good thing, right?'

Jamal squeezed her shoulder. He was so tall that his hand rested comfortably on her shoulder as they walked. Catherine always felt very small next to him.

'I hope so. It would be nice to think that Mum could have someone else in her life.'

'Someone other than you?' he asked.

'Well… yes.'

'I agree. Much as I love Diana, she relies on you far too much. You need to have your own life and you're not getting any younger. And, of course, Bob has a friend now, so why shouldn't you?'

Catherine pressed her lips together. Jamal always said exactly what he was thinking. He'd seen Catherine's relationship with her mother over the years and knew how Catherine sometimes struggled to help Diana. It was hard to be objective when they were so close. As for the comment about her age, she knew Jamal was just stating fact – she wasn't old by any stretch of the imagination, but time wasn't slowing down either.

'And on that note, Catherine, I just wanted you to know that Mark is coming this evening.'

Catherine's stomach flipped. 'What? But why?'

'What and why?' Jamal rolled his eyes. 'He's a nice guy; he hasn't got any friends here and I thought it would be good to see him again. I like him. He's got that decent aura about him.'

'Decent aura?'

'Yes. He has integrity and he's not the type to love and leave you.'

'I'm not looking for a type. I'm not looking for any man, in fact, good aura or not.'

'Did I say that was why I invited him?' Jamal affected an air of innocence. 'He was kind and patient the night of Diana's party and, Bradley and I agreed, very patient with your mother. He deserves a drink to say thank you. Besides, he might have a broad general knowledge and help us win the quiz.'

'So you have an ulterior motive in addition to your matchmaking?'

'It's not matchmaking, but yes… it doesn't hurt to have an extra team member, does it?'

'I guess not.'

'I didn't say anything earlier because you might have decided not to come, knowing that Mark would be there, plus, I didn't know how your mother would take it. She didn't seem too keen on him but then I doubt she'd approve of any man who showed you attention, unless he was gay.'

'You're probably right about that, although with the way she's changed since Bob's return, I'm not even certain about how she'd react now. Still, I'd rather not push her backwards when she seems to be taking positive steps. One thing at a time, I guess.'

They walked on in silence until they reached the shop.

'I hope Bradley's mobile *is* in there, otherwise goodness only knows what he's done with it.' Jamal pulled the keys from his pocket. 'I can't believe he didn't notice that he didn't have it with him as he's usually glued to the damned thing. I swear he even takes it to the toilet with him. It's like an extension of his arm.'

Bradley had gone up to the village pub to keep them a table for the weekly pub quiz and Jamal and Catherine were going to the salon to collect Bradley's mobile. He'd have gone himself, but Jamal had insisted, and Catherine knew that it was because he wanted five minutes alone with her.

Outside Hairway to Heaven, Jamal paused while he looked for the correct key from the bunch he had on the key ring. There were about ten keys on there that all looked the same but he refused to get rid of any of them just in case he needed them. He didn't know what most of them were for, but said that he'd clearly needed them at some point, and he just knew that if he binned any of them, he'd regret it.

'Did you leave a light on?' Catherine asked as she peered through the glass. It wasn't yet dark, but dusk had settled over Penhallow Sands and she could definitely see a glow from inside.

'What? No... I don't think so. Unless Bradley did. Forgetting his mobile and leaving lights on... I'll have to feed him more oily fish at this rate.' Jamal shook his head just as he found the shop key and slid it into the lock.

'There's definitely a light on out the back.' Catherine rubbed the glass to clear the mist created by her breath. 'And it's... moving.'

Jamal turned to her and his big brown eyes widened.

'What should we do?' she asked, concern filling her.

'I... uh... oh blimey.' Jamal looked around them as if searching for the answer.

'Could a customer have got stuck in there, Jamal? Perhaps they went to the toilet and... fell asleep, then woke up to find themselves locked inside and now they're using the torch on their mobile to look around?'

'Catherine...' Jamal put his hands on his hips. 'I always bleach the loo before we leave. There was no one in there then and besides which, who falls asleep on the loo?'

'Okay... Well, in that case... perhaps it's just a bulb flickering.'

'Perhaps.' Jamal took a deep breath. 'I hope so. Right... I'm going to have to go in and check.'

'Jamal, no one is going to want to mess with you.' Catherine looked up at him. 'It's not like you're tiny or puny.'

'What, because I'm a big black guy with a deep voice?' He shook his head. 'I know I might look a bit intimidating if you don't know me, but I hate violence, Catherine, you know that.' He shook his head. 'What would I do if there's someone in there?' He chewed his bottom lip.

'I'll be right beside you.' Catherine braced herself. She wouldn't leave Jamal alone in there; they were best friends and she'd have his back. 'Besides which, who breaks into a hair salon? Unless they're looking to steal a perming solution or a curling tongs.'

'You're right,' he said, then he pushed the door open slowly. 'I'm sure it's no organised crime gang. Let's check it out.'

Inside the shop, they tiptoed towards the doorway that led to the sinks, the toilet, the office and the small kitchen area.

'Hold on,' Jamal whispered, then picked up a hairdryer.

In spite of the tension, Catherine had to bite back a giggle.

'Jamal, what are you going to do? Blow-dry them to death. Halt, thief, or I'll freeze you with the cold setting.' She snorted and Jamal frowned at her.

'Be quiet! This isn't funny.'

'I know. Sorry, I'm nervous and you know that can make me giggly.'

Catherine glanced around the shop, looking for something to brandish, just in case there was a thief out the back, and she needed a weapon. She settled on a long-handled broom that had been propped up against the back wall. She'd watched enough TV to know that you could cause some damage with a stick. The only problem was that there was a brush at the end of it and it was covered in hair. Perhaps she could repulse the intruder with that.

The light out the back moved again and there was a loud bang coming from the office.

'Who's there?' Jamal shouted, his deep voice cutting through the gloom.

The light went out and suddenly, the sink area seemed very dark indeed.

The office door squeaked open and a figure dashed past them towards the toilet.

'Stop, thief!' Jamal shouted as he turned the light on and Catherine winced at the brightness. Jamal was standing in the middle of the sink area, holding the hairdryer in front of him with both hands like an oversized gun.

'He went that way!' Catherine pointed at the toilet door that was open a fraction.

Jamal hurried to the door and kicked it forcefully, which sent it banging against the wall of the toilet then straight back towards Jamal, hitting him in the nose.

'Ouch!' He hunched over, holding his face.

'Jamal!' Catherine rushed to him but he waved at the toilet.

'Get him, Catherine…' His voice now had a nasal quality and Catherine realised the door had hit his nose hard.

Catherine held the broom in front of her and pushed the door open slowly. It led to a small area with a sink then the toilet cubicle itself. She could hear shuffling and panting from behind the inner door and her heart threatened to burst from her chest.

'Who's there? I'm warning you… I'm armed.' She realised that she might not have said the right thing. After all, if the intruder had a weapon too, they might shoot through the door. Shoot? They were in Cornwall and whoever it was had broken into a hair salon. It wasn't exactly the likely scene of an armed robbery. Still, it paid to be cautious. 'What I mean is… I have a… a stick and I'm not afraid to… to…'

Stop talking, Catherine!

Her mobile started vibrating in her pocket so she pulled it out. Glancing at the screen, she saw Mark's name.

She swiped answer and put him on speakerphone. At least there would be an audio witness.

'Catherine?'

'Yes. Listen, Mark—'

'Are you in the salon?'

'Yes, why?'

'I was on my way to the pub and I saw you and Jamal go in but I'm outside and the lights are off.'

'We're out the back. There's an intruder.'

'What? I'm on my way in!'

'No! Don't...' But he'd gone so Catherine tucked her phone back in her pocket again and gripped the broom with both hands.

'Catherine?'

'Mark?'

He appeared in the doorway and she was so relieved to see him, she ran and hugged him.

'You okay?'

'Yes... but there's someone in there.'

More shuffling and panting came from behind the door. Was someone trying to squeeze out a big panic poo? She'd read about that happening to burglars when their adrenaline got so high that they suddenly needed the toilet.

'Let me.' Mark reached for the broom then tapped it against the door. 'Ready or not, I'm coming in!'

He pushed the door but it was locked from the inside, so he took a few steps back then ran at it. It gave under his weight and Mark staggered into the cubicle with Catherine behind him.

Right in front of them, hanging through the frosted-glass sash window that led out to the carparking space behind the shop, was a bottom and a pair of legs. Legs that were wiggling furiously but going nowhere.

Mark poked the legs.

'Ouch… Get off me!' The shout came from the other side of the glass.

'Are you stuck?' Catherine asked.

'No… I'm getting out now…' The figure moaned and the legs waggled again but it didn't budge.

'What's going on?' Jamal asked as he entered the toilet.

'He's stuck.' She pointed at the window then frowned at him. 'Where were you all this time, Jamal?'

'I thought I'd broken my nose. It stunned me for a moment.'

'Were you checking it in the mirror? While we were about to accost the criminal?' She shook her head and Jamal looked down at his feet.

'Sorry, but my nose is important. It's right in the middle of my face. Anyway, you had Mark with you, and he seems to be managing quite well.'

'Right,' Mark said to the intruder, 'I'm going to try to pull you back this way by holding your ankles.'

'No! Push me,' the voice outside said.

'What and let you run off?' Mark tutted. 'No chance, buddy. You're coming this way then we're phoning the police.'

'But I haven't done anything wrong.'

'You broke into the salon,' Jamal said, stepping forward and giving one of the legs a tug.

'The window wasn't locked and it slid right up.'

'That doesn't give you the right to climb through it,' Catherine said.

'I'll go outside and try to push him in while you two pull.' Jamal gestured at the door.

'Right.' Mark nodded. 'We need to push the window up a bit first to create more room.'

Ten minutes later, the window remained firmly wedged and pushing and pulling had made no difference. The intruder was firmly lodged in the window and wouldn't go backwards or forwards.

'It looks like a very old frame and there's probably a fault with the sash cord itself, so I'll need to take a closer look,' Mark said. 'It could have snapped or become jammed in the frame.'

'Ok?' Catherine looked at the glass. 'What do you need?'

'A screwdriver and some screws if you have any here, Jamal, and something to hold the window open once I've found the cord.'

Jamal left the toilet cubicle, then rejoined them and handed Mark a small toolkit. 'I keep one in the back for minor repairs. You never know when you'll need to change a fuse or alter the mechanism on one of the salon chairs.' He gave a small shrug.

Mark set about examining the window and Catherine stood next to him holding the tools. As he worked, she felt a bit like she was assisting a surgeon during an operation because of Mark's focus and the tense silence in the toilet cubicle. At one point she even handed Mark some toilet paper to wipe his brow.

Finally, Mark turned to Catherine and said, 'Okay, let's try it now. Jamal, do you want to go back outside?'

Jamal nodded and left the room. When he was the other side of the window, Mark gave a grunt and the window slid up then he locked the sash in place. The intruder slid into the toilet cubicle feet first and landed on the floor.

'I can't feel my legs,' he said from underneath the beanie that was pulled down over his ears with just his eyes peering out.

'They'll be all right in a minute,' Mark said then he closed the window again and locked it.

When Jamal reappeared, he grabbed the intruder by an arm and led him through to the shop.

'How did you know how to do that?' Catherine asked Mark as he tidied up in the cubicle.

'I used to do some work with my uncle who has a window sales company. I learnt to remove old windows, fit new ones and so on. Old sash windows can often cause problems, especially when there's an issue with the cord.'

'Impressive.' She smiled.

'Yeah… I knew the knowledge might come in handy one day.' He looked at the window. 'Problem is, I don't have the tools to fix it properly and it could stick again, so Jamal will probably need to get a new one fitted. The window frame is so old and rotten anyway, I'm surprised it hasn't fallen in with a gust of wind.'

He shook his head.

'Mark… I heard on the grapevine that your talents extend in other directions too.' Catherine looked up at him shyly.

'In what way?'

'Delivering babies.'

'You heard about that?'

'Jamal told me. It's all around the village that the handsome stranger staying at Plum Tree Cottage safely delivered Maggie's new baby.'

Mark's cheeks coloured and he dropped his gaze to his feet.

'Well, you know… I was the only one there. What else could I have done?'

'I doubt many people could have done what you did.'

He shrugged.

'Excuse me!' Jamal's voice boomed from the shop. 'I need a hand.'

'Better go help Jamal,' Mark said, clearly relieved to get the conversation off him.

In the salon, the intruder was sitting in a swivel chair in front of a mirror and Jamal was leaning on the back, staring into the mirror, presumably trying to intimidate the small man.

'Now… we're going to call the police and you can tell them why you were in the shop.' Jamal placed his big hands on the back of the chair.

'No… please don't call the police.' Without the window muffling the voice and the confined space of the toilet cubicle distorting it, it seemed higher, more feminine.

'Then tell me why you were in my salon.'

Catherine approached the chair and peered around at the intruder. She reached out and carefully removed the beanie.

'It's you,' she said. 'The woman who was spying through the salon window.'

Jamal gasped. 'Why were you in my shop?'

The woman's bottom lip wobbled and a tear ran down her cheek.

'Look, why don't you explain, then we might be able to come to some sort of arrangement,' Catherine spoke softly, her teacher training kicking in. This woman was clearly troubled and wouldn't have broken into the shop unless she was looking for something – probably money or something to sell to get money for drugs. That was the most likely explanation.

'I… was… searching… for…' The woman started to sob and Catherine was filled with compassion. This woman was a lost soul in need of help and support, not retribution and punishment.

'For what?' Catherine asked.

'For…' The woman met Catherine's eyes. She looked tired and thin and stressed.

'Yes?' Jamal leant forwards so his face was right next to the woman's. 'This had better be good.'

'Jamal.' Catherine shook her head quickly. Upsetting the woman further would just stop her talking.

'For… your plans.'

'My plans?' Jamal frowned, standing up straight so quickly that his spiky dreads bounced.

'Yes… for… Beach Waves.'

Jamal's mouth fell open as he looked at Catherine.

'That's why she was spying on us before.' He turned back to the woman. 'Wasn't it?'

'Yes.'

'But why?' Catherine asked.

'Because… I need to win.'

–

'You *need* to win?' Jamal asked, folding his arms across his chest.

Mark was looking from Catherine to Jamal to the intruder and back. He couldn't quite believe this was happening. If he remembered correctly, Beach Waves was the competition Jamal had said he'd like Mark to be his hair model in. Was it actually so competitive that hairdressers were prepared to break into each other's salons in order to find out their plans? Was the prize really so coveted?

'I think she needs a mug of tea.' Catherine said. 'I'll pop the kettle on.'

When they all had tea in hand, Catherine took a seat next to the woman and Mark and Jamal pulled up stools.

'Tell me why you should win.' Jamal perched on his stool, his long legs easily reaching the floor, his mug lost in his big hands.

'I know I have no more right than you or anyone else.' The woman stared into her mug. 'But I need it. See… I'm struggling. I'm a single mum…' She glanced at Catherine. 'My son starts at the primary school in September.'

Catherine nodded.

'I didn't meet you when I enrolled him but I did see you in the office. I was a hairdresser and beautician before I came here with my partner. But… he walked out on us a few weeks ago and now I'm struggling to make the rent. I have a mobile beauty business, but round here, it's like no one's interested and I can't get it off the ground. They all come here and they're loyal to you and your husband.'

Jamal nodded. 'For their haircuts, yes. But I don't offer other… beauty services like waxing and eyebrows and all that stuff.'

'I know but it's all about building a reputation and those I've given cards to have told me they have their hair done here and go further afield for beauty treatments. It's like… because I'm new here, no one trusts me.'

'It is a close village and word of mouth is important.' Jamal sipped his tea. 'It will improve as people get to know you. Unless they hear about this, of course.'

'I'm so sorry but I'm broke. I'm struggling. My son needs a uniform and supplies for September.'

'The school might be able to help with that,' Catherine said. 'We do have a kind of hardship fund for special cases.'

The woman shook her head. 'I'm not a charity case.'

'It's not charity as such,' Catherine said. 'It's only small and we raise it via fetes and raffles, but it's there to help those who need a boost when times get hard. Local businesses also contribute towards it because we want the best for our children in Penhallow Sands.'

She spoke so kindly to the woman that Mark couldn't drag his eyes from her face. Catherine was calm and patient, sweet and caring. He could see that she genuinely wanted to help if she could. And she was so incredibly beautiful and he just wanted to hold her tight, kiss her soft lips and never let her go.

He jolted as he wondered if he'd said the words out loud, but no one was looking at him so he sipped his tea and brought his attention back to the room.

'Still…' The woman sighed. 'If I won Beach Waves I wouldn't need help.'

'But why would my design plans help you?' Jamal asked.

'Because you're the best there is.' Her reply was delivered softly.

Jamal cleared his throat, clearly embarrassed at the direct praise.

'I knew that if I could top whatever you were doing then I'd be in with a chance of winning. It would mean that I'd get not only the prize money but the publicity that comes with it, and that would, in turn, boost my business.'

'Of course.' Jamal nodded.

'Please don't call the police. If you do and I get into trouble, I could lose everything. It was a stupid thing to do and I wouldn't have done it if I wasn't desperate. The window really was unlocked and I thought I could climb in, have a look around then leave without causing any harm. But when I tried to get back out the other way, it slid down onto me and I got stuck there.'

Tears ran down her face and dropped onto her jacket.

'Look…' Jamal stood up. 'I need to speak to Bradley about this before I make any decisions. He's my husband but he's also my business partner. You finish your tea and I'll ring the pub and speak to him.'

Catherine took the mugs out to the kitchen area and Mark stood up and went to the front window, not wanting to sit there staring at the woman who seemed genuine enough, but could be lying to cover her back. Although her eyes did seem filled with fear and pain. He'd seen that same pain in his own eyes every day for months. The pain of heartbreak and betrayal… it was enough to drive anyone mad or to commit uncharacteristic acts. Of course, not everyone would turn to breaking and entering, but he didn't have a child depending upon him and he wasn't desperate for money, so who knew what that could do to a person?

When Catherine returned, she handed the woman another mug of tea. Mark watched them from the window, not wanting to interrupt if Catherine was going to try to get more information. She seemed to have won the woman's trust.

'What's your name?' Catherine asked.

'Lucy Challicombe.'

Catherine nodded. 'I remember the surname. Your little boy is Ben, right?'

'That's right. So you see, if I'm lying then you'll know where to find me.'

'Where's Ben now?'

'Pardon?'

'Well, you said your partner left, so I wondered who's taking care of him.'

'My neighbour, Doreen. She has twin grandsons the same age.'

'I know Doreen.' Catherine nodded. 'And Jamie and John.'

'That's right.'

'Okay!' Jamal walked back into the room. 'I've spoken to Bradley and he's of the same mind as me about this.' He stood in front of Lucy and gazed at her.

'This is Lucy, Jamal,' Catherine interrupted. 'Her son, Ben, is starting at the school in September. She lives next door to Doreen Walker.'

'Ah…' Jamal nodded, chewing on his full bottom lip. 'Right, Lucy.'

Lucy shuffled to the end of her chair.

'For a while now, Bradley and I have been speaking about expanding the business and taking on another stylist… possibly someone who could do other beauty treatments too. We have the space here, as you can see. However, we don't know you or if you're any good or if you're reliable or... of course, if you'd even be interested. Breaking and entering is not the best reference in the world, so we'd need to know more.'

Lucy nodded.

'However, if you are interested in the possibility of a position here, which would provide the job security and consistent income that it seems you need and want, then we'd be prepared to consider giving you a chance to prove yourself. Therefore' – he released a deep breath – 'you should enter Beach Waves independently and see how it goes. Prove yourself by giving that a good go, possibly even winning, then come back and see us and we'll give you a two-week probationary period at Hairway. We can see what you can do, what you can offer to our customers and, most importantly, how we all get on. This is a small business and we need to have a good working relationship, or chemistry, as Bradley calls it. What do you think?'

'You're not going to ring the police?' Lucy asked.

'No.' Jamal shook his head. 'I like the idea of giving you a second chance. I was given one once, a long time ago, after I did something almost as foolish as this. I want to pay the good deed on now by offering you a second chance.'

'Thank you so much!' Lucy stood up and held out her hand and Jamal shook it. 'You won't regret this, I promise. I'm not normally a criminal. I'm a good person, a good mum, but getting down to the last few pounds in my bank account and seeing Ben's face when I say we've got beans on toast for tea again and worrying about how I'm going to pay for his uniform has pushed me further than I ever thought I'd go.'

'Well, I hope things improve for you, Lucy, I really do. Let's exchange numbers and stay in touch. Perhaps I can give you a few pointers for Beach Waves.'

Lucy nodded then followed Jamal through to the office.

Catherine walked over to the window and stood next to Mark, gazing out at the street. It was almost dark and the street lamps had come on. Across the road, the sea was vast and dark, the cliffs hugging the coast to the left and right. It seemed to give Penhallow Sands a feeling of security, being surrounded by the cliffs, protected from the worst of the elements. Next to him, Catherine seemed lost in her thoughts, but he didn't feel the need to speak and break the silence. He was fine with standing beside her, close enough to touch, close enough to feel the warmth emanating from her skin, close enough to smell her delicious coconut and vanilla scent.

It was a good place to be, and in that moment, Mark didn't want to be anywhere else. If Catherine were his, he would never want to leave.

Chapter 10

The following morning, Catherine went to visit Maggie and the new baby. She had popped into Newquay first and bought a small teddy bear, a pretty little outfit and a helium balloon with *It's a Girl!* in big pink letters.

Maggie lived in a cliff-top development that overlooked Penhallow Sands. It had been built two years previously and Catherine knew that the houses there weren't cheap, but Maggie's husband had a good job and they had saved for years. Maggie had confided this to Catherine when they'd put their village cottage up for sale. She'd said that she didn't want people to think she had become a snob by moving to the new housing development, but that she and Fred had saved every spare penny ready to move into a bigger property. They needed the room too, with five children.

Catherine had decided to walk to Maggie's, seeing as how it was a beautiful day and she wanted to enjoy some fresh air. She'd dressed in navy linen trousers, a white vest top and white plimsolls so she'd be comfortable for walking and hopefully not too warm. She'd also pulled her long hair up into a bun high on her head and put sunglasses on to protect her eyes.

She sent Maggie a text to check that it was a good time to visit and Maggie had replied that it was perfect, seeing as how Fred was home too and he could watch their brood for an hour to allow her and Catherine to catch up.

The walk was wonderful and Catherine savoured the sunshine on her face and the breeze that caressed her skin. Being outdoors always gave her immense pleasure and lifted her whenever she felt a bit low or disconnected from things. On her way she passed a few children from school and waved at them and their parents and exchanged pleasantries with other familiar faces from the village. She was looking forward to seeing Maggie and her new baby. It was always delightful to welcome a new life into the world and comforting too, as it was a reminder that life went on and that the next generation would be there to take over the world one day. It was one of the things that Catherine loved about teaching, knowing that she was helping to shape the future by educating children and helping to prepare them for the life ahead.

'Catherine!' Maggie opened the door and smiled. 'So good to see you.'

Catherine accepted her friend's hug, handed her the gift bag then followed her through the sunny hallway and into the lounge at the rear. She'd been to the house before but every time she came, she was amazed by the incredible view. The floor to ceiling windows at the back of the property overlooked the sea. There were ten properties on the development in total but only five had the panoramic sea view, while two had the view of Penhallow Sands and the three at the other side looked out over the next bay along.

Catherine peered out at the sea, admiring how its surface sparkled in the sunlight as if it was filled with millions of diamonds.

'If I lived here, I'd just stare out of the window all the time,' Catherine said.

'I would too if I didn't have so many children to deal with,' Maggie replied laughing. 'Coffee?'

Catherine turned back to the room.

'Yes, if that's what you're having.'

Maggie rolled her eyes. 'Mint tea for me. I'm breast-feeding and can't have too much caffeine at the moment. Not if I want the little one to sleep that is. But you can have coffee.'

They walked through to the large open-plan kitchen-diner with its sleek cream cabinets and marble work surfaces, and Maggie made the tea and coffee while Catherine sat on one of the barstools at the island.

'You look incredible, Maggie,' she said as she eyed Maggie's slim frame in black leggings and a T-shirt.

'Well, thank you. But the secret is that I've tucked my saggy belly into my big knickers.' Maggie smiled and patted her tummy. 'However, I didn't put on too much baby weight because running around after the other four stopped me piling on the pounds this time. I don't know about eating for two... I was eating for five.' She flicked her long black hair over her shoulder.

'Are you getting enough rest?' Catherine asked, 'Because I'll help out if I can.'

Maggie nodded. 'I'm fine, honestly. Fred is fabulous and my mother-in-law will take the children whenever I ask. I know I joke about her but she's good as gold really. And number five has turned out to be angelic.' She paused the added, 'Thus far, anyway. Could be that once she starts teething, she'll give us hell.'

Catherine smiled. 'I doubt it. You're always so calm that your babies emerge with perfect inner peace.'

'Ha! I wish.' Maggie placed two mugs on the island then sat opposite Catherine. She opened the gift bag and unwrapped the teddy bear and outfit. 'These are lovely, thanks so much.'

'My pleasure. It's only something small. I figured you'd have a lot from family and people in the village.'

Maggie nodded. 'Everyone has been so generous, as always.'

'Well you're an important local figure and lots of people want to show their appreciation for what you do.'

Maggie blushed. 'I only run the library.'

'And look how important a role that is.'

'I just hope Felicity will manage while I'm off. I'm wondering now if we should have considered employing another part timer.'

'You've trained her well so I'm sure she'll be fine.' Catherine nodded. 'Although… I might know someone if you are looking for more help. She's new to the village and has a son who'll be attending our school.' The idea that Lucy could help at the library had popped into her head and now it seemed like a really good one. Even if Lucy did get some hours at the salon, she could also do some at the library. It would be a good way for her to earn money and integrate into the community.

'That is worth considering.' Maggie chewed her lip. 'Let me think about it and have a chat with Felicity. She'd be able to train her while I'm off.'

Felicity Browning had moved to Penhallow Sands the previous summer. She was in her mid-fifties, well-read and sharp-tongued, but she had a heart of gold. Maggie had employed Felicity as a library assistant and the two made a good team.

'I'm just glad Felicity wasn't there when I went into labour because she'd have had a fit seeing my waters break in the reading corner.'

'I still can't believe that happened.'

Maggie's eyes widened. 'Oh, it happened. It's a good job Mark was there to help me.'

Catherine sighed inwardly at his name and realised she was keen to hear more about how he'd saved the day.

'Was he very helpful then?'

'Extremely. He said he'd researched it for one of his books.'

'It?'

'Oh, sorry, labour and childbirth. He certainly knows plenty about it now.'

'He mentioned that he writes but I didn't ask what.' Catherine chewed her bottom lip. 'I guess I should have.'

'You two getting along then?' Maggie asked as she eyed Catherine over the rim of her mug.

'He seems like a nice person.' Catherine was as non-committal as possible but the heat that was crawling up her throat and into her cheeks was sure to give her away. 'I've seen him a few times.' She raised her own mug to try to hide her face.

'Oh, he's nice all right.' Maggie chuckled. 'Poor man saw far more of me than he ever expected though. I told him to check if the head was coming, which he wasn't keen on doing, but it all happened so quickly that I had no choice.'

'Goodness!' Catherine gasped. 'But I guess that when it happens, it can't be stopped.'

'Nope. Little Molly was coming then and there and nothing was going to prevent her. Mark was, all things considered, pretty calm even when I asked him to look at my... nether regions.'

They laughed together then.

'Poor man.'

'He's coming to visit this morning too,' Maggie said. She glanced at the clock on the wall. 'He'll be here any minute I should imagine.'

Catherine stiffened. Mark was coming here? Now?

They'd had a good time last night after letting the intruder, now known as Lucy, go. Catherine had gone to the pub with Jamal and Mark and they'd met up with Bradley then filled him in with the whole story from start to finish. Bradley had heard the potted version of the story from Jamal on the phone, but he'd wanted to hear it again, especially after Catherine mentioned that Jamal had gone in with the hairdryer as a weapon. They'd agreed not to broadcast what had happened though, because they didn't want people thinking badly of Lucy or her little boy, Ben. Lucy had acted desperately in desperate circumstances and she needed support not local condemnation. Catherine just hoped that she'd keep her side of the agreement and not do anything so reckless again.

As for Mark, he'd been amazing. He'd fixed the window as easily as if it was something he did every day. If he hadn't known that the sash cord was jammed, Catherine and Jamal would definitely have been forced to call the fire brigade or the police and things would have turned out very differently for Lucy. It was a funny old life; no one had an easy time of it and Catherine was a firm believer in helping others as far as was possible. Kindness was so important.

'Here she is.' Fred walked into the kitchen holding a small bundle in his arms. Catherine put down her mug and gazed down at the baby as Fred gently put her in Catherine's arms.

'Congratulations, Fred.' Catherine held the baby carefully. 'She's so beautiful.'

Molly had a head of black fluffy hair and dark eyelashes that fluttered on her cheeks. She was warm and surprisingly solid in Catherine's arms and she realised that she had expected such a tiny baby to feel fragile. But this little girl was perfect.

'While you have her, I'm going to pop to the bathroom,' Maggie said, easing herself off the stool. 'Fred, I think I just heard a car pull up.'

Catherine was left alone in the sunny kitchen with the baby. She couldn't tear her eyes away from the peaches-and- cream skin or the little nose that turned up slightly at the end. Emotion rushed through her, making her sigh and blink hard as her vision blurred. She had always insisted, to herself and others, that she was not cut out to be a mother. She had denied ever feeling remotely maternal, except towards the children at the school, and they were already walking and talking by the time they got to her. But when things like this happened and she got to hold a newborn – which she had on a variety of occasions, when local women and old friends had given birth – she was always amazed by the way it made her feel.

As if she was seeing the world anew.

As if she was seeing something she had missed out on.

As if a part of her had some regrets that she had never done this.

It wasn't that Catherine believed that a woman's life had to involve finding love, getting married and having a family, because she didn't, not at all. But holding a baby like this, breathing in that sweet fragrance of baby shampoo, milk and… whatever it was that made babies smell so good… made something in Catherine waver. There was a yearning deep inside her that she usually didn't notice, that she effectively suppressed, that she would outwardly deny to all who would listen.

But not now, not today, not while this precious infant was in her arms.

She let the feeling envelope her and went with it, allowing her maternal instinct to rise to the surface and make itself known.

'Catherine?'

She started at her name and looked up, wondering if her feelings had been written all over her face as she gazed so intently at the baby.

'Hi, Mark.' She smiled easily, glad to see him.

'I thought it was you.' He coughed. 'What am I on about? I meant that I knew it was you but it's strange seeing you with a baby.'

Something inside her smarted. Did she look strange holding a little one? Was he trying to say that it didn't suit her?

'She looks like an expert, doesn't she?' Fred asked as he walked in behind Mark.

'She does,' Mark nodded. 'Like a natural. Perfect.'

Catherine met his eyes and something flashed there. It was gone as quickly as it had appeared but it echoed through her, making her heart beat faster. So she looked right holding a baby then and Mark had approved of seeing her like that.

'Would you like a drink, Mark?' Fred asked as he walked through and opened the bifold doors that opened out onto a verandah surrounded by a very high childproof fence.

'Water would be perfect, thanks.' Mark rubbed his throat. 'It's hot out there now. Lovely in here though with the sea breeze.'

'We've been keeping the doors closed to avoid drafts but the place needs some air.' Fred got a glass out of a cupboard then ran the tap.

Mark took the stool closest to Catherine. She could smell his fresh lemony cologne, warm skin and a hint of toothpaste. It made her stomach flip.

'Beautiful,' Mark said as he leant towards her.

She held her breath, wondering what he was doing, what he meant, then he gently stroked the baby's cheek.

'She is, isn't she?' Catherine scolded herself. He was talking about the baby – of course he was! 'Do you want to hold her?'

'Uh… okay.'

Catherine shuffled forwards on the stool and leant closer to him then gently slid the baby into his arms. As she did so, their knees touched and their heads bumped together.

'Sorry,' she said.

'It's okay. I have a hard head.'

'I know.' She rubbed her head but it hadn't really hurt, just made her more aware of his close proximity.

He held the baby as if she were made of glass and Catherine found herself touching his arm as she peered at little Molly. She was even tempted to rest her head on his shoulder; it all felt so natural in that moment.

'She's incredible, isn't she?' Mark asked. 'A perfect tiny person. I love babies at this age. They have so much potential. She could grow up to be anything at all.'

'She could.' Catherine accepted a fresh coffee from Fred, swallowing her delight that Mark had said he loved babies. She shook herself as she sipped her coffee. Had her hormones gone completely haywire today?

'Well, I hope it's something successful because I need her to keep me in style when I'm an old man,' Fred teased. 'That's the only reason we had five children, see, Mark.'

'Sorry?' Mark looked up.

'We had five children so they'd look after us when we're old and grey.'

'Oh.' Mark looked shocked.

'He's teasing you, Mark,' Catherine said.

'Of course I am.' Fred nodded. 'I don't expect them to look after me or Maggie in later life. We'll be off cruising around the world.'

'Will we, darling?' Maggie walked into the kitchen. 'Sorry about taking so long but there was an incident in the playroom upstairs. Something to do with one of our lovely children threatening to do a poo on another one's head if the Xbox time wasn't shared properly.'

'I'll go up now.' Fred kissed Maggie's forehead then left the kitchen.

'There you are, my impromptu midwife!' Maggie smiled at Mark.

'I'm actually thinking of retraining,' Mark said. 'Midwife Mark. What do you think?'

'You'd be great.' Maggie got carefully onto a stool. 'And it would be inspiration for your books.'

'What do you write?' Catherine seized the opportunity to ask.

Mark looked down at Molly and smiled.

'I've written thrillers and romantic comedies and I actually write as—'

Just then, Molly let out a squawk and Mark jumped.

'Did I do something wrong?'

'No.' Maggie shook her head. 'She probably wants feeding again. Honestly, she has a better appetite than any of the others did.'

Mark slid off the stool and carried Molly to her mum.

'I'll… uh… give you a minute.'

'There's no need. I'm not shy.' Maggie laughed. 'This is all perfectly natural.'

'I know.' Mark averted his eyes. 'It's just… I get a bit… embarrassed.'

He walked over to the open doors, leaving Catherine and Maggie with Molly.

The baby gulped loudly as she drank, which Catherine found surprising.

'I didn't realise they were so noisy when feeding.'

'Molly can be. And wait until you hear her belch!' Maggie settled herself more comfortably on the stool, holding the baby to her chest with ease.

Catherine sipped her drink, marvelling at how amazing Maggie was with her tiny daughter. If she ever had a baby, Catherine doubted she'd be so relaxed about it. She'd probably have been a nervous wreck. But then, it had never happened to her, so how would she know? Once upon a time, she'd thought that she'd be too nervous to stand in front of a class of twenty-five children, let alone a whole-school assembly, but now it was something she did without even thinking twice about it. Things that could seem daunting often became part of life when you did them every day. So perhaps Catherine would have made a good mum. It was something she couldn't imagine ever happening though, seeing as how she'd only been in one proper relationship and she knew that she didn't have the time or energy to maintain another one as well as working and being there for her own mum.

Some things just weren't meant to be.

But that didn't stop her daydreaming about having them, or occasionally wishing that things could have been different. Being around Mark also made her feel that these things were possible, that they weren't just dreams. It was silly really, as she didn't know him that well, but she did have a gut feeling that there was a connection between them.

–

Another week of the holidays had flown past and Catherine couldn't believe that there was only one week left. She'd been swimming and reading and napping and the days had started to melt into one as they often did during the summer. Most mornings, after her swim, she played with Bob and Ginger, made lunch for her and her mother, then read for a few hours before taking a nap. It was bliss to be able to relax.

Most days, admittedly, her thoughts strayed to Mark and what he was doing, but something held her back from contacting him too often. She knew it was fear of being hurt, of liking him too much and of ending up wanting all the things she'd thought for so long that she couldn't have. It had filled her mind that day after she'd visited Maggie and her new baby, when Mark had been there and she'd felt that intense connection between them. At that point, she'd felt as though things between them could go either way, as if they could continue as they were or dive into something deeper. The latter thought was the one that left her with doubts. Could she really open her heart to love and vulnerability?

This evening, Jamal had arranged a costume fitting for Beach Waves at the haberdasher's shop, which was a fifteen minutes' drive from Penhallow Sands. From outside it looked like a clothes shop, but as Catherine pushed the door and entered, the inside made her think of Aladdin's Cave. Everywhere she looked, she saw rolls of material in all colours of the rainbow and everything in between. There were plastic containers piled up in the corners of the shop and they appeared to be filled with buttons and cotton, and at the rear of the shop, behind the counter, were two headless mannequins wearing tape measures around their necks. The smell of dyed fabrics and coffee permeated the air and her stomach rolled as she approached the counter.

'Hello, there.'

The voice from behind her made Catherine jump and she turned to meet the grey eyes of a tall, thin woman with a blunt black bob and bright red lips. She was wearing an orange jumpsuit and gold platform boots that looked as though they had come right out of the seventies.

'Hi. I'm here for a fitting.'

'And your name is?' The woman went around the counter and opened an A4 book then flicked to the middle.

'Catherine Bromley.'

'Ahhh... You're with Jamal.'

'Yes, that's right.'

'He's out the back with Bradley and a very cute guy with a posh accent.' She grinned at Catherine, revealing fixed braces on her top and bottom teeth.

'Mark?'

'Yes, that's right. Follow me. I'm Libby, by the way.'

Catherine followed Libby to a curtain behind the counter that she slid aside, then they went through a short corridor and into a brightly lit back room. Jamal and Bradley were sitting on a maroon velvet sofa and they looked up as Catherine approached them.

'I told you to get a lift with us.' Jamal stood up and hugged Catherine.

'I know, but I had a few things to do before leaving so it was easier to make my own way here.' Also easier to leave if she felt the need to escape, as she had no idea what Jamal had in store for her and Mark.

And where was Mark?

'How're you getting on?' Libby asked outside one of the changing rooms. The curtain slid open and Mark stepped out.

'Hi, Catherine. What do you think?'

She pressed a hand to her mouth then pretended to cough.

'What... uh...' She looked at Jamal and he was smiling from ear to ear.

'Perfect! Exactly as I envisaged them.'

Libby glowed at his praise but Mark shifted uncomfortably.

'Do you always get your models to wear costumes?' he asked.

'It's part of the fun.' Jamal walked around Mark.

'Really?' Mark asked.

'Come on then, Catherine,' Libby showed her to a changing room. 'Your turn. Your costume is hanging up in there ready and waiting for you.'

Catherine met Mark's eyes and his widened. If his costume was that… flamboyant, she wondered what hers would be like. She knew that Jamal liked to make a statement at these competitions, but this might be going a bit far, and judging by Mark's costume, perhaps she should have waxed her bikini line before coming here today. In fact, perhaps she should have waxed everything…

Five minutes later, Catherine and Mark stood side by side under the bright lights, both trying not to fidget, but it was difficult to keep still as the sides of the costume that covered her hips kept riding up and she was worried that her friends and Libby were seeing far more of her than they would want to. Mark appeared to be having a similar problem but with the part that covered his bum.

'Don't they look gorgeous?' Jamal asked Bradley.

'They really do. With the styles you have planned, these costumes will go down well.'

'I'll let you have a chat, then if you want any alterations, let me know.' Libby said to Jamal. 'I can drop the costumes at the salon for you tomorrow afternoon, Jamal.'

When Libby had gone, Catherine sighed.

'Did you have to choose spandex, Jamal? I mean... I can hardly move because this keeps riding up and it seems like poor Mark is suffering with a constant wedgie.'

Mark blushed but nodded. 'Sorry, I have to pull it out because it feels like it's crushing my ba... man parts.'

'Don't worry about that!' Jamal laughed. 'I'll ask Libby to put in a bit more material to allow for your man parts, Mark, and to cover your rather unruly bikini line, Catherine.'

'Jamal!' she scolded. 'There's no need for that, is there?' Heat rose up her neck and raged on her cheeks.

'Sorry, honey, but you know I can't help telling the truth.' He winked at her. 'Anyway, you can wear some of those thick opaque tights if you like and Mark, don't worry, we can get that crotch adjusted. Go and get changed the pair of you.'

Catherine and Mark shuffled into their respective changing rooms and Catherine leant her head against the cool surface of the mirror. It seemed that she was to be spared no humiliation in front of Mark and that he now knew more about her personal grooming than she was comfortable with. But then, he was in a similar boat really, as his costume hadn't left much to the imagination.

Or rather, it had left Catherine with plenty to entertain her imagination while she got changed. She giggled, surprised by her own wicked humour. Laughing at awkward times was important, and she did suffer from a nervous giggle, so from now on, she would try to take herself less seriously. Hopefully, it would make the whole experience of Beach Waves less painful.

But for now, she had more pressing concerns to deal with.

'Jamal?'

'Yes?'

'Can you come in here a minute please?'

'Why?'

'I've got the costume stuck on my head and I can't find the way out.'

'Oh, Catherine,' he sighed as he opened the curtain. 'What am I going to do with you?'

And as he tried to help her to get the spandex over her head, the pair of them huffed and puffed and giggled and swore. Catherine had a feeling that there were plenty more good times ahead, especially if Mark, Jamal and Bradley were involved in them. If Mark decided to stay in Penhallow Sands long term, that was.

She hoped with every fibre of her being that he would because life was far more interesting and exciting when he was around.

Chapter 11

The next few days flew past as Penhallow Sands prepared to host Beach Waves – the big event of the summer. A large white marquee had been set up on the sand, close to the path – to allow for power cables and water pipes – and the village had buzzed for days as shopkeepers had stuck posters in their windows, villagers had hung flags and bunting from their upstairs windows, and the Turner bakery and Shell's Shack had taken in larger orders of ingredients ready to cater for the event.

Catherine had been caught up in the excitement herself as Jamal had insisted that she go to the salon for a trial the day before the competition, then comforted him as he'd become worked up about the styles he had planned; styles that he now believed were not good enough. Lucy had come to the salon too for some advice about the styles she was planning, along with her volunteer models – a young couple from the village whom Lucy had made friends with and who also had a little boy at the village school.

At seven thirty on the Saturday morning, Catherine left her cottage and made her way down to Hairway to Heaven. She'd washed her hair in the shower the night before and left it to dry naturally, because she knew that Jamal would be washing it and styling it, as well as using a bucket load of product on it, so there was no point in her doing anything else. Butterflies in her stomach made her take some deep breaths as she walked. She couldn't pinpoint one reason why she was nervous because there were several whirling around in her head – perhaps it was because she'd have hundreds of eyes on her today while wearing that elaborate costume; perhaps it was because she had promised Jamal he could have free rein with her hair (and she had no idea exactly what he would do as he'd kept the final chosen style secret from everyone, including her); perhaps it was because she would spend the day in a chair right next to Mark.

After she'd left Maggie and Fred's the week before, she'd walked home alone. Mark had stayed there for a while longer because Fred had wanted to show him his collection of mountain bikes. According to Maggie, Fred was keen to find someone to accompany him on his punishing bike rides. Catherine thought now about how she had enjoyed holding little Molly; she had experienced such a deep yearning as she'd gazed at the beautiful baby and it had unsettled her. She'd told herself for so long that she was happy and fulfilled, but times like that made her question it all again. Was she satisfied with her life as it was or did she want more? Even the thought that she might want more made her afraid. She knew that she was lucky: she had a lovely home in a gorgeous location; she had a secure job that came with a pension pot at the end of her career; she had her mother, whereas many people didn't: she had so much to be thankful for and yet…

Something was missing.

It wasn't just about babies and romance though; she missed having a dad too. She knew that had her father stayed around, her life would have been different: her mother wouldn't have become so sad and embittered, and her childhood would have lasted longer and not become one where she had to look out for her mother, sometimes even taking care of her mother when Diana couldn't cope. Sometimes, Catherine wished that things had worked out differently. She knew, of course, that wishing wouldn't change a thing but it didn't matter. Wishing didn't hurt anyone, did it? Unless wanting something else led to a deeper unhappiness and even resentment, and she didn't want to live her life like that.

And there was the anger. It was a by-product of the hurt, she knew that, but it was something she couldn't entirely let go of. Her father had walked out, selfishly left her mother in pieces, left Catherine wondering why he had gone. Was it because Catherine wasn't good enough? Didn't he love his daughter enough to stay around? What kind of person abandoned the ones who loved them? Her imagined reconstructions of that day had been a mix of him telling her he'd be back soon then hugging her tight, or him begging Catherine to go with him because he couldn't bear to leave her behind – which she declined because she had to be there for her mother – and when her pain and anger were at their worst, Catherine imagined pounding her fists against her father's chest and telling him exactly what kind of selfish pig she thought he was.

Life was complicated. People were flawed and things didn't always work out, but every day offered fresh opportunities. She had to cling to that at all times. Yesterday, she'd opened her personal email inbox for the first time in days – she'd neglected it as she'd been busy – and there had been an email from her father. She'd left it sitting there, unopened for an hour, afraid to read it. However, curiosity had overtaken fear and she'd read it, then read it again. He had asked to meet her. Soon. Her stomach had churned and her palms had become clammy. She'd made the first move this time but she'd half expected him not to reply. He had, so now the ball was in her court again. She had to decide whether to meet him; or not. She had decided to sleep on it.

And now, it was a warm August morning and she was on her way to model for Jamal. It was true that you couldn't choose your family, but you could choose your friends, and Jamal was one of the best.

–

Mark had decided to walk down to Penhallow Sands on the morning of Beach Waves because he suspected that parking would be difficult. Besides which, he was feeling rather nervous and he hoped the walk might help to calm his nerves.

Jamal had asked him to go in for a consultation prior to the competition, and he had done so earlier in the week, but Jamal hadn't done anything other than show Mark some photos of hairstyles and colours and ask his opinion. Jamal had told Mark not to worry, told him that he was in safe hands, and that the model's satisfaction with their new style was just as important – if not more important – than winning.

Mark hoped Jamal meant what he said. Still, even if he didn't like whatever Jamal did with his hair, it would grow out. Not that he really minded right now. He'd looked at his reflection in the mirror that morning before showering and he had to admit that his hair was a mess. It was too long, it was irritating having to keep pushing it back from his face as he worked out and sat at his laptop, and he would prefer to wear it shorter. He didn't mind the colour so much though, thinking that the grey at the sides that then blended in with his stubble was quite distinguished-looking. Mark didn't mind the crow's feet at the sides of his eyes, the fine lines across his brow or the changing colour of his hair and beard, because he wasn't afraid of getting older.

He reached Beach Street and strolled along, breathing in the fresh sea air and taking care to avoid the crowds that were already gathering. People were carrying deckchairs and windbreakers down to the sand, setting up for the day. Mark had a near miss with a woman carrying a tray of takeaway coffees and almost tripped over a pram when the man pushing it stopped suddenly in front of him. He was glad he hadn't brought the car because he'd probably have ended up parking as far away as his cottage anyway.

He squeezed through the bodies towards the rail that divided the beach from the pavement and gazed across the sand. There was a large marquee set up, its sides flapping in the breeze. As he watched, a seagull soared above the marquee then swooped down to land on one of the flag posts. That was where the competition would happen. His stomach flipped again. There would be so many eyes on him today, judging him not for his writing but for his hair and his costume. That bloody costume. He could only hope that Libby had added more material to it or he'd be in danger of injury when he sat down. His lips twitched as he briefly wondered what Ellie would have made of it. How would she have reacted to this situation, to Mark having his hair done in a competition and wearing a costume? Whatever she thought didn't matter now, but he did wonder – and care – what Catherine thought.

He shook himself. Today was about supporting a new friend and his business, about integrating into the community, and about moving on. He would also get to spend most of the day in the same place as Catherine, and that was a very appealing prospect indeed.

–

'Mark!' Jamal clapped his hands as Mark entered the salon and Catherine turned around in the swivel chair Jamal had pressed her into and smiled.

Mark met her eyes and she sighed inwardly. His skin was clear, his cheeks flushed from walking in the breeze, and his eyes shone. He was certainly very easy on the eye and she was secretly looking forward to being able to spend the day with him.

'Good morning,' Mark said as Jamal directed him to the seat next to Catherine.

'Nervous?' Catherine asked.

'Me?' Mark raised his eyebrows. 'Never! I can't wait to see what fate Jamal has selected for my precious locks.' He gave his hair a dramatic flick, making Catherine giggle.

'Now, now, don't be silly.' Jamal placed his hand on Mark's shoulders and looked at him in the mirror. 'All will be well. I promise not to harm a hair on your head.'

Mark grimaced at Catherine and she returned the look.

'You will both be fine.' Bradley came through from the back of the salon and smiled at them all. 'Jamal will have you looking like Hollywood stars, especially once you get those gorgeous costumes on.'

'Bradley, I'm more beautician than magician. I use a comb not a wand!' Jamal shook his head but he winked at them both. 'They'll look good but not that good. We just don't have the raw material here to work with.'

'Gee, thanks, Jamal.' Catherine pouted playfully.

Jamal rushed over to Catherine and hugged her.

'I'm teasing, my beautiful friend… you know that, right? You are both gorgeous and I am lucky to have you as such willing models. The nerves are just making me edgy and that makes me babble.'

'He always looks so sexy when he's edgy,' Bradley growled at Jamal. 'The babbling can be a bit annoying though.'

'Behave, you!' Jamal pointed his comb at his husband. 'Okay… my darling models, let's just have one more run through, then I'll make a final decision.'

'You haven't made your final decision yet?' Catherine heard the panic in her own voice.

'I thought I had, then I slept on it again and changed my mind when I took one last look at the costumes this morning.'

Catherine sank deeper into the chair.

It was going to be an interesting, and probably very challenging, day…

Chapter 12

Inside the marquee, Jamal was led to his workstation, and Catherine, Mark and Bradley followed. Bradley wheeled Jamal's work case behind him; it was filled with products that sponsors of the event had sent to Jamal prior to the competition. Catherine and Mark wore black capes to hide their costumes until the final reveal.

There were eight workstations in total, all set up with enough space for the hair stylists to work. Each stylist was allowed two models and one assistant – in Jamal's case, his assistant was Bradley.

The centre of the marquee was devoted to six sinks set in two back-to-back rows. Catherine knew that the piping for the water and the power cables ran under the decking that created the floor of the marquee. There were also large tower fans in the corners of the marquee, should the temperature inside rise to uncomfortable levels.

While Jamal set up, Bradley wrapped towels around Catherine and Mark's shoulders then settled them onto the chairs in front of the mirror at Jamal's workstation. Jamal cursed as he dropped a bottle of heat protector spray and it broke, sending product all over the floor. He bent over to pick it up and bumped his head on the shelf of the workstation, which made him stagger backwards.

'Jamal!' Bradley grabbed him by the shoulders. 'Are you okay?'

Jamal nodded. 'I'm fine. Just… butterfingers.' He held up his trembling hands.

'Come on, now, love.' Bradley took his husband's hands and squeezed them. 'You've done this before. No need to be nervous.'

'I don't know why I am.' Jamal sighed. 'Silly really.'

While Bradley comforted his husband, Mark turned to Catherine.

'I hope he's okay.'

'Me too.'

'Also… butterfingers makes me a bit… nervous.'

Catherine smiled. 'I know. Not the type of fingers you want holding a scissors near your hair, right?'

'It's not my hair I'm worried about now.' Mark raised his hands to the sides of his head. 'It's more that I'm rather partial to my ears.'

Catherine giggled, enjoying the warmth of their banter. 'They're nice ears! I'm sure he'll be fine, so try not to worry.'

There was a commotion over the far side of the marquee and Catherine and Mark turned around to see what was going on. She could hear someone panting and other people squabbling over what to do.

'What's wrong?' she raised her voice to deputy head teacher level – it was guaranteed to be heard over any commotion.

A woman turned from the huddle and replied, 'It's the stylist over here. She can't breathe.'

Catherine got out of her chair and hurried over. She pushed through the people, her black cape billowing around her, to find Lucy on her knees, her face white, her blue lips matching her hair colour as she gasped.

'Lucy! It's okay, just take your time.' Catherine turned back to the onlookers. 'Right you lot, clear away. She needs some space. And someone get some water.' The crowd of stylists and models parted reluctantly, with someone muttering about her thinking she was some sort of superhero in her black cape, then Catherine knelt next to Lucy and took her hands. 'Okay, Lucy, you're having a panic attack. You're going to be fine but I want you to listen to me.'

Lucy nodded.

'Breathe with me,' Catherine's tone was strict; she meant business and knew it would get Lucy to listen. 'Slowly, breathe in… that's it… deeply and gently… okay…' She squeezed Lucy's hands. 'And now exhale… gently does it… good! That's it, good. And again…'

She held Lucy's gaze and soon, the colour had returned to Lucy's cheeks and the blue tinge retreated from her lips. Her fingers were cold so Catherine rubbed them vigorously between her hands until they thawed out.

'You're going to be fine, Lucy. Just fine.'

'Thank you,' Lucy replied, then she took a sip from the bottle of water that someone handed her.

'I take it you're nervous.' Catherine smiled.

'Very. There's so much riding on this.' Lucy shook her head. 'I need to win so badly.'

'Lucy…' Catherine took her hand again. 'You might well win, but you might not. There are some excellent stylists here and the competition is, I'm sorry to say, fierce. But remember… even if you don't win, you still have a chance of a job at Hairway to Heaven.'

'I know and it's so kind of Jamal and Bradley to even consider giving me a chance after what I did.'

'I always tell the pupils at school that everyone deserves a second chance. People make mistakes when they're pushed into a corner. You made a mistake but you have a second chance. Plus… I wasn't going to say anything until after the competition but this might help to soothe your worries. My friend Maggie is the local librarian and she's looking for someone to work two days a week as a library assistant.' Catherine watched Lucy's face carefully and was pleased to see hope cross her features.

'Do you… mean me?' Lucy asked.

'I do. There's no pressure, but I know you said you needed work and as it's only two days a week, you could do that and your beauty treatments. Anyway, it's something for you to consider.'

'I don't know a thing about working in a library.' Lucy shook her head.

'You'd have full training and be entitled to all the benefits like holiday pay and so on.'

'Wow!' Lucy's eyes glistened. 'Thank you so much.'

'I'll send you Maggie's details later and you can have a chat with her and find out if it's something you fancy doing.'

Catherine stood up and helped Lucy to her feet.

'If you were one of my pupils now, I'd also tell you that this is your opportunity to show what you can do here. Everyone gets nervous before a test, exam, competition, performance and that's perfectly natural. But you should give it your best effort and then you can be proud of yourself.'

'I agree. You should listen to our very own superhero.' Jamal had joined them. He opened his arms. 'Now have a Jamal hug, then show these judges what you're capable of, Lucy.'

They hugged and when Lucy emerged from Jamal's embrace, she was smiling.

'I'm going to!' she said, then she turned to Catherine. 'Thank you so much.'

'No problem.'

Catherine and Jamal went back to his workstation and Catherine sat next to Mark again.

'I was going to come over and help, but then you shouted at people to give you some space, so I thought I'd better stay in my seat.' He gave a nervous laugh. 'You were quite stern.'

'It's my teacher voice. I reserve it for special occasions when I need people to really listen to me.'

'I hope you never have cause to use it on me.'

'I'm sure I won't.'

Then they fell silent as the five judges entered the marquee, the rules were read out and the competition began.

–

Catherine closed her eyes as Jamal applied dye onto her hair with a small brush then wrapped each section in foil. Soon her head was a mass of pieces of foil that stuck out, making her resemble a modern medusa. Jamal set a timer then turned to Mark.

'Your turn.'

Mark glanced at Catherine and raised his eyebrows, but Jamal took hold of his chin and turned him to face the mirror. Bradley stood next to Jamal holding his tray of styling instruments. She could no longer see Mark, so she gazed at her own reflection instead.

Behind her, stylists waved combs and brushes around, pumped chairs up and down to better reach their models' heads and ushered their models to the sinks then back. It was a hive of activity and Catherine was filled with admiration for everyone taking part. Her job was high-pressured. She worked long hours and she worked hard, often with tight or seemingly unachievable deadlines; she always had done. Hair stylists worked hard too. They were artists, trusted with people's hair, but they were also like therapists as their clients often confided in them or asked their advice on matters of the heart. They had to be able to listen and respond, to be patient and to try to create the styles that their clients desired – even at times against their better judgement. Catherine could no more cut someone's hair than she could sing in an opera, but that was fine. People were different and they all had their own skill sets, their own passions and directions.

Mark, for instance, was a writer. Catherine hadn't yet discovered exactly what he wrote, as the only answer she'd received had been a bit vague, but the fact that he was a writer made her admire him even more. Writing took patience and resilience, self-discipline and a thick skin when critical reviews came in. But it must also be a wonderfully rewarding job for someone who was creative. She'd always wanted to meet a real-life writer and now she had. And he was a pretty special person too. After all, he was allowing her best friend to style his hair as he saw fit and not many people would be up for that. Mark had patience and compassion and kindness in his heart;

Catherine had seen it in how he had behaved towards her mother and towards Jamal, Bradley and Lucy. He was the kind of man a woman could fall in love with – if she allowed herself to fall for him that was.

Catherine's thoughts strayed, as they so often did, to her mother. The past two weeks had seen another change in their life with the transformation in her mother's relationship with her aunt. It had seemed to come out of the blue, but then, when Catherine thought about it, perhaps it had been on the cards for some time. Aunty Jane had always tried to have a relationship with her sister and now, it seemed, her persistence was paying off. She had shown Diana kindness during a dark time and Diana had responded well. On more than one occasion this week, Catherine had heard her mother giggling as she spoke to Jane on the phone and it was a sound that had lifted her heart. Age was no barrier to love, whatever form that love came in, and knowing that her mother had someone else in her life lifted the weight Catherine had carried for so long. It was not a weight she resented, but it was a weight nonetheless. It was the weight of responsibility for her mother. But now, Jane had come to share it – even if just for a while. Catherine hoped that it would be permanent for all their sakes.

'Let's take a look then, Catherine.' Bradley cut into her thoughts as he opened one of the pieces of foil on the top of her head then slid the foil off. 'You are done!' He removed the rest of the foil, leaving her looking something like a scarecrow with a head of sticky straw, then gestured for her to follow him to the sinks.

But as Bradley started to massage her head, Catherine fought the relaxation she usually surrendered to. There was no way she could start moaning in the middle of the busy marquee. Not unless she wanted to be forever known as the marquee moaner or something similar. She knew from Jamal that there were forums where stylists discussed that kind of thing and the thought of gaining such a moniker made her cringe.

If only Bradley's hands combined with the warm water on her head didn't feel quite so good...

–

Mark had closed his eyes as Jamal started chopping his hair. He thought it would be better to wait until Jamal was done then check out the finished product. He also didn't want to show any disapproval, surprise or fear while Jamal was working, so closing his eyes and focusing instead on the noises of the marquee seemed the best option. He even managed to try not to wince when he heard the buzzing of a shaver approaching his head.

Bradley had washed his hair first and Mark had found it very relaxing. Bradley had massaged his scalp with shampoo then conditioner that smelt of summer fruits, and Mark had found himself drifting off. He was actually disappointed when Bradley led him back to the chair in front of the mirror.

'I'm done cutting... apart from a few finishing touches once it's dry... but you can open your eyes now,' Jamal announced, dragging Mark from his thoughts. 'Just bear in mind that it needs to be dried for you to fully appreciate the style.'

Mark slowly opened his eyes.

Well, that was different...

He could see his ears for a start and his neck felt cold without the hair hanging down over it.

Jamal shook a bottle, then squirted some product onto his hand and proceeded to smooth it through what was left of Mark's hair. Then he picked up a hairdryer and a brush and Mark couldn't hear a thing other than the drone of the dryer, so he closed his eyes again.

'It's fabulous!' Catherine said as the dryer fell silent and Mark opened his eyes again. He stared at his reflection.

'Is that really me?' he asked.

Jamal appeared in the mirror and met his eyes.

'What do you think?' He ran his long fingers through Mark's hair, sweeping it from side to side then letting it drop, then he reached for a can of spray and misted it over Mark's head.

'It's... well, I look younger for a start.'

Mark turned to Catherine.

'Not that I was bothered about looking younger but now I do. What do you think, Catherine?'

—

Catherine smiled at Mark. He certainly did look younger and, if it was possible, even more handsome than before. Jamal hadn't coloured Mark's hair but instead had worked with the shiny dark waves and the grey at the temples to create a shorter crop. It was graduated up to Mark's ears where the grey was most obvious then the top was longer, and Jamal had swept it over to one side so Mark looked like a celebrity footballer or an actor off to the Oscars. With his dark eyes and the few days' stubble, he was...

'Breathtaking,' she whispered.

'Pardon?' Mark frowned.

'She said you're breathtaking.' Bradley grinned.

'No!' Catherine shook her head. "I meant your hair style is breathtaking. Not you. Goodness, no!'

'Uh... thanks.' Mark grimaced. 'Not that I would have become big-headed or anything, but you put me right back into my place, Catherine. Please don't spare my feelings.'

She gasped. 'I'm sorry. I didn't mean it like that. You are... uh... very handsome.' Her cheeks blazed and she raised her cool hands to cover them. 'Mark... your hair looks great and so do you.'

She turned back to the mirror quickly and tried to will the blush to leave her face.

'She does think you're breathtaking,' Bradley whispered to Mark, deliberately loud enough for her to hear, so she shot him the glare that she reserved for particularly naughty children.

'Anyway!' Jamal said as he held a scissors aloft. 'Time to chop your locks, Catherine. Ready or not...'

Chapter 13

A hush fell in the marquee as the judges walked around, holding their clipboards to their chests, their sharp eyes scanning every model's head. Under the heat of their gaze, Catherine felt very uncomfortable and she hoped they would soon move on. Mark was subjected to the same scrutiny then Jamal was questioned about his techniques and the products he had used to achieve the styles.

When the judges finally went to the next workstation, Mark wiped his brow and sighed loudly.

'I thought they'd never leave us.' He grimaced.

'Me too. That was really stressful,' Catherine stretched in her chair. 'I could do with some air.'

'Not yet!' Jamal held up a hand. 'They might come back and we can't risk the wind ruining your style.'

Catherine nodded then eyed her reflection in the mirror. Jamal had added some white highlights to her blonde hair along with some silvery streaks. While he was in the process of adding the colour, she'd been worried that it would make her appear older, but the silver and white blonde actually seemed to make her eyes sparkle and added a luminosity to her skin. He had then washed and dried her hair before working a curl serum into it and pinning some of it up. The hair he'd left down had been curled with tongs. The finished effect reminded her of a painting she'd seen of an ancient Greek goddess.

'It looks good,' Mark said and she met his eyes in the mirror. He was still in his chair but leaning closer to her and if she'd put out her hand, she could have touched him. She wanted to touch him. 'It really suits you.'

She smiled. 'Far too glamorous for a deputy head teacher, though.'

'Hey, don't knock it. Nothing wrong with adding some glamour to the local primary school. Might start a trend.' Mark laughed.

'I rarely fuss with my hair before I go to work in the mornings.'

'She's not lying.' Jamal rolled his eyes. 'She scrapes it back into a bun or a ponytail and off she goes. Not exactly showcasing our efforts at Hairway to Heaven and she could be such a great advert for us with her being a respected member of the community and all that.'

'Jamal, you know I don't have the time or inclination to fuss with my hair before work. It's not important anyway as long as I'm smart and presentable. I don't need to look like some glamorous model or celebrity.'

'Catherine, you always look beautiful,' Bradley butted in. 'Take no notice.'

Catherine smiled her thanks at Bradley, and out the corner of her eye, she could see Mark nodding. Did he think she was beautiful? She hoped so.

'Ladies and gentlemen, it's time for the catwalk so grab your models and head outside!'

Everyone stood up and the stylists removed their models' capes, then in threes, they headed for the entrance to the marquee. Jamal took Catherine's hand and then Mark's, and suddenly it was their turn.

Outside, the catwalk – basically a length of red material – stretched out before them in front the marquee and down the beach in the direction of the sea. At the sides were temporary fences to stop people cutting across the material and getting sand all over it. As the previous stylist and his models returned to the marquee and went inside, Jamal whispered, 'Come on, my loves. Strut your stuff!'

And they did.

Catherine plastered a smile on her face and sent up a silent thank you to Bradley for finding her the thick opaque tights that now gave her enough coverage to feel comfortable in front of the many eyes and cameras that were focused on them. Mark had been given a similar pair, but his were black.

The costumes Jamal had chosen for them made them look like fantasy ravens. They consisted of spandex leotards with fake purple feather plumes coming from the shoulders and the behinds. Libby had added some extra material and even a kind of codpiece to Mark's after the fitting, so he didn't have to worry about revealing everything to the crowds.

As they sashayed along the catwalk, Catherine caught Mark grinning at her and she grinned back. Jamal was between them, his head held high, and she could see that he was loving every minute of it. All around them, people cheered and whistled. In that moment, Catherine felt invigorated and alive. Every fibre of her being tingled and goosebumps rose all over her skin. She knew she really was embracing life.

After they had returned to the marquee and the final stylist had come back inside, clapping from the other side of the marquee caught their attention and Bradley muttered, 'Here goes…'

One of the judges, a fifty-something man whose forehead was so smooth someone could have skied down it, held up a hand. 'Thank you for your patience, everyone. What a day it has been!' He pushed up the sleeves of his beige linen shirt then smoothed back his brown quiff – the only hair on his otherwise shaved head. 'This year's entries are incredibly impressive, and stylists, you have set the bar high. From chic to sexy, retro to futuristic, you've covered them all. Every hairstyle was perfectly matched to a costume, so an extra well done on that. But… there can be only one winner…' He looked around the marquee for effect then clicked his fingers. 'The winner is… Jamal Wilson of Hairway to Heaven!'

Applause erupted around the marquee, along with a few gasps, and Jamal covered his mouth with both hands then grabbed Bradley and hugged him. Catherine and Mark stood up and clapped loudly then Jamal pulled them into hugs too.

The judge held up his hands again for silence. 'It was a close one, because, as I said, there are some wonderful styles here but what Jamal has done with his male and female models was turning them from ordinary Joes into delicious Delilahs… or should I say ravishing ravens. I especially like the codpiece!' He looked over and winked at Mark.

Catherine frowned at Mark and he mouthed *Delicious Delilahs? Ravishing ravens?*

She shrugged but her chest shook with laughter and happiness. Jamal had won again and it would be good for his business and good for Penhallow Sands, as the more business the village brought in, the better for all concerned.

As champagne corks were popped, photographs were taken and people came to congratulate Jamal and to take a closer look at Catherine and Mark's hairstyles, Lucy also approached the workstation. Catherine watched as she shook Jamal's hand then he pulled her into a hug and whispered something into her ear. She nodded and smiled, her eyes shining. Catherine knew how kind and generous Jamal was, and suspected that he'd probably just reassured Lucy and told her that she'd still have a trial at the salon, probably even a permanent job if she wanted it. After all, Lucy's models looked amazing and she was clearly a talented hair stylist, so if she could provide beauty treatments too, then she'd be an asset to the business.

An hour later, Catherine's head was fuzzy from the champagne, excitement and having dozens of photographs taken and all she wanted was to get out into the fresh air.

'You feeling okay?' Mark asked, gently touching her elbow.

'A bit warm to be honest. It's making my head spin.'

'Shall we go outside? I think they've finished with us now.'

She nodded and followed him out to the beach.

The afternoon was bright and the beach was busy. The catwalk had been removed and people made their way across the beach unhindered. For as far as she could see, there were people: on beach towels, deckchairs, in the sea and walking along the seafront.

'I wish we could go for a swim.' She gazed wistfully at the water.

'We can… if you like.'

'It's too busy and I don't have my costume.'

'You are kind of wearing a leotard,' he said as he gestured at her outfit.

'Oh we can't swim in these. Jamal will probably want to put them in a display case at the salon.'

'I hope I haven't perspired too much in mine then.' Mark plucked at the clingy material. 'You fancy getting out of here? Perhaps come up to Plum Tree?'

The idea appealed enormously.

'Where were you thinking?'

'I could make us some lunch. I have some cold beers in the fridge and we're guaranteed peace and quiet. I could also take you to this secret place I discovered recently.'

'Secret place?' Catherine frowned. 'What secret place?'

'If I tell you, it won't be a secret. I'd prefer to show you.'

He looked away then, as if he was almost embarrassed to ask her, and Catherine found his uncertainty endearing. He wasn't at all arrogant or pushy and he didn't make her feel uncomfortable or threatened the way some men did just by looking at her. She felt very comfortable with Mark and reassured by his behaviour and actions. She knew she could decline his offer and he wouldn't be offended at all; he'd just go about his business and that would be that.

But she was curious to know more about him, to find out more about who he was, about what he wrote and about his life before Penhallow Sands. She wanted to get to know him better and that thought made her both nervous and excited.

'That sounds perfect. I'll just let Jamal and Bradley know that we're leaving. We'd should probably get changed at Hairway first though, as I don't fancy keeping this costume on all day.'

'That sounds like a very good plan.'

—

Catherine and Mark had walked up to Plum Tree Cottage along country lanes with their high green hedgerows full with summer growth, then they'd cut across fields of corn, rapeseed and wildflowers. It was a beautiful day and it felt good to be alive, to be able to enjoy the breeze on her face and in her hair and the sun on her skin. After being cooped up in the marquee all morning, being outside was wonderful and even though most of the walk was uphill, and at times the muscles in her legs burned and her breath came quickly, it was still enjoyable.

When they were about ten minutes from the cottage, Mark stopped walking and turned around. Catherine did the same and gasped, because there, spread out in front of them was the breathtaking view of Penhallow Sands, of the coastline that curled away around the rest of Cornwall to their left and right and the dark mass of the sea with white breakers rising and curling then disappearing again.

'It's an incredible view, isn't it?' Mark said and Catherine nodded.

'The best there is.'

She glanced at him, admiring the flush in his cheeks after the exercise and his new, fancy haircut that made him look younger and even more handsome. Being with Mark made her feel funny, a mixture of excited and nervous, and that reminded her of what it felt like to be a teenager. Not that she'd ever want to go back to that age when everything was so emotional and challenging and she had no idea what life held in store for her – other than that she had to be there to support her mother – but it was still nice to feel the anticipation that came with the unknown. And Mark was the unknown.

Catherine didn't know what he was thinking, what he wanted from her or even if he'd be around this time next month let alone next year, and it was stirring something inside her that she hadn't felt before. It was a rebellious emotion, a side to her that wanted to be a bit reckless, to enjoy living in the moment and not to worry about the consequences for once. She was always so sensible, so aware of how her actions impacted upon those around her and it could be exhausting being the one everyone else could rely on all the time – from pupils to teaching staff to the school governors to the head teacher and to her mother. For one day, one moment, Catherine wanted to live selfishly. To do something just for herself.

'That's a lovely smile.' Mark broke into her thoughts. 'What were you thinking?'

She shrugged. 'Oh… just about what a great day it's been so far.'

'It has been a lot of fun.' He nodded. 'I'll be honest though… I'm glad to get you away from everyone else.'

'You are?'

She met his gaze, his intense dark eyes with their dark lashes and something inside her flipped over.

'I am. I want to get to know you better.'

'You do?'

'I do. Every time we've tried to have a conversation up to this point, something has got in the way. Now it'll just be you, me and some ice-cold beers.'

'Sounds perfect.'

'Not far to go now.'

They started walking again and Catherine knew that she was still smiling like the cat that got the cream. She couldn't help it and she didn't care. Mark wanted to get to know her better. She almost started to skip...

–

Ten minutes later, they'd reached the cottage and Mark led her around the back. Catherine had walked past Plum Tree Cottage a few times but never been inside. Set in its own land, it was a lovely private location and she doubted many people actually came this way because they'd use the road or the cycle paths and the walking routes. She knew it wasn't that far from Greenacres House and Vineyard, but it was still a good walk and it was unlikely that Holly or Rich would arrive unannounced. It added to her sense of anticipation, knowing that she really was going to have some time alone with Mark.

The back garden was pretty and neat with borders bursting with colourful flowers and roses climbing up the cottage and around a small pergola. Their scent filled the air, rich and sweet and Catherine inhaled deeply, appreciating the uplifting, heady scent. White sheets and a few T-shirts swayed back and forth in the breeze on a rotary washing line off to the left and to the right, in the far corner of the garden was a summer house with its doors wide open. She wondered what it would be like to live here, to wake up in the morning and head outside to eat breakfast. Would she ever want to leave again, even to go to work? It would probably be very difficult, especially if Mark was here, warm and welcoming, handsome and sexy as hell.

Mark let them into the kitchen and placed his keys on the kitchen table. The room had aromas of wood smoke, spices and coffee. It was delicious and homely.

'Is it all right if I use the bathroom?' she asked.

'Of course. It's upstairs. You want me to show you?'

'No, it's fine, I can find my own way.'

She went through to the hallway then climbed the stairs, taking in how clean and tidy everything was. Mark had either cleaned up recently or liked to keep his house in order. If she'd come here to find smelly socks on the floor and dishes in the sink, then it wouldn't have put her off Mark, but it might have made her question what she already thought about him. Just a bit, anyway.

She found the bathroom, used the toilet then washed her hands and met her eyes in the mirror above the sink, surprised by her reflection. Her hair did look good but it didn't look like her; it was as though she was looking at a more polished version of herself that she might see after she'd been airbrushed in a photograph. She smiled, showing her white teeth then pouted the way that people often did in selfies, and that made her laugh and shake her head. Catherine had never thought of herself as sexy or even particularly attractive, and she knew that wasn't about to change now just because she had a new hairstyle. She'd always believed that she was presentable enough and she did her best to maintain what she'd been given. She washed and conditioned her hair and had it cut and highlighted when she could find the time; she cleansed and moisturised her skin daily; she drank plenty of water and she walked and swam to keep in shape and to keep her heart healthy. She'd never seen any point in doing more because she was a busy person and because she couldn't see how it would impact upon her life anyway. Who would care if she had fuller lips or a line-free brow? Who would know if she had a cellulite free bum and thighs or a flawless bikini line?

But now she did wonder what Mark thought about her appearance. Did he find her relatively attractive? She had to assume so because she was here, in his cottage, wasn't she? Was there a possibility that he saw more than she did? It was her face and she had looked at it every day for years, so perhaps he saw it differently. In the romance novels she read, especially in the Alex Radcliffe ones, the hero always saw the heroine's beauty both inside and out, and he appreciated everything about her, including her quirks and idiosyncrasies. But did that happen in real life? Was she the type of woman Mark could desire and want to grow old with?

Catherine shook her head. Now she was getting carried away and it was silly. She should just take the afternoon as it came and enjoy herself. She didn't want to be disappointed by letting her imagination run away with her.

She left the bathroom and looked both ways along the landing, wanting desperately to have a peek inside the bedrooms but knowing that it was rather nosy and that, if Mark caught her or heard her, then she'd be mortified, so she suppressed her curiosity and headed for the stairs instead.

Mark was trying to stay calm but he couldn't help feeling a flicker of excitement that he had a whole afternoon alone with Catherine. It had been a good morning down at the beach but he hadn't expected Catherine to agree to come up to the cottage with him; he hadn't even known he was going to ask her until he did, but now she was here and he wanted to ensure that she had an enjoyable afternoon.

It had been so long since he'd been alone with a woman. In fact, the last woman he'd been alone with had been Ellie and they'd known each other for most of their lives. Catherine was still basically a stranger to him in so many ways. Yes, he knew her, but there was lots he didn't know about her. They could spend time together this afternoon and find that they didn't like certain things about each other or that they disagreed on topics like relationships, politics and even what music they enjoyed. He hadn't really ever dated because Ellie had been his girlfriend from such a young age, and he didn't think he'd be any good at that whole dating app, swipe left or right process. Mark certainly wasn't the type to ask a woman out in a bar or a club, or in any other situation for that matter. He knew that he needed to have some sort of friendship with a woman first and that anything akin to a blind date would throw him headfirst into a boiling pot of nerves and insecurity. Today, he'd invited Catherine to Plum Tree Cottage because he did want to be alone with her, to speak to her and find out more about her. The fact that he thought she was beautiful, that he already loved the way her smile lit up her face and the way she played with her hair when she was feeling anxious or doubtful, was something he couldn't ignore, of course. But then he couldn't see why it wasn't okay for them to spend some time alone together. They were both adults, capable of making up their own minds and Catherine had seemed happy to accept his invitation.

He heard her enter the kitchen so he turned and smiled, trying to relax his shoulders and to act normally. It was possible that Catherine saw him as a friend and nothing more, that she had come here to enjoy the afternoon with him away from the village, that she really did just want some peace and quiet. But he hoped it was more than that, and sensed that it was. Mark was happy to go with the flow, to enjoy her company and see what happened. There was no point worrying about anything, because that would just place pressure on him and then he'd be tense and unnatural, awkward and goofy.

'I've got the beers out of the fridge but I thought we might as well have some lunch too. Is there anything you don't eat or don't like?'

She shook her head. 'I'm not a particularly fussy eater.'

'Okay, well do you want to go and sit outside and I'll make us a picnic?'

'No.'

His heart sank.

'I'll stay right here and give you a hand.'

Her broad smile warmed him right through.

'Okay then. Let's see what I've got in the fridge, shall we?'

And as they stood side by side gazing into the large fridge, Mark felt happier than he had done in quite some time. It was good to have company, especially the company of an intelligent and very beautiful woman. In that moment, he realised exactly how much he'd missed having someone around and he was very glad that Catherine had accepted his invitation.

If only he could stop thinking about kissing her. Unless, of course, she was thinking about kissing him too.

Chapter 14

'I have an idea,' Mark said as he stood looking at the food he had prepared with Catherine's help. 'Let's pack this up and take it to the secret place I told you about earlier. I thought we could go there after lunch, but now I'm thinking that we could have a picnic there.'

Catherine's eyes widened. 'That sounds wonderful.'

Mark grabbed some sandwich bags and they packed all of the food carefully then he loaded it into a rucksack along with some chilled beers and two bottles of water.

'I'll just grab a few more things then we can head off.'

He left Catherine in the kitchen and padded up the stairs. He got two towels, some clean T-shirts and two pairs of swimming shorts as well as suncream and a rolled-up picnic blanket. He tucked them into a smaller rucksack that he had under his bed, then returned to the kitchen.

'Ready?' He asked Catherine.

'I am.' She smiled and he was filled with warmth. He hoped she would like the spot he'd decided upon for their picnic.

Mark wanted to carry both rucksacks, but Catherine wouldn't let him, so he took the one with the food and she the smaller one. He led the way across the field and along the path, telling Catherine to be careful of the brambles and stinging nettles.

'I've never been to a secret location before,' Catherine said.

'I thought you might have been here, being a local.' Mark slowed his pace when they emerged from the leafy canopy into the sunshine.

'Are we having a picnic here on the clifftop or in a field?' she asked.

'No, it's better than that,' he said, then he held out his hand.

Catherine slid her hand into his and he held her tight. The sensation of skin on skin, the security of their palms meeting and their fingers entwining made his heart beat faster. Human connection was so powerful – physical, intellectual and emotional and he felt it with Catherine. He wanted her on more than one level, wanted to know her in so many ways.

They walked down to the stile then he held Catherine's hand as she climbed over and he followed.

'Plums!' she exclaimed.

'Want some?'

'Are we allowed to pick them?' She looked around.

'I wondered about that before but there are so many on the ground rotting that I think they've been forgotten about. I'm sure it's okay to take a few of the ripe ones.'

They picked four and Mark slid them into the rucksack on top of the rest of the food.

'Right, there's a steep path the descend then we'll be there.'

'Plum Tree Bay?' she asked, smiling.

'You read the sign.'

'I've heard of it but not in a long time. When I was at school, some of the kids used to go there but it wasn't accessible without a boat, and I wasn't exactly in the "in" crowd so I was never invited. I knew there was meant to be a path near the vineyard but it would have never occurred to me to come here alone because that would have taken bravery and it also seemed kind of sad.'

'You are brave, Catherine. Look at what you've done with your life.'

She shrugged. 'I have a stable job at the school in the village I live in. I still live with my mother and I'm in my thirties. I don't travel and I don't take risks... with anything.'

'I think teaching is an incredibly challenging career and you have moved from classroom teacher to deputy head. I bet you'll be a head teacher one day too. That's brave, Catherine. Some people run away from their problems but you stood and fought for what you believed in. You stayed and supported your mother. Don't ever dismiss how brave that is or how strong you are.'

She looked away and a blush stole over her cheeks.

'You're too kind.'

Mark reached for her hand again.

'Hey, I'm not being kind; I'm being honest. So many people get away from their families and put distance between them because it's easier than seeing them every day. Not all people have close relationships with their parents or siblings. You've been your mother's rock. I haven't been here long but even I can see that. As for the other stuff... about when you were growing up...' He shrugged. 'Kids can be cruel. So what if you weren't in the so-called popular crowd. Neither was I. I loved reading and making up stories and I was always the dorky kid who preferred reading hour to football.'

'Really?' Her eyebrows raised.

'Really. It's a shame you didn't get to see the bay but in a way I'm glad.'

'You are? Why?'

'Because I get to show it to you.'

Catherine pressed her lips together then a smile lit up her face.

'You know what? So am I.'

'Let's get down there then.'

They took their time, carefully negotiating the steep path and Mark kept checking on Catherine. He enjoyed looking out for her and he was delighted that he'd be the one to show her the bay. It would be something they could share, something that he could give to her.

At the bottom of the path, they linked hands again then walked out onto the small beach. The tide was on the way in and the small bay looked like a perfect crescent moon hugged by the cliffs that created the secluded beach.

'It's so beautiful, Mark.'

He smiled down at her. 'Just like you.'

-

Catherine helped Mark to set out the picnic blanket then they spread the food out. He opened two of the beers and handed one to Catherine.

'Cheers!'

'Cheers!'

They clinked bottles then sat on the blanket.

'I'm really glad I came to Penhallow Sands.' Mark leant back on his elbows.

'You are?'

He nodded. 'I've had a wonderful few weeks and done things I never would have imagined doing before.'

'Like what?'

'I delivered a baby; I found out that cats like having friends; I took part in a hairstyle competition as a hair model and I've been able to accept that my own company's not that bad.'

'You didn't like being alone before?'

'Well, I did like some peace and quiet, but here, staying in Plum Tree, I've had proper time alone to think and to work through some things. I feel like I've been able to let go of my past and to look to the future again.'

'That's good.'

Catherine sipped the beer that was still cold from the fridge. It was light and refreshing and the alcohol was relaxing her.

'It makes me wonder what else I'll get to do here.' His cheeks flushed as he looked up at her from under his dark lashes and heat spread over her own skin. He looked so good reclining there with the sun on his face and his new short haircut. His eyes were dark green pools, inviting her closer.

'You're not at all dorky.'

'Thank you. I think. But it's not really a label I mind.'

'Okay, then you're a… sexy dork.'

She giggled then sipped her beer again.

'Now *that* I like.' He nodded. 'Are you hungry yet?'

Catherine bit back the comment that sprang to mind about a different kind of hunger and instead nodded.

'How about a dip in the water before we eat?' Mark asked.

'I don't have my costume.'

'I brought shorts and a T-shirt.' Mark patted the smaller rucksack.

'Will they fit?'

'They'll be big on you but at least you can go into the water then.'

'I would like a swim. It does look inviting.'

Mark set his beer down then opened the rucksack and handed Catherine some shorts and the smallest of his T-shirts that he could find. She took them behind some rocks and changed quickly while Mark did the same.

The T-shirt was big but she tied a knot in the front of it and folded the waistband of the shorts over a few times to tighten them. When she stepped back out, Mark gave a whistle.

'You look amazing.'

'Hardly!' She looked down at herself. 'But thank you anyway.'

'Shall we swim?'

'Oh…' She paused.

'What is it?'

'What about our hair?'

'I don't think Jamal will mind now, will he? Unless you were planning on sleeping sitting up tonight, the style would be ruined anyway.'

'True.' She nodded.

They held hands and walked down to the water then let it lap over their toes before wading in to their knees.

'Are you one for going in gradually or a "rip the plaster off quickly" kind of swimmer?' Mark wiggled his eyebrows.

'Uh… it usually depends how cold the water is.'

'And today how is it?'

Catherine tilted her head. 'It's not bad.'

'I'll help you make your decision, shall I?'

'What?'

He stepped closer to her and she stiffened. 'What are you going to do? Mark?'

He leant forwards and scooped her up in his arms and she squealed.

'No! Not like this…'

'You mean you don't want to be dunked?' He smiled.

Catherine slid her arms around his neck and held on tight.

'Only if you keep hold of me.'

'You've got yourself a deal.'

He waded slowly into the water and it washed over them as they clung together. Soon they were immersed to their chests, but Mark didn't let go of her and Catherine kept her arms around him. As Mark held her gaze, his eyes softened and something inside her shifted. This man was special and she wanted to be with him.

–

When they finally released each other, they swam for a bit, but Mark found that he wanted to hold Catherine close again. Her weight in his arms, her arms around his neck, all made him feel uplifted and alive and he was keen to experience that again.

They floated back into the shallows and Catherine reached out a hand. Mark took it then smiled as he held their hands up.

'Our fingers are getting wrinkly.'

'I know. Shall we go and eat? I'm quite hungry now.'

They waded out of the sea and he watched as Catherine squeezed water out of his shorts and T-shirt. He'd neglected to mention his naked solo swims to Catherine, not wanting to make her uncomfortable, tempting as it was to raise the idea. The T-shirt clung to her curves like a second skin and her long blonde hair was slicked back from her face. She had such pretty features and a beautiful figure that Mark's desire roared inside him.

As they sat back on the picnic blanket, he removed the food from the bags and opened two fresh beers.

'Enjoy!' he said as he handed Catherine a beer then gestured at the food.

'Oh I will. This all looks amazing.'

—

They ate in a comfortable silence, tucking into the picnic of plump bright green olives, carrot sticks and hummus, smoked salmon and cucumber sandwiches, mini puff pastry cheese and onion tarts and a light lemon cheese-cake with a buttery biscuit base. When they'd finished, Catherine smiled lazily at Mark.

'Do you always eat this well?'

'I'll let you into a secret…' He tapped his bottle against hers. 'I just can't resist the bakery or Shell's Shack. Every time I'm in Penhallow Sands, I have to pop into both establishments and buy something, whether it's a cake, pie or whatever's their daily special.'

'Is that why you run?'

'Yes.' He nodded. 'Otherwise I'd be twice the man I am. Literally!'

'This is a perfect spot, Mark.'

They hadn't seen or heard another soul for hours and it was as if they were completely cut off from the world in Plum Tree Bay, just two people enjoying each other's company without fear of being disturbed. Catherine had left her mobile phone in her bag in Mark's kitchen and hadn't missed it at all, which was refreshing because normally she was a slave to it – whether to keep a check on work emails or, if in work, to check for messages from her mother. Now she thought about it, she was constantly on call for other people and never really got to switch off. Her time, her life, were never her own and that couldn't be good. She noticed that Mark didn't have a mobile on him either, and assumed he must have left his at the cottage too. It was good to exist without any interruptions from the outside world and Catherine realised that life must have been like this before mobile phones became so popular.

'I love it here in Penhallow Sands. I thought I'd always be a die-hard London fan but after… after my life changed, I guess what I wanted did too.'

'How did your life change?' Catherine asked, then realised it was probably something he didn't want to discuss. 'I'm sorry. I understand that you might not want to share.'

'No… it's fine.' He sipped from his bottle then set it down on the sand. 'I was in a long-term relationship. And by long-term, I mean that we got together when we were very young. Just sixteen, in fact.'

'Wow!' Catherine sat up. 'That is very young. And you only broke up recently?'

'About six months ago officially.'

'You had an unofficial breakup?'

He gave a wry laugh. 'Yeah, I guess. See… this is quite embarrassing, but about a year ago, I took Ellie to Paris to celebrate her birthday and… we went up the Eiffel Tower and I… proposed.'

Catherine bit her lip. 'I'm guessing she didn't accept?'

He shook his head. 'Nope. And it wasn't the first time.'

'You proposed more than once?'

Catherine watched him carefully, wondering why a woman he'd been with for so many years would refuse to marry him. Of course, it might have been that Ellie wasn't keen on marriage… but surely, Mark would have been aware of that. So it must have been something else. Perhaps she just hadn't loved Mark the way he loved her.

'I know that proposing at the top of the Eiffel Tower can be seen as being a bit cheesy, perhaps, and I could have come up with something more original, but I guess I'm just an old-fashioned kind of guy.'

'An old-fashioned romantic.' Catherine sighed. She would love to have met someone like that who'd wine and dine her, whisk her away to romantic locations and make her feel special the way the heroes in romance novels did.

'I know, right? Cheesy, isn't it?'

'Not at all. I think it's lovely.'

'You do?' The uncertainty in his eyes made her want to hug him.

'Definitely.'

'Ellie didn't. And when she turned me down for the third time, I realised that something wasn't right. I mean, I knew before that but I kept trying. I didn't know what else to do. I'm not the type to play the field and I thought we had something special, something worth fighting for, but Ellie proved me wrong.'

'I'm sorry.'

'It's certainly not your fault.' He rubbed his hands over his face. 'And the worst thing about it was that she walked off and left me there, on my knees, Paris spread out before me and a diamond ring in an open box in my hand. People were staring at me as if I was mad, some shaking their heads in pity.'

'Oh Mark, that's so awful.'

'Tell me about it. I just stayed there for ages. I knew that if I got up and left the Eiffel Tower, then it would be over for good. Of course, I did get up eventually and I went back to our hotel room and found her packing. She said she had doubts about us and had done for a long time and that she needed some time to think.'

'What did you do?'

'Went back to our London flat, packed my bags and went to stay with a friend. I thought that she might miss me if she had some time away from me. I sound pathetic, don't I?'

'No, you don't. You sound like you really cared about her.'

'I did care. I was also afraid of what breaking up would mean. There I was, heading towards forty, about to be single and homeless. Not exactly what I thought I'd be dealing with at that age.'

'Life can surprise us all.'

'Indeed it can.' He cleared his throat.

Mark gazed out at the sea and Catherine watched him from the corner of her eye. He'd been through such a lot. To be turned down by the woman he'd been with for so long – and three times – must have been very hard indeed. And he was such a gentle person, so kind and self-deprecating, funny and sincere. He deserved better and Catherine hoped he would have a happier future.

Mark pulled the rucksack closer then reached inside and pulled out a box of truffles.

'I thought you might be peckish.' He handed her the box.

'Peckish?' She laughed. 'Well, my blood sugar *had* dropped a bit seeing as how I hadn't eaten for about five minutes. Best keep eating, I guess.'

She opened the truffles and popped one into her mouth then handed the box to Mark. As the cocoa-dusted chocolate dissolved on her tongue, the rich truffle was revealed, cool, creamy and sweet.

'These are good.'

'Also purchased in the village.'

'I'll have to get you to do my shopping,' she teased.

'Any time.' He met her gaze and her insides fluttered.

'So what happened after you moved out?'

'I stayed with friends for a few months, you know, the sofa surfing that I told you about, then Ellie asked to meet up. I thought perhaps she'd changed her mind but no… it was to tell me that she was in love with someone else and had been for months.'

'She was cheating?' Catherine picked up her fresh beer.

'It seems that way.'

'Goodness, Mark, that's awful.' Catherine squeezed his arm.

'It's okay. At the time I was furious, upset, lost, but you move on. It's still early days, really, I suppose, but I'm doing okay. Better than okay since I moved here.'

'I'm so glad. What's she like?' Catherine was curious to know more about the woman Mark had loved.

'She's a tennis coach so she's very fit and energetic, usually running around, never sitting still for long. My mother always warned me it could be the sign of a restless heart. She has red hair in one of those elfin cuts and bright hazel eyes that can draw you in or cut you off cold, depending on her mood.'

'She sounds… nice.'

He laughed. 'She's very striking physically, even I could see that after twenty years together, but she can also be quite hard and cold.'

'How do you feel about her now?' Catherine almost didn't want to ask but Mark seemed to want to talk about it.

'Well, we've settled our joint finances and she bought me out of the flat. She moved her lover in and I think that finally sealed it all for me. It was the kick up the bum I needed to pull myself together. It hurt but it's fading, especially since I left London. It was like severing the final cord, really and it has definitely helped.' He sipped his beer. 'The worst thing has been the writer's block.'

'Of course, you're an author. Come on then, I want to hear more about this writing!' Catherine tucked her legs under her then leaned closer to him. 'Please tell me more. What do you write? How successful are you? Do you have an agent and a large following of devoted readers and bloggers?'

'At the moment, I'm struggling to write, because since Ellie and I split up, something has been stopping me. It's like I've had a concrete block at the front of my brain and nothing can move it. I've had some ideas and inspiration but I can't get much down on the page.'

'That must be very frustrating.'

'It is.' He nodded. 'Writing is my job and although I've got royalties coming in every quarter, I also had an advance for my next book, and I have deadlines which at the moment, I don't think I'm going to meet.'

'Well, keep talking and perhaps it will help. Perhaps we can work at freeing your mind and giving your creativity a boost.'

'That would be amazing.' He flashed her a smile. 'So… when I started writing, I wrote thrillers. You know the dark, gritty psychological books that seem to dominate the charts?'

'I do.'

'But something was off.'

'How so?'

Catherine popped another truffle into her mouth.

'Well, they just flopped. My agent liked them, as did the publisher I was with at the time, but for some reason, the readers didn't. Then, based on some of the elements of my thrillers, my agent suggested a change of direction.'

'And?' Catherine was fascinated.

'I had an idea so I ran with it and before I knew it, I had written a full romance novel. I sent it to my agent and she loved it. She said it was perfect for the women's fiction market and she had an editor in mind for it.'

'And they snapped it up?'

'Yes, and contracted more.'

'I love romance novels but I haven't read any of yours, at least I don't think so. I don't recall seeing your name anywhere. Sorry.'

'You might have done but not realise it. In fact, I know you have done because you were checking one of them out of the library when I first saw you.'

Catherine frowned, trying to remember what books she'd taken out that day.

'No… you're not? It's not possible. Is it?' Goosebumps rose on her arms.

'I'm Alex Radcliffe.'

Catherine gasped.

'No!'

'Yes.'

'But I thought… well… I used to assume that Alex Radcliffe was a woman, but more recently I had started to question my assumption, but… are you really?' She shook her head and her mouth fell open. 'I can't believe this!'

'I know. Most people assume I'm a woman, like you did. We kept it a mystery because my earlier books had flopped and we didn't want to reveal my actual name in case we had reviewer comments along the lines of "*Should have stuck to crime*" and all that. My agent and publisher thought it would be better to build my reputation and brand first, then have a big reveal at a publication party and in the book magazines and so on. That way, I'd have a loyal readership first and hopefully sell even more books by announcing the fact that Alex Radcliffe is a man. They even mentioned possible TV appearances as a way to generate publicity, like early morning television and Friday night chat shows. I was getting quite excited at the thought of sitting on Graham Norton's sofa along with actual celebrities. It hasn't happened yet and we're still building the momentum, but I have to accept that it won't happen if I can't get my brain into gear again.'

'Goodness me.' Catherine shook her head. 'I'm stunned.' She glanced at him and her heart ached at the uncertainty in his expression. 'Not in a bad way. You're... you're one of my favourite authors, Mark. I love your books. The stories always get me right here.' She held her free hand over her heart. 'I've spent many hours wishing there were men out there like the men in your books. I mean... I know they're just fictional characters, but a woman can dream, right?'

She was sitting with the author of her favourite books. This was the man who had written as though he could see right into her heart, as if he knew exactly how she had always longed to be loved.

'They are fictional, but they do have an element of me and male friends of mine in them.'

'Of course!' She nodded. 'The old-fashioned romance, like taking the women flowers and romantic dates and all that.'

'And the women are romantic too.'

'They are. Just how I always imagined I would be if I...' She cut herself off and looked away.

'If you what?' he asked.

'Well... if I was in a long-term relationship.'

'That's something I can't get over with you, Catherine. You're incredibly lovely and yet, you're single. And please don't take that the wrong way. I don't think relationships are compulsory, and in no way do I think that being in a relationship or getting married is the only way to live, because I don't. Not at all. However, if you meet someone who makes you smile, who can be there for you when times are tough and who can be both lover and friend... then that's when a relationship can be a good thing.'

Catherine smiled. 'Exactly that.'

'But you've never… felt that?'

'Once. I did have a relationship when I was younger. I fell in love with a fellow PGCE student named Damon Looe. He was going to be a primary school teacher too. He was sweet and handsome and excited about life. We got on well and had plenty in common. He treated me well.'

'But?'

'At the end of the course, I got a job at Penhallow Sands Primary School as a classroom teacher and Damon got a job at a school in Weymouth. You have to take jobs where they arise, really, or risk not being employed. One of us could have done some supply teaching or waited until something closer to the other one came up but there were other things happening too. His older sister lost a baby and needed him around and I had things here… my mother, and then my job, and both took up so much time. Before I knew it, I hadn't seen Damon in weeks, then months and then… we knew it was silly to try to keep it going between us. It had fizzled out and we were friends and nothing more.'

'Do you keep in touch?'

'Christmas cards and the odd birthday card but he's married now and has two young children. Since then, I've had a few dates with other teachers that I've met on courses and the like but nothing ever felt right. Besides which, I'm always so busy here, and relationships take commitment and energy… I don't know… I guess I knew that my mother needed that energy, as did my job, and it would have been unfair to expect a man to deal with what was left.'

'I'm sorry.'

Catherine shook her head. 'What are you sorry for?'

'You've had a difficult time of it too.'

'Not as bad as you. I just gave up on the one relationship I could have worked at because I felt I was needed here. I made what I thought was a sensible choice. You were... badly let down.'

'So we've both lost out.'

'I guess we have.'

They clinked bottles.

'But you know what?' he asked, moving closer to Catherine on the blanket.

'What?' she asked, her heart thudding so loudly she thought he might hear it.

'I'm kind of glad.'

'You are?'

He nodded then placed his beer back on the sand, took Catherine's and put it next to his. When he turned back to her, she held her breath, because the look in his eyes made her whole body tingle.

'If we'd both stayed with the people from our pasts, then we wouldn't be here today, together, like this.'

'We wouldn't.'

He gently stroked the side of her face and she sighed. Her whole body responded to his touch and she felt breathless with anticipation.

'Catherine?'

'Yes?'

'Is it all right if I kiss you?'

'I'd really like it if you did.'

Her voice was husky with desire and as he moved closer, cupping her chin in his big hands, she went weak.

When he brushed his lips against hers, gently at first and then with more pressure, she slid her arms around his neck and surrendered to sensation.

Sometimes, denying herself was the right thing to do. She had responsibilities, people relying on her and her position in the community to think about. But today, it was about her and Mark and the spark that had been lit between them. Catherine wanted to be with him and it was clear he felt the same.

This was about the here and now at Plum Tree Bay.

Chapter 15

When Catherine woke the next morning she stretched and yawned, then her relaxed state turned to surprise when she realised that she wasn't in her own bedroom. She turned her head slowly to the right and there he was.

Mark. His breathing was slow and steady, his presence next to her in the bed solid and reassuring.

Then doubts crept in, stealing away her desire to snuggle closer to him, dampening the temptation to press a gentle kiss to his lips.

What time was it? How long had she been asleep? After they'd made love, she must have fallen into a deep slumber. It was the best sleep she'd had in a long time.

She went to reach for her mobile then remembered she'd left it downstairs in her bag. Judging from the grey light in the bedroom, it could be late evening. Or early morning.

Panic prickled her armpits.

If it was late evening, then fine, it would be easy enough to make up a reason for her mother as to why she'd disappeared all afternoon, but if she'd spent the night at Mark's then she would have a lot of explaining to do...

She shuddered. This was ridiculous. She was thirty-four but still worrying about what her mother would think about her staying out overnight with a man. Diana's disapproval could still get to Catherine and she wished it didn't, wished she could shrug it off, but time and conditioning had led her to this state and only a change of circumstances would change that.

She slid the quilt off slowly and shuffled to the edge of the bed then sat up. Where were her clothes? If she woke Mark up, then chances were that she wouldn't end up leaving now. Twice since they'd headed upstairs at Plum Tree Cottage after a glorious afternoon at the secluded bay – giggling and kissing like teenagers – she'd got up to leave and he'd pulled her back down and… well… they'd spent even more time appreciating each other before finally passing out. But now, she had to find out the time and get home.

Once she found her clothes, she sneaked across the landing to the bathroom then dressed and washed her face. The cottage was still and silent, making her every move feel exaggerated, her every breath seem far too loud.

Downstairs, she grabbed her bag and pulled out her mobile. Three text messages. One from Jamal and two from her mother – the first one asking when she'd be home, and the second telling her that Diana was off to bed and would see her in the morning, so could she ensure the milk bottles didn't get knocked over when she came in as they were on the doorstep.

Darn it!

And the time…

Double darn it!

Five forty-five.

A.M.

Typical that Catherine's good sleep had meant that she'd slept through until morning. Now she'd have to try to get home and sneak in before her mother awoke. Otherwise, she'd have to tell Diana where she'd been, and although she knew it was her business and so on, she didn't want to have to endure her mother's frown and muttered comments that would quite likely lead to a tirade of anger and a sulk that would go on for days if not weeks.

Catherine had enough to think about without having to digest her mother's opinion on the matter too, and she also hated it when Diana refused to speak to her. It made being at home so awkward and the tension leaked into every aspect of her life.

But she also didn't want to leave Plum Tree Cottage without saying goodbye. She wanted to head back upstairs and slide back under the covers then into Mark's arms. To press her face to his warm skin and breathe him in.

A flush crept into her cheeks as memories of last night flashed through her mind. How had they been so comfortable with each other? So passionate? So delighted in each other that they'd fallen into bed as if they hadn't a care in the world.

It just wasn't what Catherine did. She never behaved like that. But Mark had made her feel appreciated and attractive and she had felt liberated by their mutual desire.

There was a notepad on the fridge, stuck there with a magnet, so she scribbled a brief note to Mark and signed her name underneath. Then she added a kiss. It didn't feel good sneaking off like this, but it would take her twenty minutes to half an hour to get to the village and it was likely she'd be seen on the way as it was – and the news would no doubt get back to her mother – so she couldn't delay any longer.

She hesitated in the hallway as she glanced up the stairs. The choice was there, open for her to make. Stay or leave.

She sighed. She really had to get home.

—

Mark stretched out his arm, expecting to find Catherine's warm body in the bed next to him, her skin soft and sweet, her lips ripe for kissing. Instead, the other side of the bed was empty and cold.

He sat up and listened carefully. She'd probably gone to use the bathroom or even downstairs to make a cup of tea. He lay back down and smiled. It had been a long time since he'd enjoyed a cup of tea in bed with company. In fact, even when he'd been with Ellie, they'd rarely had the time to enjoy a morning cuppa together. Ellie was always rushing off somewhere, to teach an early morning tennis lesson or to a yoga session or even swimming. There were numerous times when Mark stirred to find Ellie leaving or woke to find himself alone, and he had tried not to care, tried to explain it to himself as part of being in a long-term relationship or being with a sporty partner, but it didn't mean that he hadn't sometimes wished things could be different. Even when they'd managed to get away for the odd weekend or on holiday, Ellie would find a reason to be up and out early. It had often made him wonder if she didn't actually want to lie in bed with him, to greet the day together with a cuddle and a chat. But of course, now he knew that the latter was, in fact, the case.

Last night had been amazing. He hadn't had any plans for when Catherine came to the cottage; there'd been no prerequisite for her visit or expectation other than a desire to get to know her better. But they'd had a lovely afternoon, then one thing had led to another and he'd enjoyed the best night he'd had in years. They had found comfort in each other and plenty more. Catherine was sweet and slightly shy at first, but as passion took over, she became more confident and they had become lost in each other. Mark had always thought that was how desire should be, that it should be about revealing your whole self to the person you were with, to allow yourself to be consumed by what you felt for them and how good it was to be with them.

He had laid himself bare before Catherine. Completely. Utterly. Undeniably and deliciously.

He needed to see her. Right now. He was missing her already...

He swung his legs over the edge of the bed, grabbed his pyjama bottoms and pulled them on.

The bathroom was empty, so he padded down the stairs but he couldn't hear anything other than the birdsong from outside. In the kitchen, the kettle was cold and there was no sign of Catherine. He checked the lounge too then even popped his head out the back door in the hope that she might have been enjoying a glass of juice in the summer-house, but she wasn't there either.

A deep sense of loss and foreboding crept through him. Had he done something wrong or misread the situation? He'd been certain that Catherine liked him too – her actions and words last night had suggested as much – and yet, here he was: alone. Goosebumps rose on his skin and he rubbed his arms as if he could wipe them away.

Back inside, he looked around and spotted a note stuck to the fridge door. He ripped it from the pad:

Dear Mark,

*Thank you so much for a lovely afternoon swim
and picnic, as well as a very enjoyable evening. I
had a wonderful time with you. Sorry to leave so
early but I didn't like to wake you.*

Speak soon,
Catherine X

He exhaled slowly. So she had enjoyed herself and she had
left without saying anything because she needed to get
home. He wished she had woken him because he would
have liked to say goodbye and he could have given her a
lift to save her from walking back so early in the morning.
However, she had gone and he had slept through her
departure. But, she had put a kiss at the end of the note
and said she'd speak to him soon.

She'd speak to him soon.

Hope was not lost.

She hadn't abandoned him. It was okay. She just
needed to go home.

He ran the words through his mind a few times, then
pushed back his shoulders and tried to relax.

So many times throughout his life, he'd heard all about
how men slept with women then moved on to the next
one, and about how sex was just sex for men and most of
them didn't want commitment, but for Mark that wasn't
true at all and he guessed it probably wasn't true for most
men. Mark didn't sleep around; there hadn't been anyone
since Ellie and she'd been the first. He had always known
that for him there needed to be an emotional connection as well as a physical attraction, and last night, with
Catherine, he'd believed there had been both. He'd never

have gone upstairs with her if he hadn't thought there was more than lust between them because he respected her – and himself – more than that.

What was Catherine thinking and feeling right now? He found it difficult to imagine that she'd had some fun and wouldn't want anything to do with him again. Their kisses had been so tender, their lovemaking so slow and sensual. She'd got inside his head and he knew she had started to break down the walls he'd built around his heart. He had thought it wouldn't be possible, that he'd never love again, but Catherine had reached him and he wanted to hold on to what they had started.

Mark made a mug of tea and a piece of toast then took them out into the garden. He sat on the sofa in the summerhouse with the doors open and closed his eyes, breathing in the sweet scents of summer and listening to the birds singing, savouring the gentle warmth of the morning and memories of the connection he'd experienced last night. Something inside him had changed and he felt that he could breathe again, as if a weight had been lifted…

His eyes sprang open and excitement jolted in his chest.

He wanted to write! An idea was forming in his mind, and as he drank his tea, it fleshed out, bringing characters and dialogue and subplots and themes. He tried not to rush to his computer, knowing that this could be a false alarm and that by the time he got inside, it could disappear like smoke on the breeze.

He'd give it some time to percolate first, like a good coffee. Allow his brain to work it through, to turn it over and check for plot flaws or inconsistencies or ways it could fall short of being a full novel.

Then he'd go inside, casually turn on his computer and see if he could, at last, begin to write again.

Catherine, it seemed, had been the key to unlocking his heart, to awakening his creativity, and he couldn't wait to let her know.

–

Catherine stirred her coffee then carried it into the garden and sank onto the wicker sofa. Her walk home from Plum Tree Cottage had been fraught with anxiety as reality had crept in. Last night, she'd thrown caution to the wind and allowed herself to enjoy being with Mark. In the time she had been with him, she'd been lost on a sea of desire and pleasure, savouring every second of existing in the moment. It had been exquisite, sweet and fulfilling in a way she hadn't realised making love could be.

But now, in the cold light of day, it dawned on her exactly what she'd done and what the repercussions could be. She had made herself vulnerable, had opened her heart and her body to a man who would now have the power to hurt her. And she had responsibilities. How could she love Mark and be there for her mother? How could she divide her time and her loyalty between two people when one of those people – her mother – would surely hate the fact that Catherine was sharing her love and her attention between them?

She'd done something completely out of character, like the female lead in an Alex Radcliffe novel, and all because she'd wanted to spend some time with Mark, to let her hair down and make love to him.

What on earth had she been thinking?

She sipped her coffee, wincing as it burnt her tongue.

When she looked up, her mother was standing in the doorway gazing out at her. Did she know Catherine had stayed out all night? Could she tell just by looking at her that Catherine had been with Mark?

She held her breath, waiting to find out exactly how their conversation would go.

Chapter 16

'Honey, you got laid?' Jamal gaped at Catherine from the opposite side of the table at Shell's Shack. She'd sent him a text begging him to meet her that morning for breakfast. 'Why didn't you tell me yesterday?'

Catherine laced her fingers together and rested her elbows on the table. The final week of the summer had arrived and instead of feeling relaxed and ready for September as she usually did, she was a boiling pot of nerves and anxiety.

'Jamal… I couldn't. I had to deal with my mother and try to get my head straight.'

'But I'm so happy for you!' He clapped his hands. 'We should be having champagne.' He frowned. 'Except it's Monday and I have a client scheduled in for a cut and dye at ten. Best not have any alcohol with breakfast, I guess. But tell me *everything* and let me share in your special time.'

He leant forwards, his brown eyes fixed on Catherine and for a moment she felt like jumping up and running away. She could pack her bags, get on a train and leave Penhallow Sands for ever. She could do it, if she wanted to. She had savings and she could get a passport and just keep on moving around, go from place to place and never be hurt by anyone. If she was the one to leave, then no one could leave her.

'Hey.' Jamal reached across the table and took her hands. 'It's okay. You haven't done anything wrong.'

'But I have.' She shook her head, still outraged at herself for behaving so rashly. 'I can't just go around sleeping with... with tourists whenever I feel like it.'

Jamal squeezed her hands.

'Now listen to me, Catherine Bromley. You are being ridiculous. Mark is more than a tourist. He's a warm, friendly man who clearly likes you a lot. You haven't hurt anyone by spending the night with him. You haven't done anything wrong at all. It's not like you shot someone or went out in your thong and danced in the rain.'

Catherine snorted in spite of her distress.

'In my thong?'

'Yes, you know, singing *It's Raining Men* or something like *The Time of My Life* with your baps flopping all over the place.'

'My baps?' She giggled. 'What are you on about?'

'Well, if you were just wearing a thong, your boobies would be out and then everyone would see them and that dreadfully unruly bikini line of yours.'

'Jamal!' She forced her mouth closed. 'You are outrageous sometimes.'

'I know.' He grinned. 'But admit it, that image did make you smile and let's be honest, that would have been far worse than enjoying some long-awaited sex.'

'Firstly, my boobs don't flop around. They're quite... firm, I'll have you know. Secondly, Mark didn't even seem to notice my bikini line... not negatively, anyway. And thirdly, yes, the thong and boobies scenario would have been a lot worse, I guess. Although, I do wonder if I would feel this vulnerable if I had danced naked. I don't think much could top this feeling of insecurity that's now bubbling away inside me.'

'Aw honey, I'm sorry you're feeling insecure. Making love to someone can make you vulnerable but not if they care about you. I'm sure Mark does care. I'm convinced of it.'

Catherine watched her friend's familiar face carefully. He seemed to believe what he was saying about Mark but even so, she would never know exactly what Mark was thinking or feeling. It was impossible and a relationship needed trust. Catherine didn't know if she could ever trust someone enough to love them fully.

'I just don't know, Jamal. How can I be sure? How can I trust any man after what happened between my parents?'

'I'm a man and you trust me, don't you?'

'Yes, but that's different.'

'Not that different. I love you, Catherine. You're my girl and I'm here to support you and make you smile. Always. Give Mark some credit. If you allow yourself to trust him then he might surprise you.' His eyes widened. 'So… how was he?'

'Jamal, I'm not going to tell you that.'

He pouted. 'Your first romantic encounter in… goodness knows how long and you won't even tell your best friend.'

'It's… kind of private.'

'At least tell me that you had a good time.'

Catherine sighed as she recalled the sensations of Mark's hands in her hair, his soft kisses on her lips and the scent of him on her skin that she hadn't wanted to shower away.

'He's lovely.'

Jamal released her hands and sat back then tilted his head.

'You love him.'

'I do not! And shhhh, people can hear you.'

Jamal glanced around them. Apart from Shell, who was behind the counter staring at her mobile phone and an elderly man in the corner reading a newspaper, they were alone.

'But you do, don't you? I can see it all over your face. You have that post-coital glow and that bright shine in your eyes that says I've been done and done good and now I love him.'

'Jamal, it's Monday, and I spent Saturday night with him. How can I have a post-coital glow?'

'You do. Trust me. He must have done a good job.'

He giggled and Catherine shook her head. It was clear that her best friend wasn't going to listen to her. Jamal wanted her to be happy and in love and for a short while, she found herself wanting to believe in hope as much as he did. She picked up a menu and tried to read it but the words swam in front of her eyes.

'Have you heard from him since?'

'He sent a text yesterday afternoon, just to check that I was okay and asking what I was doing.'

'Did you reply?'

'Briefly. I didn't know what to say to be honest, so I just thanked him again for a good evening and said I'd see him soon.'

'Catherine, you gave him the brush off?' Jamal glared at her.

'No, I didn't. I just… I couldn't have asked him to mine, could I, and I didn't like to invite myself back to Plum Tree.'

'It sounds like he wanted you to suggest something. The poor man!'

Catherine groaned. 'I'm not good at this whole romance thing. I don't know how to act or what to say. Besides which, yes, I like him but I don't know if I want anything else from this, us, you know?' She said the words but they sounded hollow. Part of her was begging her to give Mark a chance, to at least find out how he felt after Saturday, but the stronger voice in her head – that sounded remarkably like her mother – was telling her not to be so foolish.

'I despair of you, woman.' Jamal fanned himself with his menu. 'He's hot, sweet and talented. You're both single. What have you got to lose?'

'According to my mother… quite a lot.'

'She knows?' He raised his eyebrows.

'She knew I'd been out all night and she was a bit… concerned.'

'Catherine, I love you and Diana, but you are a woman past thirty. You aren't a teenager anymore and your mother has no right to tell you how to live your life.'

'The thing is, Jamal, I know that. I've known it for years deep down but living with her makes it difficult to deal with. She can be so kind and loving and my heart aches for her and for what she's been through.'

'But she's your mother, not your responsibility. Bloody hell, Catherine, my parents disowned me when I told them I was gay. They never wanted anything to do with me after that, but, as I told them before I left their house, I am who I am and if they couldn't accept me for me, then I didn't want them in my life either.'

'I know how hard that's always been for you, Jamal.'

He nodded.

'I want better for you, Catherine. I want you to have happiness without having to sacrifice who you are. You deserve to be happy.'

'I don't need a relationship to be happy, Jamal.'

'You don't *need* one, no, but you've met someone special, a man who likes you for who you are. I've seen how Mark looks at you and I know that he's right for you. If you just give him a chance, give yourself a chance, you might find a happiness you've never had before. Look at Bradley and me and how happy we are.'

Catherine smiled sadly. Jamal was such a romantic at times, so much so that she sometimes thought he must read more romance novels than she did. But he'd always believed in the power of love and that there was someone out there for everyone.

'Look… I could have a word with Diana. Not wanting to overstep the mark here but she does like me and she might listen to me.'

'There's no need, but thank you. 'I think that she's mainly worried because she sees this as rushing into a love affair and she'd prefer me to take it slowly rather than end up regretting sleeping with Mark in the heat of the moment. To a certain extent, I have to agree with her. It was a bit irresponsible and uncharacteristic of me.'

Jamal smacked his palm against his forehead.

'Slowly? Regret? I'm not going to get through to you, am I? You do know what you're doing, don't you?'

'What?'

'Using all these excuses to avoid dealing with the real issue here.'

'Which is?'

'You really like Mark and know that he likes you, but you're afraid to let yourself enjoy being with him in case you do have to admit that you're falling for him. Being single, being the strong, introverted deputy head teacher with daddy abandonment issues is easier than opening your heart to love. Love could hurt you so you think it's better to avoid it.'

The sadness in his eyes made Catherine's breath catch in her chest. She had her reasons for wanting to avoid being vulnerable to pain. After all, men didn't always hang around, even when there was a child involved. Her dad hadn't so why would any other man be any different?

'Catherine…' Jamal took her hands again. 'Mark isn't your father.'

She swallowed hard then replied, 'I know. But I don't know why he would want me anymore than my father did.'

She thought of the polite emails they'd exchanged after she'd emailed her father. She had so many questions she wanted to ask him but she was also afraid of hearing the answers. Who wanted to hear that their father hadn't loved them enough to stick around? Was it better not to know and to leave their relationship in the past?

'Your mother has damaged you, Catherine. I don't think she meant to but she has scarred you, honey. You need to take a step back and think about what you're doing, analyse why you feel the way you do. You are amazing and any man would be lucky to have you for so many reasons.'

A tear trickled down Catherine's cheek.

'But' – Jamal stood up and came around to her side of the table then crouched down and hugged her – 'until you're ready to let love in, I'm happy to be the man in your life.'

Catherine buried her face in his neck and closed her eyes. Jamal was a good friend and sometimes he knew her even better than she knew herself. Perhaps it was time to make some changes, but first she needed to work out where to start.

–

Mark stared at his phone. He was tempted to fling it across the kitchen just to hear it smash, but he knew that would be foolish and that he'd regret it immediately. However, the text he'd just received from Catherine had left him reeling.

For the past three days, he'd been glued to his computer screen. He'd only got up to wash, eat, drink and pop to the loo. After he'd woken to find Catherine gone, he'd been compelled to write and the urge had been overwhelming. Inspiration had struck and he'd been afraid to delay in case it left him again. Having experienced writer's block, he didn't want to stop writing in case it returned. It had been months since he'd been able to get more than two thousand words (that he'd often delete) written in one sitting, but in the past three days, the story had poured from his fingers and he now had the best part of half a novel.

And it was all thanks to Catherine.

She had become his muse.

And he wanted to thank her for inspiring him, as well as to see her, so he'd sent a text that morning inviting her out for dinner, or, if she preferred, to have dinner at Plum Tree Cottage. He hadn't heard from her since the text she'd sent on Sunday and that had been brief and non-committal, but he'd thought she might need some time to get her head around things, just as he did. Their time together had been brief but intense and Mark didn't want to rush Catherine or himself. Plus, he wanted to write while the urge was upon him.

She hadn't replied to his invite immediately, so he'd assumed she was busy, but the reply he'd received just now, as dusk was falling, made his heart heavy. She'd said that she didn't think it was a good idea, that she liked him but she thought what they'd done had been a mistake. She apologised for telling him in a text but said she was too upset to speak to him right now.

Mark read it through again, hoping he might have misread it or that he would detect in it a sign that she did care. But there was nothing to give him hope.

He pressed the button at the top of his smart phone then swiped the screen to turn it off. He had three choices right now: sit here and wallow in his disappointment; head into Penhallow Sands, find Catherine and have it out with her; or get back to his book.

He hated sitting around feeling sorry for himself. He also knew he shouldn't rush to see Catherine right now as he might say the wrong thing and she clearly needed some space to think. So that left writing. The one thing he'd had as a constant in his life. The one thing he'd always been able to rely on before as a way of escaping. It was like free creative therapy, cathartic and constructive, so that was what he'd do.

He made a coffee, grabbed a bottle of water from the fridge, loaded a plate up with snacks then placed them all on the coffee table in front of the sofa in the lounge. He grabbed his laptop, got his quilt from the bed upstairs and returned to the lounge, flopped on the sofa and snuggled up. He had everything he needed; he just had to let the words flow.

And they did.

Deep into the night.

Chapter 17

Catherine had always loved the start of September school term. Usually, after a restful summer holiday, she felt ready to greet the pupils, from the youngest as they started in reception to the children in year 6, about to begin their final year at primary school. September was a fresh and exciting time, and the academic year ahead seemed filled with potential.

However, even walking through freshly painted hallways, peering into classrooms with new wall displays and hearing the happy murmur of conversation from her colleagues in the staffroom failed to raise her spirits this year.

She went into her office and closed the door then sat at her desk. The morning sun was already warming the small room and her desk was bathed in stripes of sunlight that made their way in through the vertical blinds. The shadows between the stripes of light made her think of how her life had been since she'd met Mark. She'd had moments of warmth and clarity but they had been separated by times of insecurity and doubt, times of worry and darkness. Everything good came with something bad, but then didn't that mean that it worked the other way too? For every dark moment, a lighter one would come along too? Ups and downs, highs and lows. It was all about finding balance.

The last week of the summer holidays had been one of deep reflection and although she had come into school before the weekend to attend to emails and paperwork ready for today's INSET, she still felt as if the summer shouldn't be over yet. And she was pretty certain she knew why. She had ended things with Mark via text. It was cowardly and she was ashamed, but she knew that she couldn't have done it face to face or in a phone call. She just couldn't seem to find the strength to speak to him, and it was as if, by keeping her distance, she could almost pretend that nothing had happened. Apart from her mother and Jamal (and, because of Jamal, Bradley) no one else seemed to know that she'd spent the night with Mark and therefore, it was as if she'd got away with it. As if it hadn't happened. As if she could continue as before. Life could continue as before. The problem was, that she wasn't sure that she wanted it to.

Catherine had tasted happiness, had savoured time with a man she liked and respected, a man she was incredibly attracted to, and she had enjoyed it, in spite of all her fears and worries. Before this summer, she had been content with her life and with how it had turned out. She hadn't really imagined that life held anything else in store for her, but then Mark had come along and turned it all on its head and now, she was at odds with herself and her safe, if somewhat mundane, existence. She wanted more time in the sun, more moments in the light and less time in the shadows.

What was she to do?

For now, nothing. She would head to the staffroom, make a coffee, speak to her colleagues about their holidays and deflect questions about her own. Most of them didn't live in Penhallow Sands anyway, so unless they'd come to the village or the beach during August, they wouldn't be any the wiser about what Catherine did with her time.

Her time.

Her life.

Her future.

What on earth was she doing with her life?

She needed to speak to her mother when she got home. Diana had chosen to spend her life single, hidden away avoiding men and relationships, but Catherine didn't want to. She wanted to seize the day, to have more than an existence, but before she could do that, she had to have this out with her mother. She should have done it years ago, but there had never been enough of a motive to risk rocking the boat, to risk upsetting her mother and their settled life. But now... things had changed and Catherine wanted more. She doubted very much that Mark would want to know her now, that he would even want to speak to her after how coldly she'd turned her back on him, but she knew she owed him a lot. He had opened her eyes to how she'd been hiding away and how much life could offer if you just took a chance.

He was a good man and she would need to find a way to apologise to him. She owed him that at least. And she owed it to herself to seize the day and finally start to live the life she wanted.

-

It had taken a week of early starts and late nights, but Mark now had a big chunk of his novel written. He'd forgotten over the past year how enjoyable writing was, how much he loved seeing the words flow onto the page and how exciting it was when the characters filled out and became like real people who talked to him day and night, telling him what they were going to do and why.

Yesterday afternoon, he'd sent the first half of the manuscript to his agent, asking her to let him know what she thought. With it being a Sunday, he hadn't expected to hear from her but she'd replied just after lunchtime today, telling him she'd opened the document, intending on taking a brief look, and she'd been hooked. She'd read the entire partial he had sent and wanted to read the rest.

Mark had sat in front of his laptop, reading her email over and over. This was a good sign. A few weeks ago, he'd been worried that his lack of work combined with his despondency about it was starting to affect his relationship with his agent, but now he had something to show her at last. And she loved it. This was a very good sign. He'd replied to her email to say that he hoped to finish the story within the month, if not before, and that he'd send it as soon as it was done. She could let his editor know and that would take the pressure off regarding his contract and his deadline.

He felt enormously relieved. After Ellie had broken off their relationship, he'd thought that his life would never be the same again, but now, for the first time in a long while, it looked as though it could well improve.

And it was because he'd come here to Penhallow Sands and spent the summer relaxing, exercising and replenishing his creative stores. Ultimately, he was very aware that it was being with Catherine that had lifted him from his writer's block, that had rescued him from the quagmire of self-doubt and apathy. He would always be grateful to her for that.

Even though he wished she had wanted to see him again.

Even though he had been hurt by her rejection.

Because being with her had sparked hope inside him again, a hope he'd thought Ellie had extinguished forever.

But now he needed to complete the story and he'd hit a snag, because he wasn't sure how it ended. It could go in two or more possible directions. He knew which way he'd like it to go, but the section between that ending and the point he had reached was still hazy. It was something he'd encountered before and often a run or a good night's sleep would help and he'd find that the characters had worked out exactly what should happen next and he'd get the next few scenes written. So it would be a good idea to take a short break and let his subconscious work its way through everything.

He'd print out what he'd written so far then head down to the village for a walk to clear his head. After days at the computer, his face was pasty, his hair was greasy and he had bags under his eyes that he could have packed for a holiday. So first he'd shower, dress in fresh clothes, eat, then walk.

The prospect of fresh air and stretching his stiff legs was very appealing indeed.

-

Catherine had gone home after work, but found the cottage empty. It was unlike Diana to go out for long, so Catherine had made two mugs of tea, expecting her mother back at any time. When she hadn't returned and the tea had gone cold, Catherine had rung her mother's mobile but it had gone through to voicemail. She'd texted Jamal to see if he knew where her mother might be and he'd replied saying that Diana was at the salon. Catherine had decided to have a long soak in the bath, followed by a nap if she still felt so tired. The first day back at work was always exhausting and it usually took her a good fortnight to get back into the swing of her work routine.

While lying in the bath, she heard the door closing downstairs, so she knew that her mother was home, then the landline started ringing almost immediately. Diana's enthusiastic greeting made Catherine think that it must be her aunty again.

Catherine was glad that her mother seemed to be getting on so well with her sister. She was surprised, certainly, but also happy that the two women had over-come whatever had led to their estrangement. She hoped it would continue and that Diana would, at last, start to rebuild her life. It would make it easier for Catherine to say what she needed to say.

After another ten minutes, Catherine dried and dressed in her pyjamas then lay down on her bed. She'd take a nap before dinner, then snuggle on the sofa and watch some mindless TV. She had wanted to speak to her mother about everything this evening, but she needed to pick the right time, and seeing as how Diana was still on the phone, it would have to wait.

She closed her eyes and stretched out, and as she drifted, she heard a gentle purring at her side and reached out to stroke Bob's soft fur. He rubbed his small head against her hand and another small head nudged her feet.

Bob and Ginger. Together like a sweet feline team. Letting her know they were there.

–

It was dusk by the time Mark reached the village, so he stood in front of the railing and gazed out at the beach. A few people were still walking on the sand and on the horizon he could see the silhouette of a small boat that was probably on the way to the harbour of the neighbouring village. He zipped up his hoodie against the cool evening breeze. It was only September but the air had already changed from the heady warmth of summer to the cool of approaching autumn. Mark had always liked autumn with its cooler temperatures, changing colours and the darker evenings. It was the perfect time to snuggle in front of an open fire and to read and enjoy hot chocolates or fine wines. Of course, those things weren't quite so enjoyable alone, and he wondered how Catherine would feel about spending such evenings with him. He'd really like to find out.

The air was laced with the scents of fish and chips, frying onions and ocean brine. A quiet sadness settled over him as he thought about the scene on the beach just over a week ago, when summer had felt like it would last forever and he'd been inside the large white marquee with Catherine at his side. Did such exquisite moments always pass so quickly? He wished he could snatch that time back and treasure it, hold it with him and take it out to look at it whenever he wanted to see Catherine's smile and hear her laugh. He wondered what she was doing right now, if she was working or watching TV or even thinking about him. Did she think about their afternoon at Plum Tree Bay when they had taken the steps that turned friendship into something more? Did she long to see him as he did her?

He turned from the beach and crossed the road then began to walk up the road that led to Catherine's cottage. The street was quiet and as he passed other cottages. TV screens flickered in lounges and the savoury aromas of people's evening meals drifted out into the air. These people all had someone in their lives, people to share dinner with and to watch TV with, to snuggle with as the evening wore on. There were couples, families and pets, settling down for the evening in their cosy homes, oblivious to the outside world.

When he reached Catherine's cottage, he paused and peered up at the bedroom windows. The curtains were closed both upstairs and downstairs, but the glow of a light could be seen coming from inside and he could hear the murmur of a television.

Should he really do this? Was it the right decision to make?

At this point, he didn't have much to lose, and it was something he needed to do.

He opened his rucksack and pulled out the envelope containing what he'd written of his novel so far. He'd paper clipped a note to the first page that read:

Please read this then let me know... How does the story end? Mark X

His stomach churned as he placed the envelope on the doorstep. He'd never done anything like this before, but then the whole situation was unfamiliar territory to him. It was, he knew, quite possible that Catherine would never read the story, that she'd see it was from him and throw it into the bin. It would be devastating if that happened, but it was a risk he had to take.

He was about to walk away, but he realised that if he left the envelope there it could get picked up by someone walking past or rained on, or worse if a passing dog decided to water it, so he took a deep breath then knocked on the door.

He waited. Heard a noise as someone inside approached the door. Then ran for it.

At the end of the street, he ducked down behind a parked car and peered back the way he'd come. Catherine's front door was open and light flooded out. A figure stood glancing back and forth along the street but he couldn't make out if it was Catherine or Diana. At least the envelope had been found. Now he had to hope that the woman he loved would read the contents.

Once the door had closed again, he got up and hurried down to the seafront then padded down the steps to the sand and towards the water. He needed to feel the sand between his toes, the cool water lapping over his feet, to reconnect with nature. It usually had the ability to soothe and calm him, as it always did. But he didn't know if it could do that tonight as he waited to hear from Catherine. All he could do was hold on to hope.

Chapter 18

Catherine had made it to the end of the first week of the autumn term. She switched off her computer then stood up and stretched. It had been a busy week and one in which she had been so tired by the time she'd returned home that she'd eaten, soaked in the bath then gone to bed, accompanied by Bob and Ginger, of course.

She hadn't seen much of her mother though, and when they had been in the same room, Diana had seemed tense and agitated, as though she wanted to speak about something but couldn't quite find the courage. Catherine certainly wanted to speak to her mother, but hadn't yet found the right time and hoped that the weekend would provide it. This couldn't go on indefinitely, that was for sure. She knew that something was simmering away between them, that it would soon come to the boil and that, hopefully, the air would be cleared for once and for all. Her mother was probably preparing for this, waiting for the right time to have a proper discussion.

Catherine grabbed her bag and jacket then went out into the hallway. She wished the staff who were still there a good weekend, waved at Jowanetta through her office window, then headed for the entrance. As she crossed the car park, her mobile buzzed in her bag, so she pulled it out to find a text from Jamal asking her to pop by the salon on her way home. Hairway to Heaven wasn't exactly on her way, but she could do a detour and walk home via the seafront. The exercise would do her good and the walk would give her time to clear her head.

Twenty minutes later, she pushed open the door to the salon and found Jamal and Lucy standing behind a client who was sitting in one of the black swivel chairs.

Jamal turned to greet her.

'Hello, stranger!' He hugged her. 'I hate when you go back to school because I don't see as much of you.'

'I know what you mean.' Catherine nodded. She had missed him too but knew he'd be busy at the salon, as Lucy had started her trial that Monday.

'Hello, Catherine.' Lucy smiled.

'Love the hair!' Catherine looked at Lucy's bright pink crop.

'Thanks. Jamal did it for me yesterday because I said I fancied a colour change.'

'It's fabulous.'

'I'm hoping that Maggie will think so too.'

'You've spoken to her then?' Catherine asked.

'Yes. I went in for a chat earlier in the week and Maggie and Felicity were both lovely. Maggie said that she can certainly offer me two days' work at the library, so as long as things go well here too… then I'll have two jobs.'

'I'm so glad for you, Lucy. That's wonderful news.'

'Are you all right, Catherine? Please don't take this the wrong way but you look… tired.' Lucy frowned.

'I am exhausted and I feel physically wrecked by this week. It's always the same with the first week back at school.' Catherine slumped onto the sofa in front of the window.

'Tell you what,' Jamal said, 'I'll dry Mrs Lawrence's hair, Lucy, and you can give Catherine a manicure. Show me and her what you can do.'

'I'd love to.' Lucy turned to Catherine.

'No, it's okay,' Catherine shook her head. 'No need for that.'

'I'll throw in a pedicure as well.' Lucy held out a hand. 'I have my beauty station set up at the back with the sinks, so come on through and let's spoil you. It's my way of saying thank you.'

Catherine was about to argue but Jamal walked over to her and pulled her to her feet, so she allowed herself to be led through to the back of the salon and settled into a chair with a foot rest and reclining back. If someone wanted to spoil her, who was she to argue?

—

By the time Lucy had soaked Catherine's feet in warm water, sloughed off the dead skin with a peppermint foot scrub, then massaged lots of lovely smelling lotion into them, Catherine was almost comatose. Lucy went through a similar routine with Catherine's hands then asked her to choose a colour from her range of nail polish. Catherine settled on a silvery blue that made her think of the sky on a summer's evening, and Lucy got to work.

'Catherine, do you realise that you made the same noises as Lucy was massaging your feet that you make when Bradley washes your hair?' Jamal asked as he stood next to her chair.

'I did not.'

'You did, darling. You just can't help yourself. Makes me wonder what you're like when you're, you know what–ing.'

'Jamal!' Catherine shook her head and scowled at him. 'You're unbelievable sometimes.'

He smiled.

'Thank you. I shall take that as a compliment. Anyway, how do you fancy coming to the pub for a drink when we close up?'

'Oh… I can't really. I told Mum I'd be home early and she said something about cooking a nice dinner.'

'Have you managed to speak to her yet? About a certain complicated topic?'

'No. It's been busy this week and I need to find the right time.'

'Well, try to get it done tonight or over the weekend.' He held her gaze until she looked away. 'It won't do you or her any good if this continues.'

'I will.'

When Catherine's nails were dry, she tried to pay Lucy but the woman shook her head. 'It's fine honestly. It's part of my trial.'

'But I want to pay. You completely relaxed me and I owe you.'

'No, it's fine, honestly, and you don't owe me a thing. It's more the other way around.'

'Well, I'll be back and I'm definitely paying next time.' Catherine smiled. 'How has your little boy settled in at school?'

'Really well, thank you. He already has a lovely group of friends and he's excited getting up in the mornings. It's such a relief.' Catherine knew from years of experience that seeing your child settle into their new school was a big deal for most parents and the staff at Penhallow Sands Primary strove to make the transition for all pupils as pleasant and seamless as possible.

'That's wonderful. Any issues or questions, just give me a call.'

'Thank you, I will.'

'Life has a way of working out, doesn't it?' Catherine squeezed Lucy's hand.

'It really does.' Lucy's eyes shone. 'Thank you so much for everything you've done.'

Catherine shook her head. 'I just pointed you in the right direction.'

'Are you sure you don't want to come to the pub just for one?' Jamal asked as Catherine slid her arms into her jacket. 'Have a drinkypoo to help steady your nerves.'

'Better not. I think I've put this conversation off long enough.'

'Okay, then. Let me know how it goes.'

'Will do.'

Jamal pulled her into one of his bear hugs then kissed her cheeks and Catherine tried to take strength from him. She had a feeling she was going to need it.

-

When Catherine opened the front door, she was met with the delicious aroma of garlic, onions and freshly baked bread. Her mother had always been a good cook but she tended to keep their meals simple these days, citing heartburn and indigestion as reasons not to eat anything too flavoursome. It seemed that perhaps she had decided to ignore those complaints today and to create something delicious for dinner.

Catherine kicked off her shoes and tucked them under the stairs then slid her feet into her slippers, but not before admiring her pretty painted toenails. Her feet felt so sensitive after her pedicure, as if the hard skin that had grown there had dulled the nerves, so it was nice to feel the softness of her slippers again. She'd been loath to put her shoes back on before leaving the salon in case she ruined Lucy's hard work, but the young woman had reassured her that she'd left plenty of time for her nails to dry and that the effects of the pedicure should last for a week or two.

'Mum! I'm home.' She went through to the kitchen and found Diana standing at the stove.

'Hello, Catherine. How was your day?'

Catherine approached her and held out her hands.

'What lovely nails.' Her mother smiled.

'I had them done at Hairway on the way home. Jamal is giving Lucy Challicombe a trial there. She does beauty and hair and she's very talented.'

'He did mention something the other day about a new stylist who's also a beautician. I'll have to book an appointment.'

Catherine swallowed her surprise.

'That's a great idea. She did my feet too and it was so relaxing. You should have some pampering, Mum.' She peered into the deep frying pan that her mother was stirring. 'What are you making?'

'Five bean chilli with home-made garlic bread.'

'It smells delicious.'

'Good. It'll be ready in about forty minutes. There's wine open on the table.'

'You went out?' Catherine asked as she walked over to the kitchen table and picked up the bottle. 'To Greenacres?'

'I walked there and back. The exercise did me good.'

'Mum... you walked all the way to the vineyard?'

'Don't worry, I took my time and had a little rest while I was there. In fact, I had a cup of tea with Glenda and it was lovely to catch up.'

Catherine put the wine down and sank onto one of the chairs. Her mother had not only walked to Greenacres, which was a fair old way, but also had tea with Glenda Morton. Glenda and her husband had owned the vineyard for years but after her husband had passed away, her son-in-law and granddaughter had taken over the running of the vineyard and the on-site shop. It was so unlike her mother to go anywhere, let alone all that way. Yes, Diana was fit and healthy, but she always chose not to go far. Until now, it seemed.

'I'm happy to hear that, Mum,' Catherine poured wine into two glasses then took a sip. 'This is good.'

'Yes, Catherine, I know you like their red.'

'Thanks. Do you want a hand with anything?'

Bob appeared then with Ginger and they both wound their way around Catherine's legs, purring when she leant over to stroke their heads.

'No, it's all under control. Why don't you have a bath and change, then dinner will be ready when you come down?'

'That does sound wonderful, Mum, but... first, I think we need to talk and I don't really want to do it while we're eating.'

'I agree that we need to talk. I just wanted you to relax after what has probably been a tiring day. But… if you think we should talk first, then that's fine with me.'

Her mother turned the heat down under the chilli then came and sat opposite Catherine. She took a sip of her wine then folded her hands on the table in front of her.

'Do you want to go first?' Diana asked.

Catherine met her mother's eyes, eyes that could sparkle and smile when Diana was happy, but those moments were so fleeting and had been for as long as Catherine could remember. She mostly saw them as they were now: slightly bloodshot with deep lines etched around them and dark shadows underneath. It always made her heart lurch and she wished her mother could have had a happier life.

'This is difficult, Mum, and I want to tell you first how much I love you. I always have done. I know that you've had a hard time of things over the years and that Dad leaving almost broke you… *did* break you for a while… and I have wished so many times that I could ease your pain.'

'Oh my darling, you have always been a wonder to me.' Diana reached out and took Catherine's hand. 'From the moment I found out I was expecting you, I loved you. To become a mum at forty-one, when I'd all but given up any hope of having a child, was incredible for me. You have been my ultimate joy.'

Catherine smiled. 'However, I haven't been able to heal your hurt, in spite of how hard I've tried, but… sometimes… I don't think you wanted to be fixed.'

Her mother sighed and lowered her gaze to the table then gently pulled back her hand and steepled her fingers.

'Catherine… you are, I am afraid, so right.' She sighed. 'I've been remiss in many ways and I know that I have held you back.'

Catherine watched her mother carefully. She hadn't even needed to say what she'd prepared in her head, as her mother seemed to already know. Had Jamal spoken to her about it all without telling Catherine? Had her mother been watching those American chat shows she secretly loved, the ones she denied watching but always appeared on the recording line-up for the week ahead?

'Why do you say that?' Catherine asked.

'I knew deep down, I really did, but I told myself that I was protecting you from pain. After losing your father… after he left, I wanted to spare you the similar pain that could arise if another man was to let you down. But in doing so, I've prevented you from living your life.'

'Mum…' Catherine's throat was aching now. 'I have never blamed you for any of that.'

'I know that, my sweetheart. You have such a kind and generous heart and I worried for you, that a man might come along and take hold of it then crush it by leaving you for another woman, or because he didn't love you enough. For me, no man would ever be good enough for you.'

'I can't deny that I have been afraid of getting hurt. Recently, especially over the summer, I've thought about this a lot. I could have stood up to you and told you that I wanted more freedom, but I think that I was, in some ways, glad to have *you* to hide behind. I always had the excuse that you needed me, and you'd be lost without me if I met someone or moved away.'

'That's no way for a young woman to live, though, Catherine. I mean… look at Bob and how much happier he is having a companion. You could have been happy too if I'd just let you live your life. I am deeply ashamed of what I have done and I would understand if you couldn't forgive me.'

'Mum, if it had been just you, then I might feel anger towards you, but I have to take some of the blame. I was wrong in not getting out there, in letting Damon go when I did. I failed to make sufficient effort to keep our relationship alive, and I can't blame you for that. He loved me in his own way; I know he did. We were young and maybe it wouldn't have worked out between us long term, but I didn't give us a chance to find out.'

'And I told you to let him go.' Diana covered her mouth with both hands then dropped them to the table again. 'What I should have done was tell you to go and fight for him.'

They gazed at each other in silence, digesting what they had admitted. Catherine had thought that this evening would bring a difficult discussion but had no idea that her mother would already be prepared to accept that things hadn't been right in their life.

'There's something I haven't told you, Catherine, and it's time.'

'There is?'

Diana worried her bottom lip and wrung her hands together.

'I… I always let you believe that your father left me for another woman, that he was in the wrong. But… he actually left… because he was hurt.'

The room seemed to dip and sway, and Catherine gripped the table.

'What do you mean?'

'It was me, Catherine. Not your father. I was the one who had the affair. Before we had you, we came very close to breaking up because our love had fizzled out under the pressure of trying for a baby. It became an obsession for me and all I could think about was getting pregnant. Your father felt pushed out, unloved and unappreciated and that wasn't fair. We still cared about each other deep down, but we were always arguing and we often slept separately and it wasn't looking good for us. Then I found out I was pregnant. I spent nine months terrified that something would go wrong and that I'd lose you, but you were strong and resilient and when you were born, I thought my heart would burst with joy and love.'

Catherine opened her mouth to speak but Diana shook her head.

'Please, Catherine, let me finish.' She took a deep breath then carried on. 'Becoming parents should have brought your father and me closer together, but it didn't, because I pushed him even further away. As you grew, we stayed together because we wanted you to have a family with your parents living under the same roof, but then I met someone else one night at the pub. I was out with some friends – yes, I did have friends back then, and this man… Thomas, his name was… turned my head. It had been so long since I'd felt desire or felt desired, and we had a brief fling. Your father found out. I wasn't really that careful about hiding it. When I consider it now, I think I wanted him to know, to kick start him into some sort of action, and it did. But he told me he wanted me to leave, and that he would raise you alone.'

'My dad wanted to bring me up? He didn't want to leave me?'

Catherine shook her head. How had her mother kept this from her all this time?

'No. He asked me to go but I couldn't leave my child, the baby I'd longed for, and yet we knew we couldn't stay together either. Your father did the honourable thing… putting me first, and he left. He couldn't bear to stay around here as it was too painful for him. I know I told you that he was the one who cheated, but I was too afraid to tell you the truth in case it changed how you saw me.'

Catherine's head pounded and her mouth was dry. She stared down at her hands on the table but they didn't feel like they were a part of her. She tried to make sense of what she'd just been told but her mind was filled with a dense fog of confusion.

'Catherine? Are you all right?'

She looked up at her mother.

'Am I all right? What a stupid question!' She pushed her chair back and stood up. 'All these years… most of my life, in fact, I've blamed my father for leaving us. At times I have hated him. Because of you, I believed that men couldn't be relied upon. It was the narrative of my childhood… that men cheat and leave you, that they abandon you and your child. I can't believe you did that to me. *How* could you do that to me?'

'I'm so sorry. I didn't lie about being hurt by him leaving. I had hoped that we might have found a way to move on from what I'd done but he just couldn't trust me again.'

'You lied to me all that time. You are a liar!' Catherine's voice cracked and her eyes burned with tears. 'You know what… we've exchanged several emails recently and that poor man never once tried to tell me the truth in his emails. Not once! Even now, he's thinking of you and protecting you!'

'Catherine, I am so, so sorry.' Her mother's eyes were red and she kept shaking her head, as if she couldn't believe what she had done.

'Why now, though, Mum?'

'What do you mean?'

'Why have you realised all of this now and decided to come clean?'

Her mother looked down at her hands before replying.

'It wasn't just one thing that made me see sense. Partly, talking to my sister again and hearing about her son and grandchildren and how happy they all are started me thinking about what you don't have. Yes, they have their ups and downs but they also have many good times. They all live their own lives but also spend lots of time together too. The main reason we fell out was because she disapproved of what I've done to your father and of the fact that I let you believe it was him who'd done wrong. I kept you here with me, afraid of letting you go in case I lost you. I am a bad person for deceiving you and I feel dreadful. I always felt guilty about it but I didn't know how to make it better without turning you against me.'

'You said *partly*.' Catherine growled, her voice dangerously low. The word had stood out and Catherine wanted to know what her mother meant. She tilted her head, wondering what else could have brought about this revelation. She paced the length of the kitchen, taking deep slow breaths to try to stop her heart from racing.

'I did. As I said, there was seeing Bob and Ginger too and even though they're only cats, they still make each other so happy. Plus,' – Diana took a shaky breath – 'there was something else, you see. On Monday evening, something was delivered to the cottage. I hid it away because I wanted to take a proper look at it.'

'What was it?'

'An envelope containing a manuscript.'

'A manuscript?'

'Yes. For a romance novel. When I saw what it was and who it was from, my first reaction was to destroy it, or to hide it away so you'd never see it. But, after reading the novel – or what there is of it, because it is unfinished – I realised that I couldn't do that to you.'

Fury blazed now in Catherine, kindled by knowing her mother had lied about more than one thing, that her mother had spent her life hiding things from her and deceiving her, that her poor father had been forced to leave his home and his family because of what Diana had done.

'Was the envelope addressed to you?'

Diana hung her head. 'No.'

'You mean it was addressed to *me*?'

'Yes, and I am so sorry. I should have given it to you immediately, but I wanted to check what it was first and then… once I started reading it, I couldn't stop.'

'Let me get this right! You opened and read something that was left here for me… even after you had already started thinking about how you'd wronged me all those years. You are unbelievable.'

'You have every right to be angry, Catherine. But please, let me explain about the manuscript. It's... beautiful, painful and... it taught me what I needed to know.'

'About what?' Catherine stopped pacing and glared at her mother.

'About what I've done wrong all these years. About what a wonderful person you are and about how you deserve to have a life away from me.' A sob escaped from her mother and a tear trickled down her wrinkled cheek. 'Catherine, I only hope you can forgive me.'

Catherine picked up her glass and gulped down the wine. Forgiveness seemed like a very big ask right now and although part of her wanted to reassure her mother that everything would be all right, anger and hurt dominated her heart and mind and in that moment, she couldn't even try to make her mother feel better. She was too tired, too worn down and too bewildered to discuss it all further.

'Where is the manuscript now?'

'I'll get it for you.'

Her mother got up slowly, as if everything had suddenly weighed her down and aged her further, and she left the room. When she reappeared, she was holding a thick brown envelope. She placed it on the table in front of Catherine.

'You should read this. It's your story.'

'My story?'

'Not told with your name or mine or even Mark's... but I know that it's based on us. Between that and Jane, I've been taught a valuable lesson. I only hope it's not too late. I'll turn the chilli off, shall I? It can be reheated tomorrow or frozen for another time.'

'Where are you going?'

'To finish packing.'

'Packing?' Catherine could barely take in what her mother was saying.

'I have a taxi booked first thing in the morning to take me to the station. I'm going to stay with Jane for a while.'

'With Jane?'

Diana nodded. 'It's high time. And it's time for you to have some breathing space. That man… Mark… he cares about you, Catherine. He sees you how I always hoped you would be seen.'

'He does?'

'Read it and you will see.' Diana crossed to the kitchen doorway. 'Catherine, I do love you and really did only ever want the best for you. But in trying to protect you, I made mistakes and actually became the one thing that was quite likely keeping you from having the life you could have. I believe that you need some space to think everything through, but please know that if you have any questions or need to talk things through further, I will be there to talk to you or if you want me to come back, then I'll do that too. But… now, you have a chance of happiness. Please try to take it. Don't make the same mistakes I did.'

Alone in the kitchen, Catherine stared at the envelope in front of her. She ran a finger over her name, knowing that Mark had written it. He'd left this on her doorstep at the beginning of the week. Did he think she was ignoring him? That she'd read it and hated it? Was he going through a pain similar to that which her father must have suffered all these years? Two men in Catherine's world, hurt by Diana and her selfishness. And to think that Catherine had always tried to look out for her mother, to think that she had felt bad when she'd inadvertently upset Diana by being caught watching something romantic on TV or reading a romance novel.

Her heart ached to think of Mark sitting in Plum Tree Cottage, wondering if she'd read the story and decided to stay away. She wanted to let him know right away that she hadn't known about the manuscript, but she also wanted to know what she was dealing with. Diana might have got it wrong; this might just be a story, a fictional work that Mark wanted her to read because she had told him she loved all of his other books. If she contacted him now, she could say or do the wrong thing based on her mother's interpretation of things, so she needed to read the story and find out more. Even though her head ached and her eyes were burning, she had to know what this was about before she did anything at all.

She refilled her glass then opened the envelope and pulled out the thick wad of A4 paper. There was a note pinned to the top page:

Please read this then let me know… How does the story end? Mark X

What did he mean? How would Catherine know? Unless it really was their story.

She turned the page over and began to read, with a deep sense that she was about to set something in motion that would change her life forever.

Chapter 19

It had been a tough week for Mark as he waited to hear from Catherine. He knew she would be busy with work and that she might not have had time to read the book yet, but even so, just a text message or some acknowledgement would have been nice. Unless she had read it all and hated it and wanted nothing further to do with him. Alternatively, of course, it could be that she hadn't received the manuscript. Perhaps Diana had intercepted it. But would she stoop that low? He shook his head. Surely, not.

It was, of course, possible that Catherine had read the book and didn't like what he'd done, that she disapproved of him using their situation as inspiration for a story and that she could even be angry. Then there was the detail about him that he'd weaved into the male character's backstory. He'd poured out a lot of what he'd been through onto the page. The names had been changed and some of the details, such as his ex-girlfriend was a swimming coach, not a tennis coach, and they'd lived in Nottingham, not in London, and he was an artist not a writer, but the basics of the story remained the same. It was about a man and a woman whose lives had held them back in several ways, but when they met, everything seemed to slot into place. And that was how he felt about Catherine. She had opened his eyes, enabled him to see what he had long missed out on and he felt as though he was properly awake for the first time in his adult life.

But, if Catherine didn't appreciate what Mark had done, and if she didn't want him to use their stories as inspiration, then he would respect her wishes. The last thing he wanted to do was to hurt or embarrass her or make her uncomfortable, even though no one need ever know that the novel was based on them and how they'd met. Then there was the mother issue in the novel, the overbearing elderly woman who had ruled her daughter's life for years and stopped her finding true love. Writing her into the story could have upset Catherine, and perhaps she wasn't even fully aware of how her mother manipulated her, in which case, Catherine could become quite angry at how Mark had portrayed the older woman.

But, at the end of the day, it was a work of fiction inspired by real life, not a biography, and that was his defence. People inspired people to paint, to sing, to dance and to write. He had been inspired, but his main inspiration was Catherine and she had unlocked the door to his heart and allowed the words to flow freely.

He checked his mobile again.

Nothing.

He'd go for a run to let off some steam then try to get back to the story. He had managed to compose a few different versions of the ending but wasn't sure which one he preferred, although he knew which one he didn't like and hoped he wouldn't be compelled to use that one. Mark liked his romance novels to have a happy ending; he just wished there was a guarantee that real life could be the same.

Catherine woke on the sofa with a stiff neck and a pile of paper in her arms. She'd been reading deep into the night and must have passed out. At times like this, having Bob's soft warm little body to cuddle up to was such a comfort, and now that she had Ginger too, she had a perfect little footwarmer.

A noise from upstairs snapped her from her sadness and she sat upright then placed the novel on the coffee table. She didn't have many pages left, and although she was keen to keep reading, she also didn't want to finish the story because she was enjoying it so much. Besides which, her mother had said that she was leaving this morning and Catherine had to deal with that issue first.

There was a bumping noise coming down the stairs then her mother appeared in the doorway with her suitcase on wheels.

'Oh… You're awake. But of course you are with all the noise I just made. I was going to try to leave quietly but this is quite heavy and I couldn't lift it down all the stairs.'

'You're going now?'

'Yes.'

Catherine stood up and looked at her mum, at the woman who had loved her fiercely since before she was born and who had always been there for her, no matter what. Her love for Diana rose in her chest and into her throat and threatened to choke her with pain. Whatever Diana had done, she'd done it thinking she was doing right, even if she had been very wrong. She was still furious with her mother and incredibly hurt, but she couldn't let her go without saying goodbye.

'Why's your suitcase so heavy, Mum? How long are you going for?'

'I'm not sure yet, Catherine. It could be a while. As long as Jane doesn't mind having me there.'

'I'm sure she'll be glad to catch up.'

'And I'll be glad to have some time away from here. I've let myself get stale and let my anxiety get the better of me, but telling you the truth has been like shedding a very heavy weight. I feel dreadful knowing how much I have hurt you and how I've kept you and your father apart, but now the truth is out, I hope you and he can find a way forward with your relationship.'

'I hope so, too.'

Her mother nodded. 'I'm not saying my belly isn't fluttering wildly at the thought of getting on a train, mind you, or that I'm not nervous at the thought of staying somewhere strange, but I figure that it's now or never. I'm not getting any younger, am I?'

Her mother held her chin up and pushed her thin shoulders back and it was all Catherine could do not to burst into tears. Her little mum was heading out into the world, alone and with such pain and doubt in her heart. Her anger was something she would need to work through and she hoped that she'd be able to forgive her mother in time, but for now, she had to offer her mother some reassurance.

'Come here.' Catherine hurried over and hugged her mother tight. 'I love you, Mum.'

'I love you, too, Catherine. All I want is to see you happy.'

'I know. It's a shame that it took you so long but...' She bit her lip, not wanting to indulge in recriminations now. There would be time for that once Catherine had been able to work things through in her own mind. 'I'm working on it. You should too.'

A beep from outside signalled the arrival of the taxi.

'Right then…' Diana's voice wavered. She cleared her throat. 'I should go, my sweetheart. Don't want to miss my train, do I?' Diana released Catherine and met her gaze.

'Take care, won't you?'

'I will. And you too, Catherine. Follow your heart, and let go of all doubt and fear. Life's too short not to go for what you want and you have been held back for long enough.' Her mother reached out and placed a cool palm on Catherine's cheek then she nodded sadly and turned away.

Catherine opened the door and the taxi driver took the case from Diana and put it into the boot then opened the door for her.

'Goodbye,' Catherine called as her mum waved from the back of the cab. She knew that this was no magical cure for all the years of lies and sadness, for losing so much time believing her mother was right and her father was wrong. Nothing could get that time back and she would probably feel angry with her mother for a long time. But it would pass eventually, and she knew that there was no point regretting what hadn't been. She had to look forwards now and rebuild her life with her newly found knowledge. At least Diana was giving her the space and time to do that.

Then she was alone, at last, and she had some reading to do.

–

Back from his run, Mark showered then dressed in lounge pants and a baggy T-shirt. He jogged downstairs, running his hands through his short hair, and went into the kitchen.

His mobile was on the worktop charging, so he checked the screen to see if his battery was full yet. There was a message from his sister, Summer, on the display, but he could only read the first line. He also had three missed calls. He swiped to unlock the phone then opened the message.

> *Mark,*
>
> *Have tried to phone you but can't get through.*
> *So sorry to be the one to tell you this — if you don't know already — but didn't want you to find out from someone else as think it's a bit of a shocker…*
> *Brace yourself…*
>
> *Ellie is getting married. It's all over her social media.*
>
> *Sorry, bro, and hope you're okay with this.*
> *Ring me if you want to talk.*
>
> *Love you! Xx*

Mark dropped his mobile back onto the worktop and stared at it as if it had burnt him. Ellie was getting married? He knew Summer only meant well in letting him know, but even so, he wished she hadn't.

Didn't he?

He went to the backdoor and opened it then leant over and rested his hands on his thighs. His chest felt tight and despite his recent run, it was as though he was struggling to get enough air into his lungs.

Ellie was getting married to someone else. Someone who wasn't Mark.

He went over to the summer house and sat on the wicker sofa then lowered his head into his hands. Life really could change in an instant. He'd known Ellie was with someone else – hell, she'd been with him before Mark had even walked out their front door – but for some reason he hadn't spent much time thinking about how he'd feel if she did get married. Mark had proposed to her three times and three times she'd refused him, then this guy she'd been with for all of five minutes had proposed and she'd said yes. That was, of course, if he had been the one to propose. Perhaps Ellie had proposed to him. All those years they'd been together, had she been stringing Mark along waiting until someone better came her way? Had she ever cared for Mark at all?

The news was a bit of a shock, although he didn't know if he was hurt or angry. Until recently, he would have expected to be both, but recent events had changed his perspective. Catherine had changed his perspective on just about everything.

And now he was waiting to hear from her. He wished he could phone her and speak to her about this, hold her and be comforted by her, but he didn't want to push her, didn't want to seem desperate for her love and attention.

Ten minutes later, he was back outside with a bottle of gin that he'd stashed in one of the cupboards. He didn't drink much gin but it had been on offer at the supermarket and he'd picked it up in case he ever had guests, or, actually, in case Catherine liked it and happened to be at the cottage. He also had some small cans of elderflower tonic water and had filled a glass with ice cubes. He poured a generous measure of gin over the ice then added a can of tonic.

Mark knew that drinking alone wasn't the greatest of plans, but he wanted to take the edge off his unease. He knew that he could deal with whatever came his way, that he would process whatever happened and, if Catherine didn't want to be with him, that it would hurt less over time, but in this moment, he wanted it to go away. And fast.

He sipped the drink and was surprised to find that he liked it. The tang of the gin went well with the floral tonic water and as he swallowed, it warmed his stomach. Soon, the glass was empty and a gentle warm buzz filled Mark's veins.

That was better. He might just as well have another.

His mobile started to ring inside the cottage, but he didn't want to speak to anyone right now. If it was Summer, calling to see how he'd taken the news, then he couldn't face explaining that to her now, let alone explaining that he'd already lost his heart to someone else. He knew his parents would be concerned too, so he'd drop them all a text message a bit later on to let them know that he was fine about Ellie. It was unlikely to be his agent or editor phoning, as it was the weekend. The only other person he could think it might be was Catherine, and he couldn't have spoken to her now even if he'd wanted to because he felt suddenly very vulnerable. Perhaps it was the gin, perhaps it was knowing that he hadn't been good enough for Ellie and now, it was possible, that Catherine didn't want him either.

Mark just wanted to lie on the sofa in the September afternoon sunshine and to listen to the birds, the distant hum of a tractor and to savour the isolation of Plum Tree Cottage. Catherine had filled his heart with love; she had shown him that what he'd had with Ellie wasn't good for him and that life could be good again. If Catherine didn't want to be with him, he had a rough road ahead.

–

Catherine sat up on the sofa and sniffed. She grabbed a tissue from the box on the table and dried her eyes.

Wow! Wow! Wow!

She had just finished reading Mark's book and she was overwhelmed. He was such a talented writer and this story was beautiful, poignant and so close to home. He had perfectly captured some of the elements of her life and their relationship, without seeming at all judgemental. There were also lots of details about the hero and his past that she assumed were actually about Mark, and it had given her a deeper understanding of him and why he behaved as he did. The artist in the novel had been hurt by his ex, to whom he'd proposed three times, only to find out that she'd declined his proposals then gone off with another man as soon as the hero had moved out of their shared home. The pain that the hero had suffered had brought tears to Catherine's eyes. *Poor Mark.* And that fact that the ex-girlfriend had been ashamed of the artist and his paintings made her sad too. How could his ex have been so ashamed of him that she asked him to continue to paint (or, in Mark's case, write) under a different name? What kind of woman would be ashamed of her partner's creativity? Catherine would shout it from the rooftops if Mark was her partner; she'd be so proud of him and his talent, of his sensitivity and understanding of life and love, of his ability to create a vivid scene and to show a character's undulating emotions.

Mark was a very special man indeed.

But what now? Should she let him know that she'd read his story and that she loved it? A week had passed. Would he even want to know? Her mother had kept the manuscript secret, but he didn't know that.

Also, the story wasn't finished. He had asked her in the note how it should end. She wasn't sure. What did she want from Mark? What did he want from her? Could they find a way to be happy together?

Before she made any decisions, she needed to speak to someone else about it all.

—

'So what do you think?' Catherine asked Jamal and Bradley as they sat in the back garden of their cottage.

Jamal flicked through the pages of the novel that Catherine had brought to show them. She needed them to see the book, not just take her word for it, and Jamal had scanned through, reading odd words and phrases, but Bradley had settled down with the first chapter and was glued to it.

'I think that he really likes you. From what I've seen and what you've told me, Mark wants to know what you'd like to happen between you two.'

'Gosh, he's passionate, isn't he?' Bradley asked. 'The way he describes the hero carrying you from the sea after he rescued you.' He fanned his face with a page of the story. 'Did you know he was feeling so... excited to hold you close?'

Catherine's cheeks filled with heat. Mark's writing hadn't been explicit but it was clear that their close encounter had impacted upon Mark physically and emotionally. He had also written about the night they'd spent together; not in detail, just enough to make her heat beat faster as she'd read it. She'd been embarrassed that her mother had read it too, but then Diana hadn't said anything about it to her, so thankfully she'd been spared the humiliation of discussing what had happened that night at the cottage. Catherine had removed the pages before bringing the rest of the book to show Jamal and Bradley because she'd wanted to keep those details to herself. Mark had described her as being so utterly beautiful that she had been overwhelmed with a variety of emotions. A man had never spoken, let alone written about her, like that before and she liked how he saw her; he made her feel special and she had always thought that true love was about seeing someone as Mark had described her.

'I felt the same,' Catherine said in reply to Bradley.

'I'm not surprised,' Bradley said. 'He's gorgeous and he's smitten with you.'

'What do I do?' she asked.

'There's only one thing you can do.' Jamal stood up and nodded. 'You need to go and see him.'

'But I'm afraid.' Her voice wavered.

'Why?' Jamal's dark brows met above his nose.

'Because… I could end up getting really hurt if this goes wrong.'

'Catherine' – Jamal shook his head – 'this man loves you and he wants you to tell him how your story ends. Get your backside in your car and drive up there. Right now! I don't know about Bradley but I can't stand the suspense any longer. It's driving me mad.'

'He's right, Catherine.' Bradley stood up and went to Jamal then slid an arm around his waist. 'We love you and want you to be happy but it's up to you now. You need to go and speak to Mark.' He added softly, 'But leave the book.'

Catherine got up and went to them and they hugged, then she grabbed her bag and went to the door.

'Wish me luck.'

'You don't need luck, Catherine. You just need to go grab that gorgeous man, hold him tight and never let him go!'

Jamal smiled at her and she smiled back. Then she got into her car and made her way to Plum Tree Cottage, wondering exactly how the story would end, knowing only how she wanted it to.

Chapter 20

Catherine knocked on the door again and waited, but there was still no answer. Mark's car was there though, so he'd either gone for a walk or a run, or he must be inside. After plucking up the courage to come here, she didn't want to leave; it would be harder if she left and had to come back. Perhaps she could wait for him to come home.

She heard a noise from around the rear of the cottage, so she let herself through the side gate and walked slowly around the cottage and into the back garden.

And there he was.

Sitting on the ground in front of the summer house, rubbing his eyes.

'Mark? Are you all right?'

She hurried over to him, concerned by how pale and disorientated he looked.

'Uh?' He peered up at her. 'Catherine?'

'Yes, it's me. What happened?'

He shook his head then winced. 'Ouch.'

'Have you hurt yourself?' She asked, then she spotted the half empty gin bottle on the table and the glass next to it, along with four small tonic water cans.

'I had a... a text message and I came out here for a drink and must have... dozed off.'

'Let me help you up.' Catherine held out a hand and Mark got to his feet. 'Are you okay to walk?'

'Yes.' He nodded. 'It's just my head that hurts. A lot. What time is it?'

'Gone six.'

'Ahhhh. I've been asleep most of the afternoon.'

'After drinking gin?'

'Mmmm.' He winced. 'And lying in the sun. I'm very thirsty.'

In the kitchen, Mark sat at the table while Catherine ran the tap then filled a pint glass with water. She found some aspirin in a drawer and handed Mark the packet along with the water. 'I'll make some tea.'

'Thanks.'

Mark took the tablets and drank the water while Catherine boiled the kettle and made two mugs of tea which she carried to the table.

'Shall we go and sit in the lounge?'

He nodded. 'Good idea.'

When they were comfortable, she sipped her tea then set her mug on the table.

'So, what was the text message about?'

He frowned.

'The one that sent you head first into the gin bottle.'

'Oh… that one.' He sighed. 'I have to confess that it wasn't just the text message… there are other matters that I wanted to… kind of… forget for a while… But, uh… My ex is getting married.'

'Ah.' Catherine nodded. 'Did she tell you herself?'

'No, my sister told me. Apparently it's all over social media and she didn't want me to see it… not that I've spent much time on any of those sites in quite a while…

but she was worried it would be a shock. And it was. But it came via text from Summer.'

'She didn't try to ring you?'

'Yes. Several times, but I'd gone for a run. I saw it when I got home and it was just… strange.'

'Did it…' Catherine mentally crossed her fingers. 'Did it make you realise that you still have feelings for her?'

Mark ran a hand over his brow then through his dark hair.

'At first, I thought I might have. I was surprised and I expected to feel angry, hurt… and so on… but then… the more I thought about it, the more I realised that I really don't care. It was the finding out that stunned me initially. But then, as I sat there in the summer house and thought about everything, about all that happened over the years between Ellie and me, and about all that's happened since I came to Penhallow Sands, it became clear that whatever I did feel for Ellie has long gone.'

Catherine bit her lip and blinked hard. Mark felt that he was over Ellie and that was a huge relief. She'd come here hoping to tell him how she felt about the book and about him and then seeing him in such a state and hearing how he'd reacted to Ellie's news made her feel very afraid. Driving here, she'd envisaged throwing herself into his arms but now, something was holding her back again.

'Mark,' she said softly.

'Yes?'

'I read the book you left for me.'

'You did? I hadn't heard from you… and thought that perhaps I scared you away.'

'It wasn't that. See, my mother found it and kept it from me until yesterday when I got home from work.'

'Your mother read it?'

'Yes. It really had an impact upon her.'

'I bet it did.' He grimaced.

'Not in a bad way. Not at all. In fact, it made her think about everything.'

'She was okay with what she read?'

Catherine nodded. 'She was. We had a good talk last night… well, she told me some things and I ranted at her. She apologised for a few things she'd done and said that she feels she's held me back all my life. She also told me something rather… big, that I had no idea about.'

Mark nodded, so Catherine continued.

'She said that my father didn't actually leave her for another woman and that it had been her, not him, who cheated in the first place.'

Mark's eyes widened. 'Your mother had an affair?'

Catherine explained what Diana had told her and Mark listened carefully.

'That's one hell of a revelation. Are you okay?' He reached out and took her hand.

'I am. I can't deny that I'm angry… well, furious, actually, with her for keeping it from me, and for blatantly lying to me about it all, but at least now I know the truth. Finally.'

'How are things between you?'

'She's gone away for a while.'

'Your mother's left Penhallow Sands?'

'I couldn't believe it either. She never goes anywhere, but she's gone to stay with her sister. They were estranged for a long time but they've been in contact recently and Mum said she thought it would do her – and me – good if she gave us both some space.'

'Wow.' He whistled. 'I hope I haven't caused problems for you.'

'Not at all. You've actually been the wake-up call we both needed.' She looked down at their joined hands and smoothed her thumb over his. 'I'm really glad you came into our lives, Mark.'

'Me too.' He smiled then he shuffled down on the sofa and leant his head on her shoulder. 'I wish my head wasn't pounding so badly though. I feel like my skull is about to burst open.'

Catherine gently stroked his forehead then ran her hand down over his cheek, needing to touch him and hoping that he would find her touch soothing.

'What will you do about your father now?' Mark asked.

'I've given him the brush off a few times but now I know the truth, I want to tell him and to apologise for not realising that he wasn't the bad man my mother made him out to be.'

'I don't think you need to apologise to him, Catherine. You didn't know and why would you have suspected that your mother was lying? She repeated the same lie for years, from when you were a child, so of course you'd believe her.'

'I feel so bad that he suffered for so long.'

'It's not your fault, Catherine. It was Diana's and you have to let any guilt you feel about this go.'

'I know you're right, but it's all so hard and confusing.'

'At least you know the truth now and can try to have a relationship with him.'

Mark slid his arm around her waist and held her tight.

After a while, the weight of his head became heavier on her shoulder and his breathing slowed, and she knew he'd fallen asleep. And that was fine. It was good to hold him, good to be held. She needed comfort right now and so did he.

Catherine was glad that Mark had come to Penhallow Sands and glad that she had come here today to see him. There were things they both needed to work through, but they could also offer each other a lot too. She closed her eyes and let herself think about how she'd like their story to end, because she could finally allow herself to imagine that they could have a future.

–

The next two weeks passed in a very enjoyable haze with Mark writing the rest of the book – inspired by Catherine – while Catherine worked during the day then came back to Plum Tree Cottage most evenings. They took turns to make dinner, enjoyed long walks and early swims, spent hours in each other's arms getting to know each other and Mark was so happy he thought he might burst.

When Mark was satisfied with the draft of his manuscript, and Catherine had read it through to check if she was happy too, he emailed it to his agent. She replied quickly, asking him to come to London, as she wanted to have lunch with him and his editor.

Mark read the email through twice, knowing that in the past, lunch with his agent and editor would have been something he'd have looked forward to immensely, but now, things had changed. It would mean leaving the bubble of him and Catherine and Penhallow Sands, and venturing back to the big city where his life had been so very different. He was aware that he was also reluctant to leave Catherine behind, even for just a few days, as he looked forward to waking up next to her every morning and to holding her when she returned to him after school most evenings.

Catherine seemed different without her mother's domineering presence around; she'd been set free of a weight she'd carried for a long time. Their time together was relaxed and enjoyable, as if Catherine could finally be herself. Mark knew that Catherine loved her mother deeply, but also that Catherine was annoyed with Diana for deceiving her for most of her life, and it would take some time to heal from that, if it could ever be fully overcome.

Mark was now convinced that he was madly in love with Catherine. Her smile, her laugh, her presence in his home all lifted his spirits and he no longer felt the shadow of loneliness. For some time before Ellie had told him it was over between them, he'd felt alone anyway, as if he was the only one in the relationship, and it had hurt immensely and left him quite despondent. But having Catherine in his life made everything brighter and he was filled with hope for the future. He felt that they could have a life together, a wonderful life, and he'd be very happy to settle in Penhallow Sands and to spend his life with Catherine. They hadn't yet spoken in detail about exactly how that would happen, even though she'd helped him to write the happy-ever-after for his book, but they had discussed the possibility of building a life as a couple.

After having the sunshine that was Catherine brightening in his world, Mark didn't think he'd manage if he lost her. It would certainly plunge him into a dreadful darkness. Of course, the fact that she had impacted so dramatically upon his life and that he now needed her around, did scare him. There was so much to lose, but there was also so much to gain. He was prepared to take the risk because Catherine was worth it.

However, he also knew that life couldn't stop just because he wanted to stay here with Catherine. He needed to earn a living, to continue to grow his career as an author and to promote his books, and going to London was part of that.

He checked online for tickets and booked one for the Thursday of the following week, aiming to get up there and back within two days so he could spend the weekend with Catherine. It would be something to look forward to.

—

Catherine sat on the bed and watched as Mark packed his small suitcase. They had eaten a light dinner of salmon and salad and shared a bottle of white wine. She felt relaxed and content, although she knew she would miss Mark, even if he was just going away for two days.

For more than two weeks, their lives had become entwined. Catherine stayed at Plum Tree Cottage most nights, popping back to feed and cuddle Bob and Ginger several times a day. They swam and walked and cooked and made love. In the evenings, when Catherine had work to do, they sat at the kitchen table together and Mark worked on his book. He had also put together a synopsis for the next book he planned to write, as he said that his agent and editor would want to know what he intended on writing next. Catherine hadn't asked to read it because he'd told her that the synopsis stage was one that was fraught with insecurity, as he wondered if his agent and then his editor would approve, and he didn't want to jinx it by sharing just yet. That was fine with Catherine; everyone had their own way of working and if Mark needed to fine-tune his synopsis before showing it to her, then he should do what he needed to do.

'Have you packed your toothbrush?' she asked as he stood in the middle of the bedroom looking confused.

'Not yet. Need it tonight and in the morning.'

'Of course you do. What about clean socks.'

'Check!' He smiled.

'Pyjamas?'

'Check!'

She took a deep breath. 'I'll miss you.'

'I wish you could come.'

'Me too, but I can't take days off in the week.'

'And my agent and editor don't work weekends.' He frowned. 'We can go away together soon, though, perhaps? If you fancy it.'

He sat next to her on the bed and took her hand.

'What do you think?'

Catherine smiled. 'I think that would be lovely. In the past, I couldn't really go away because of my mother, but now... it's actually possible. As long as Jamal and Bradley don't mind looking after the cats.'

'I'm sure they won't mind. We could book a romantic getaway at a hotel or go glamping in one of those yurts.'

'A yurt?'

'Yes, you know, those big round tents. All the rage now, so I've heard.'

Catherine giggled. 'I think a hotel sounds more my kind of thing. To start with at least.'

'Hotel it is then. Five stars, I take it?'

'Definitely. And as long as I'm with you, it will be wonderful.'

'Let me think on it while I'm away and we can take a look at some possible locations when I come home.'

She hugged herself inwardly because he had called Penhallow Sands *home*.

He shuffled down then pulled her into his arms so her head rested on his chest. He was warm and solid and there for her.

Catherine listened to his strong heartbeat and she was overwhelmed by how precious Mark had become to her. His mind, his heart, his body, everything about him meant so much to her now, and the thought that she could lose him was too much to bear.

'Mark?'

'Yes.' His breath tickled her cheek.

'You will come back, won't you?'

'What?' He tilted her chin and met her eyes.

'I just… I've enjoyed being with you so much but… what if you went to London and realised that you didn't want to return to Penhallow Sands? It would be so awful.'

He shook his head. 'Of course I'll come back, Catherine. Now I've found you, I'm never letting go.'

She blinked away the tears that blurred her vision and swallowed her fears. She couldn't live being afraid any longer. She had to trust Mark, although she knew it was something that would take time. Belief in another person wasn't born overnight and she didn't exactly have a good track record with her parents and their behaviour, so trust was something she would have to learn.

'Catherine, you make me happier than I've ever been. I promise I'll come back as quickly as I can. I'd prefer not to go at all, but it's my job and—'

She silenced him with a kiss.

Then another. And another.

And soon, all worries and cares floated away and they were lost in each other.

Chapter 21

Lunch had gone well and Mark was smiling as he left the restaurant and made his way to the nearest tube station. His agent and editor loved the book as well as his proposal for the next one, so once he was back in Penhallow Sands, he could make a start on writing the next book.

London was exactly as he remembered but even busier. Thursday afternoon traffic crawled around the roads and people hurried along the pavements, their eyes locked on their phone screens, their feet carrying them in familiar directions. Mark had once been one of them but it felt like twenty years or more had passed. It made him aware of how his time in Penhallow Sands had affected him. It had changed something within him, enabled him to relax and let go of what had been holding him back from his writing and from himself, and from what he really wanted. London was an incredible place and he'd always want to visit, but he no longer wanted to live there.

He wanted to be wherever Catherine was. Catherine was his home now.

'Mark?'

The voice cut through his thoughts and he turned slowly, knowing who it was and yet wishing it wasn't.

'Ellie.' He met her questioning hazel eyes, took in her delicate elfin features, her cropped red hair (darker red than he remembered) and the cute spattering of freckles on her nose. She was wearing skinny black jeans with heeled leather boots and some kind of wrap thing that swept over her left shoulder. She looked like a catwalk model or a celebrity.

'Mark!' She rushed towards him and kissed his cheeks. 'I thought it was you. My goodness, *where* have you been?'

He took a steadying breath. The last time they'd spoken it had been acrimonious and her current effusive display was unsettling. And yet, so Ellie.

'I've been away. I went to Cornwall.'

'Cornwall?' Her perfectly shaped brows rose up her smooth forehead. 'What are you doing there?'

'Taking some time out.'

She placed a hand on his arm and he glanced down at it, his eyes drawn to the sparkling diamond on her ring finger. 'But you're back now?'

'Not for long.'

'Then we must do lunch!'

'I've just eaten.'

Her familiar perfume, a heady jasmine scent that he'd once loved was cloying, burning his throat, and he averted his face to avoid breathing it in.

'Well, how about a drink? Oh do let's have a drink, Mark. Please? For old time's sake.'

Mark looked at her, at the woman he'd known since he was a teenager, at her pretty face and striking eyes, at the mouth he'd kissed hundreds of times and the head he'd buried his face in as they'd hugged.

She had been everything.

Then she had pushed him away.

He no longer had feelings for her and it was liberating. She was nothing compared to Catherine. Nothing at all.

'I don't know, Ellie. It's probably not a good idea.'

'Nonsense!' She waved a hand. 'It's exactly what we need. A way of making peace with what happened between us.'

He bit back the comment that it was her betrayal that had happened to them, her deceit that had kept them together even though she could have freed him from their relationship a long time before she in fact had. He could have got on with his life a long time ago. But perhaps the timing had been as it was meant to be, because he'd gone to Penhallow Sands and found Catherine. Thinking about her must have brought a smile to his face, as Ellie misread it as acceptance, slid an arm through his and led him towards a bar.

'Come on then, Mark, let's get a drink, shall we?'

He nodded reluctantly, although the reflection in the glass doors of the pub wasn't the one that he wanted to see. He didn't belong with Ellie anymore; it was Catherine he wanted to see on his arm.

Ten minutes later, they were sitting in a booth as strains of a Lionel Richie song filled the air and a waitress arrived to take their order. Ellie asked for a bottle of red wine and two glasses, without checking if that was what Mark wanted. He kept quiet, not seeing the point in calling her out over her inability to understand that he was a person in his own right who might have wanted something different. It wasn't something that would have even occurred to her.

She removed the dark grey wrap to expose a fitted pink T-shirt with some glittery logo on the front.

'So, Mark, what took you to Cornwall?' she asked innocently, as if she had no idea why he might have wanted to leave London in the first place.

He took a deep breath before replying. This was going to be a challenging afternoon…

–

Catherine was clock watching. She had tried to keep busy to take her mind off Mark but she couldn't help it. She knew when he'd be on the train, when he'd arrive in London, when he'd be having lunch, but after that, she wasn't sure what would happen.

Her day had involved a whole school assembly with a beautiful presentation from Year 6 about kindness, a meeting with the Alternative Learning Needs Coordinator, a meeting with a parent and playground duty. The school day was almost over but this evening, unlike every other evening recently, Catherine wouldn't be heading up to Plum Tree Cottage to see Mark.

It was a strange feeling because she looked forward to seeing him – it gave her days a lift – and knowing that he was so far away triggered a physical ache in her chest. She'd reprimanded herself several times during the day, reminding herself that she didn't need a man to complete her life, but it wasn't that. Mark had become her friend and companion and she liked him, enjoyed being with him. In a short space of time they had become so comfortable with each other that they could sit and talk, watch TV, work or just be. Catherine didn't feel that she needed to put on a front with Mark; she felt that he liked her for who she was, and that was something very special indeed.

She had grown very fond of him and the thought that anything could ruin that was dreadful.

She took a deep breath and stood up then tucked her chair back under her desk. Mark had to go to London and it was something that would happen again in the future, but it didn't mean that it had to impact negatively upon their relationship. She just hoped that he wouldn't see anything there that made him long to return to the city life he'd had before and that he didn't find that he missed it. Catherine's whole life was in Penhallow Sands and if Mark decided to leave, she wondered if she'd be able to leave with him, or if he would even want her to go.

–

Mark bit his tongue as Ellie went on and on and on. She'd always liked the sound of her own voice but once she had a few glasses of wine inside her, she liked it even more. He'd sat there listening to her talk about her job, her looks, her family, her friends and her hair – which had prompted her comment about how she liked his new style – and her latest (and rather bizarre-sounding) vampire facial. She was, he realised, very high maintenance. How had he never noticed this before? Or had he simply been blind to it, not wanting to believe that the woman he loved needed to do so much to feel good about herself?

Because that was what Mark could see now. Not the confident, glowing woman he'd loved but a woman in her late thirties who was, actually, quite insecure. She was very attractive, had a toned physique, and knew how to sit and stand to show her figure to optimum advantage, but all the time she was speaking, she kept searching Mark's face for signs of approval. She had even asked him twice what he thought about her hair and nails, if he thought she had changed in the past year, if he agreed that she'd lost a little weight. Mark had gone along with her, not wanting to hurt her, even after what she'd done to him. As the red wine had relaxed her and her flawless façade slipped, she'd shown signs of vulnerability, and he actually pitied her. Ellie clearly had some anxiety about herself and her life, about what people thought about her and how they perceived her, and Mark was glad that he didn't care about those things himself. Yes, he wanted to be a good person and yes, he wanted readers to enjoy his books, but as for pleasing people in other ways, it didn't appear on his radar.

There had been a time when Mark had wanted to please Ellie, her family and her friends and for her to love him, approve of him and need him, but that time had passed and he was, delightfully, free.

'Mark, what do you think?'

'Sorry?'

She'd asked him a question and he hadn't heard it.

'I asked what you thought about us.'

'Us?' He grimaced.

'Yes, of course. I mean… I do care about Fernando but he's not… not that mature.'

'Hold on.' Mark held up a hand. 'You're talking about the guy you've been living with, the one you moved into our home and were – apparently – sleeping with before we split up?'

'Don't say it like that, Marky baby.'

'"Marky baby"?' He cleared his throat. 'Ellie, you're engaged to be married and only recently engaged at that.'

'But I think it might be a mistake.'

She pouted at him, her hazel eyes roaming his face.

'But you love Fernando.'

She rolled her eyes then sighed and sagged in her seat.

'I thought I did, but hey... accidents happen.'

'Accidents happen? Are you saying that Fernando and the past year were accidents?' His heart was thundering and blood rushed through his ears.

'Oh, Mark, love, I miss you. Bumping into you today wasn't an accident at all. I knew you'd be here and when. Guess how?'

Mark sat and listened as she explained and his alarm grew with every second.

Finally, he shook his head and stood up. 'Oh dear. Uh... I think I need... the toilet. Back in a bit.'

He ran the cold tap and slid his hands under it then splashed water over his face. In the harsh lighting above the mirror, he looked haggard, his eyes wild and confused. He hadn't expected to bump into Ellie today and it had been a shock, and when she'd suggested going for a drink, he definitely hadn't expected to hear all that. But in a way he was glad he had. It wasn't that he didn't want Ellie to be happy, because he did, and he wished her well. But hearing that she had accepted another man's proposal and believed it was a mistake meant that it hadn't been just down to Mark getting it wrong in their relationship. In fact, it seemed that Ellie wasn't cut out for marriage, not to him nor Fernando. Now that she'd accepted a proposal from another man and realised it wasn't right for her, she apparently wanted Mark back. But for how long? How long until she tired of him again and replaced him with someone else? Five minutes going by her current track record. She seemed to crave attention and approval and didn't like anyone to move on. She had wanted Mark to love and need her and when he no longer did, it seemed that she felt the need to get him back.

Six months ago, Mark might have weakened and gone back to her, been happy with whatever fragments of love and affection she would throw him. But no longer. He was different now. Having time and space had freed him from whatever hold she had had over him and, of course, there was Catherine. She was Ellie's polar opposite and it lifted his heart to think of her.

Also, knowing that it hadn't so much been him that Ellie was rejecting as marriage itself, cleared up another mystery from his past. Ellie had yet to find her Mr Right, but Mark had found the woman he wanted to be with and it wasn't Ellie.

He dried his hands then returned to the booth and sat down.

Ellie held a finger to her lips and winked at him then gestured at the mobile she was holding. Mark blinked. Was that *his* mobile? He patted his pockets. It was. It must have fallen out of his pocket when he was sitting down and he'd rushed off to the toilets without realising. And now Ellie was speaking to someone on it.

Who?

'Yes, that's right. He's with me now in London.' Ellie nodded. 'We're sharing a bottle of wine and, do you know what? I think we're going to have another one. Bye for now.'

She cut the call off then handed Mark his mobile.

'Who was that?'

She shrugged.

'Some woman called Catrin.'

'Catrin?'

'Or was it Catherine?' She drained her glass.

'Catherine?' He swiped his phone screen and checked recent calls. Catherine had called him five minutes ago. That meant Ellie had been speaking to her for that long.

'She seems nice if a bit highly strung.' Ellie held out a hand and admired her nails.

'What did you say to her?'

'Not a lot. But she seemed to think you'd be with your agent and editor.'

'I was.'

Mark's stomach churned and he looked at his mobile as if trying to undo the conversation that had just happened.

'How did she seem?'

'I don't know, Mark. Who is she anyway?'

'She's—'

'Don't worry about her anyway.' She cut him off before he could say *she's my friend, my lover, my happiness*. 'Let's talk some more about us.'

Mark needed to speak to Catherine but he couldn't do it here. He needed some space.

'Ellie, there is no us.'

He stood up, pulled some notes from his wallet and dropped them on the table.

'I wish you well, but I have a new life now and you're not a part of it. Goodbye, Ellie.'

Her mouth fell open and she gaped at him then colour filled her cheeks. She was about to blow but Mark had no intention of being there to watch.

He marched out of the bar and onto the street then hurried back to his hotel with only one woman in his mind.

Catherine.

Chapter 22

Catherine got through the next day in a daze. She'd blamed her swollen eyes and red nose on early autumn hay fever when questioned by colleagues and some of the pupils, but she knew they weren't convinced. She looked truly awful and her head had throbbed all day.

She had rung Mark yesterday after work, keen to hear his voice and to find out how his lunch meeting had gone. She knew it could still have been going on, so only let the phone ring four times and was going to try later, when a woman answered Mark's mobile. She had told Catherine that Mark was busy so couldn't take the call right then, before asking Catherine what her call was concerning. The woman on the other end of the call couldn't have known who she was to Mark. And that was fine; after all, they hadn't yet made their relationship official in any way other than their declarations to each other. Now she wished they had, that everyone knew they were together because then she might feel more secure. But Mark had gone to London, away from Penhallow Sands and away from the bubble they had created around themselves and perhaps he had forgotten the things he had said to her, the things he had felt. It was possible that he would change his mind, that he would forget Catherine, that he would see all the attractions of his old life back in London. As fear had filled Catherine, she hadn't wanted to announce who she was because Mark clearly hadn't told anyone about her. Perhaps she just wasn't important enough to him. Then, the woman had told her that she was Ellie, and Catherine's heart had sunk. Mark was with his ex. In a pub, according to Ellie, enjoying a bottle of wine and about to have another.

Catherine had stuttered out a goodbye then turned her mobile off and dropped it onto the sofa. Mark was with his ex in London. He'd said he was meeting his agent and editor but had he even done that? It would have been a big lie if he hadn't been meeting them. So had he arranged to meet up with Ellie afterwards? But why? Ellie had hurt Mark and moved on, so why would he arrange to see her? Unless he had gone to London hoping to meet her. And the fact that Ellie didn't know about Catherine hurt her deeply. Why hadn't he told his ex that he was in love with Catherine?

She had rubbed her cheeks hard. This could all be completely innocent and perhaps it was coincidence that he'd bumped into Ellie, and Catherine could be worrying about nothing. But… the horrid churning in her stomach and the ache in her heart worried her. She had begun to trust Mark, to lower her barriers and let him in, which meant that she was open to hurt. And she didn't like it. She could phone him, hope that he'd answer, but it would mean putting her heart out there and she might hear things she didn't want to hear. Worse, perhaps, was that he could lie to her about it and then everything that her mother had ever told her about men would be true. Of course, Catherine wouldn't know if he was lying, but she would have her doubts and her fears and she couldn't bear to face them head on right now.

Catherine liked being strong and impenetrable; she didn't like being vulnerable and didn't want to be in a position where she could be hurt. Mark had that power. Unless she put a stop to it now. There would be other Ellies, other trips to London and other times when Mark might realise that Catherine was not the woman he wanted to be with. His feelings for her could change at any time. She was no manicured, polished city woman, no manipulator of people and not very experienced in the ways of flirtation and seduction. Catherine was just Catherine. Perhaps Mark wanted more and she had been a temporary distraction for him. The idea of asking him if this were true was impossible for her: how could she humiliate herself like that?

A sob burst from her and she bit down on her fist.

This would not do. She could not hurt like this.

Tears rolled down her cheeks and plopped onto her blouse and she let them. She couldn't pretend that she didn't care about Mark because she did, but right now he could well be sharing another bottle of wine with Ellie; right now he could be holding her in his arms and forgetting all about Catherine.

Her mother had always told her that men couldn't be trusted, and while Catherine had her doubts now about her mother's anti-male mantras, she couldn't quite shake the way that had penetrated her heart and mind, and how, whenever she felt vulnerable, they resurfaced, taunting her as they circled like dark storm clouds.

Whether or not Mark was reuniting with his ex wasn't the issue here.

The issue was that Catherine didn't know if she could ever fully trust anyone. And she didn't know how to change that. Or if she would ever be able to do so.

–

Mark had tried to get through to Catherine all night but he kept getting her voicemail. Hearing her personal cheery greeting was of no comfort though and he had become more and more frustrated as the evening had worn on. He had tried to call her as soon as he'd arrived at his hotel room and then all night, but she hadn't answered or returned his calls or text messages, in spite of the amount he'd left. In the end, he'd given in and called Jamal to see if Catherine had gone to his, but Jamal said he hadn't seen her that day. Jamal hadn't sounded worried but Mark had asked if he could check on Catherine in the morning and let him know that she was all right.

A text had come through from Jamal to say that he'd driven past the school early this morning and seen Catherine in the playground, so she must be having trouble with her mobile, then he'd given Mark Catherine's home number. It wasn't something Mark ever asked people for these days because everyone he knew relied on their mobile phones to communicate, but he could see why in instances like this, it would be useful to have another number to dial.

Mark couldn't face breakfast so he grabbed a coffee on his way to the station. He was booked onto a later train and would lose the money he'd paid, but he didn't care; he just wanted to get back to speak to Catherine and to find out why she had ignored his calls. To make sure that she was all right.

He couldn't wait to get back to Penhallow Sands.

-

Catherine opened the door and blinked.

'What are you doing here?'

'Can't I come to see my favourite woman on a Friday after work?'

'Well, yes, of course. Come in.'

Catherine led Jamal into the lounge then realised what a mess it must seem to him. Without her mother there, and with her frequent comings and goings to Plum Tree Cottage, she'd let things get a bit more relaxed at home and not maintained Diana's meticulous standards. Plus, Bob and Ginger had the run of the cottage now and there was cat fur on the sofa and some of their toys were strewn across the floor.

'Cup of tea?'

'Please.'

They went through to the kitchen and Catherine made tea while Jamal sat at the table.

'Everything okay?' he asked.

'Yes, why?'

'Well, you look like crap and I've had Mark calling and texting every hour or so, to find out if I've seen you and if you're okay.'

'Really?' She turned to him and saw the concern in his big brown eyes.

'Really. He said he was worried because he couldn't get through to you, so I told him I saw you in the yard this morning, then I gave him your landline, but he said he'd tried that this afternoon and still couldn't get through. What's going on?'

She carried two mugs to the table and sat opposite her friend.

'I've been such an idiot.'

'Tell me.' Jamal shook his head. 'And tell me quick because I'm fairly certain that as soon as Mark is back in Cornwall, he's going to be knocking on your door.'

Catherine's stomach clenched.

'But he was catching an afternoon train. He won't be back until late tonight.'

'He tried to get an early morning one, but there were some delays then he managed to get a seat but with a change or two. However, I do know that he said he's coming straight here.'

'Goodness.' Catherine stood up. 'I'm a mess.'

'True but I don't think he's going to care about that.'

'Okay.'

She sat back down, then she told Jamal about her doubts and fears, and about Ellie and how it had made her feel. He listened to her, passed her tissues then gave her a hug.

'Catherine, this doesn't mean it's over between you.'

'But I'm scared.'

'Some fear is a good thing. It means you care. It's very early days for you both but if you like him as much as you say you do, then you need to give him a chance to explain.'

'I know and I want to, but… I'm just scared of getting hurt.'

'Relationships come with risk, but when you love someone they're worth taking a risk on. So ask yourself, Catherine, although I'm sure you already know… Is he worth it?'

She sniffed then sipped her tea.

Was Mark worth it?

Was he worth making herself vulnerable for?

Could she take a chance on loving him?

That was what she needed to decide. But deep down, she already knew.

–

Catherine had gone upstairs to wash her face and brush her hair – at Jamal's instruction – when she heard a knock at the door.

Her heart flipped and she crept to the top of the stairs to listen.

Two voices, both deep and low. One was Jamal's and the other was Mark's.

She hurried back to the bathroom and looked at herself in the mirror. This was it, make or break. Mark either cared and had come to tell her that, or he'd come to tell her that he didn't want her and possibly, that he was back with Ellie. Either way, she had to be strong.

She padded down the stairs and into the kitchen, where Jamal was making tea, but in spite of her determination to be strong, when she saw Mark standing by the French doors, looking out into the garden, all she wanted to do was run into his arms.

'Hello.'

He turned at the sound of her voice and she gasped, because he looked awful, as if he hadn't slept in days.

'Catherine.' His familiar voice, his smile and his handsome face all made her knees weaken.

'Right, here are two mugs of tea. I'm off so you two can talk in peace, so take care and speak soon.'

Jamal patted Mark's shoulder then hugged Catherine and left them alone.

'Do you want to sit down?' Catherine asked.

'In the lounge, perhaps?' Mark asked.

'Of course.'

They went through to the lounge and as they sat down, side by side, Catherine noticed Mark's suitcase by the door.

'I came straight from the station. I tried to get back sooner but there were delays and I had to change twice. I've been so worried about you and I couldn't get through to you on the phone so I rang Jamal.'

Catherine nodded.

'Look… I know that when you rang me yesterday, which seems like years ago, you spoke to Ellie. Bumping into her was an accident. At least for me.'

'What do you mean?' Catherine held her mug tightly and tried to maintain her composure.

'She admitted to me that she'd known I was in London. She has one of those "find my friends" apps on her phone so she can see where they are, and she saw that I was in London and bumped into me on purpose.'

'But why?' *Unless she wants you back.*

'I met with my agent and editor then was on my way to the tube when I heard her calling my name. She suggested that we go for a drink and… against my better judgement, I agreed. I didn't want to have a drink with her but I was curious to know what she had to say and also… I know this sounds bad, but I'm not great at saying no to people.'

Catherine inclined her head. It wasn't great, no, and what if he was unable to say no to anything else Ellie might want.

'I don't mean in terms of anything other than going for a drink, you know?' Mark's voice wobbled. 'I wouldn't have done anything else with her. I just didn't want to be rude. I guess it's the Brit in me that feels a need to be polite.'

'Okay.' Catherine didn't trust herself to say more until she'd heard everything. She was torn between fear, sadness and anger and didn't know which one might win.

'We went into a pub; she ordered wine – even though I was going to have a coffee – and we were there for about an hour. I went to the toilet and my mobile must have fallen out of my pocket, which was when you rang.' He rubbed a hand over his face. 'I am so sorry that you had to listen to her. She really has issues, you know.'

'Mark, I can't do this.' Catherine shifted her position on the sofa to tuck her legs underneath her and she wrapped her arms around her waist. 'I'm so afraid of being hurt.'

'I would never hurt you.'

'How do you know? I was hurt just knowing you were having a drink with your ex, let alone anything else. I know that sounds silly and immature and awful, but how do I know that a drink won't turn into something else? You might realise you still have feelings for her... or for someone else at some point or you might just change your mind about me and not want me anymore and... and...'

'I'm telling you that won't happen, Catherine, and you can trust me. Besides which, I wouldn't have a drink with Ellie again. When I saw her, I realised that I needed to speak to her, to find that final closure and I did.'

'You did?' She gazed into his dark eyes and found only sincerity there.

'I did. Ellie is so self-absorbed, so in love with herself and yet so insecure in many ways. She needs to talk about herself because she wants to try to impose a certain image of herself in other people's minds. I felt almost sorry for her as I was listening to her but it didn't make me want to get back with her. I didn't feel anything really other than relief that it's over.'

Catherine sipped her tea to give herself time to digest what he'd said.

'I thought... when she told me who she was... that perhaps you'd gone to London to see her.'

'London is a big place, Catherine, and bumping into someone is unlikely. I hadn't hoped to bump into her or to hear from her or anything. Ellie has things she needs to work out for herself, but being with me is not one of them. She doesn't have a choice in that because I don't want to know.'

'Are you sure?'

'Of course I'm sure. But I'm sorry you were worried about it.'

'I'm sorry for being so insecure and not trusting you.'

'Look... I don't think it's just about trust at this point. Trust takes time to build and it has to be earned; it will hopefully grow and develop with time. You can trust me and you will see that, but I understand why you felt vulnerable. I'm here though and I'll be here for as long as you want me.'

'You're staying here?'

He nodded. 'I'd like to stay in Penhallow Sands. I'd like to be with you. I want to commit to you and to us.'

Catherine put her mug on the table and reached for Mark's. He gave it to her then pulled her onto his lap and they sat like that for a moment, their foreheads touching, their breathing in sync.

'Mark?' Catherine sat back to meet his eyes. 'I do want you to stay. More than I've ever wanted anything.'

'That's what I needed to hear. I have something for you.'

He reached into his jean pocket and pulled out a piece of paper.

'It's the dedication for the new book.'

Catherine unfolded the paper and her eyes filled with tears. She had to blink a few times to clear her vision.

For Catherine, you are my inspiration and my world. Thank you for fixing me. X

'Mark, it's beautiful. I've never had a book dedicated to me before.'

'Well, that's just plain wrong, but hopefully,' he said as he tucked her hair behind her ears then kissed her cheeks. 'It's the first of many dedications in which I thank my muse.'

He lifted her then and lay her down on the sofa then covered her body with his. As they kissed, Catherine felt her fears melt away and her heart fill with love.

Mark wouldn't hurt her and she could put her trust in him.

She could let go of the past, relinquish her need for control over her life, and look to the future. And now, it looked very bright indeed. She could have her own happily-ever-after.

Epilogue

The autumn afternoon was fresh and bright. Catherine stood on the back doorstep of Plum Tree Cottage gazing out at the fields beyond. The leaves on the trees were changing from green to red and gold, and the air was cooler now as October settled over Penhallow Sands. The breeze was fragranced with the autumnal flowers that grew in the garden and with the salty tang of the sea, and Catherine thought it was the most beautiful thing she had ever smelt.

A meow from behind her made Catherine turn and she smiled at Bob and Ginger. Mark had suggested that she bring them to his cottage seeing as how she was spending most nights there, and after a few days of worrying that they might run off, both cats seemed settled in their new home. Catherine's mother would be returning to the village at the end of the month, and Mark had suggested that Catherine and the cats move in with him. Bob and Ginger wandered past her into the garden and Catherine watched as they found a patch of sunlight to lie in then proceeded to wash each other.

She hugged herself. After so many years of being afraid and holding back on life, she was now living with a man. She had made the leap and taken the chance because Mark had told her that he loved her and cherished her and would never hurt her. She still had wobbles when she worried that he might change his mind, but she was learning how to cope with those times and knew that she could always seek reassurance from Mark, which she was learning she would always find in his words and in his arms.

'Hey you.'

She turned at his voice and smiled.

'Hey yourself.'

'How're you feeling?'

'A bit nervous.'

'It'll be okay. You know that, right?'

She glanced at the clock on the kitchen wall.

'I hope so.'

'Are you sure you want me to stay?'

She stepped forward and wrapped her arms around his waist the pressed her face into the curve of his neck.

'I definitely want you here with me, Mark. I don't want to do this alone.'

'I'm here and I love you.'

'I love you too.'

He pressed a gentle kiss on her mouth and she sighed with contentment.

A knock at the front door made them jump and Catherine's heart pounded against her ribcage. Frequent emails and several phone calls had brought her to this point.

'I'll get it,' Mark said. 'Deep breaths, now. I've got you.'

He squeezed her shoulders then left the kitchen.

She heard two male voices then Mark returned to the kitchen followed by an older man. As soon as she saw him, her eyes filled with tears.

'Hello, Catherine,' he said, his deep voice now familiar, then he crossed the kitchen and took her hands.

'Hello, Dad.'

For a moment it was strange, gazing into the eyes of the man she had loved as a child, seeing how life and time had changed him, and she felt a bit shy, a bit awkward, but then he opened his arms and she stepped into his embrace. This was a starting point and the conversations might not be easy, but with Mark at her side, Catherine knew that she wouldn't be afraid any longer. She was learning how to put her faith in people again and it was, unexpectedly, liberating.

And she was home now, with the man she had fallen deeply in love with, the man she trusted and adored more each day, and they were about to begin a whole new adventure at the cottage at Plum Tree Bay.

Acknowledgements

My thanks go to:

My husband and children, for your love and support.

My warm and wonderful agent, Amanda Preston, at LBA.

The fabulous team at Canelo. As always, your enthusiasm and hard work are deeply appreciated. Special thanks to Louise Cullen for help with the edits on this story.

My very supportive author and blogger friends.

All the readers who come back for more and who take the time to write reviews and share the book love.

Cornish Hearts

The House at Greenacres
The Cottage at Plum Tree Bay
The Christmas Tea Shop